About the Editor

Ama Ata Aidoo is a distinguished writer, consultant and scholar on gender and developmental issues. She graduated from the English Department of the University of Ghana, Legon where she served as a Junior Research Fellow of the Institute of African Studies. She has taught in many universities worldwide, including Stanford and Brown in the USA. While lecturing in the Department of English at the University of Cape Coast in the 1970s she was also appointed to the Board of Directors of the Ghana Broadcasting Corporation, The Arts Council of Ghana and the Ghana Medical and Dental Council. She was the first woman Minister of Education in Ghana serving in the 1980s and is currently the Executive Director of Mbaasem, a foundation to support African women writers and their work. She now divides her time between Ghana and lecturing in the USA.

Her publications include the dramas *The Dilemma of a Ghost* (Longman, Harlow, 1965) and *Anowa* (Longman, Harlow, 1970); the short stories *No Sweetness Here* (Longman, Harlow 1970); the novels *Our Sister Killjoy or Reflections from a Black-Eyed Squint* (Longman, Harlow, 1977) and *Changes* (The Women's Press, London 1991); the poetry *Someone Talking to Sometime* (College Press, Harare, 1985) and *An Angry Letter in January and Other Poems* (Dangaroo Press, Coventry, 1992); and the children's books *The Eagle and the Chickens & Other Stories* (Tana Press, Enugu, 1986); *Birds & Other Poems* (College Press, Harare, 1987); *Birds & Other Poems* (Pedacons, Teshie-Nungua Estates, Accra, 2002). Most recent releases include *The Girl Who Can & Other Stories* (Heinemann African Writers Series, Oxford, 2002) and a novel *Changes* (Heinemann African Writers Series, Oxford, 2004).

Ama Ata Aidoo's many awards include the Nelson Mandela Prize for Poetry in 1987 for *Someone Talking to Sometime* and the Commonwealth Writers' Prize for Africa for *Changes* in 1992.

AFRICAN LOVE STORIES

an anthology

Edited by Ama Ata Aidoo

An Adinkra symbol meaning
Ntesie maternasie
A symbol of knowledge and wisdom

For my Mother

This edition published by Ayebia Clarke Limited
7 Syringa Walk
Banbury
OX16 1FR
Oxfordshire
UK

First published in the UK by Ayebia Clarke Publishing Limited, 2006
Ayebia Clarke Literary Agency & Publishing Limited

And distributed outside Africa, Europe and the United Kingdom exclusively by
Lynne Rienner Publishers, Inc.
1800 30th St., Ste. 314
Boulder, CO 80301
USA
www.rienner.com

British Library Cataloguing-in-Publication Data
A catalogue record of this book is available from the British Library.

Cover design by Amanda Carroll at Millipedia
Cover artwork © of Adil Badawi Ali Elsanousi, 1997 at www.sunartists.org
Picture research by Amanda Carroll

Typeset by FiSH Books, Enfield, Middlesex.
Printed and bound in Great Britain by Cox & Wyman Ltd., Reading, Berkshire.

The publisher wishes to acknowledge the help of Arts Council Funding

ISBN 978-0-9547023-6-6

Available from www.ayebia.co.uk or email info@ayebia.co.uk
Distributed in Africa, Europe & the UK by TURNAROUND at
www.turnaround-uk.com

Contents

Introduction

One clear problem with love stories is that the moment you describe anything as such, readers and audiences begin to look for the frivolous and the sentimental. Yet we have all heard of profoundly serious love stories: documented or not. By 'serious', we do not necessarily refer to the intensity of the emotions of the protagonists, or the levels of their commitment to one another. Rather, it is a label that speaks of the enormity of the consequences of loving, especially its impact on the lovers themselves, their families, and the entire society in which they live and love. Within the Western European tradition, and as professionals of the word and the book, we should have read/heard of Troilus and Cressida, Heloise and Abelard or, at the very least, Romeo and Juliet, even when literature may not have been our special discipline.

It is indisputable that, apart from what nature endows humans and occasionally visits on us in the form of disasters and destruction, love is at the bottom of nearly all earthly happenings: great achievements, as well as mischief, murder and mayhem. Indeed, what we may choose not to remember is that love is not only the most serious literature, but one of the only three human tales that are. The other two being our quest for and worship of the Creator, and politics.

As far as the English-speaking world is concerned, the rise of the [true!] romance novel and the very vigorous marketing of it to teenage girls and young women did not help the 'silly' image of the love story. Publishers of Mills and Boon Halcyon romances and their kind saw to it that love was parcelled into some sort of dreamy fluff and treacle, which got sold to successive generations with few questions raised as to their suitability for the health of growing minds. All the while, however, other writers and publishers were weaving real magic for boys and young men, with more energetic stories of adventure, discovery and derring-do!

The fact that for most women, the reality often turned out to be more banal at best, and at worst, quite brutal than we could ever have imagined, never seemed to wake us up from the dream, tarnish its pristine attraction or the longing it kept burning in us. For average white Western females, as they grew up, so did what they were served. Juvenile pulp fiction gave way to adult romantic tomes with older protagonists, and steamier possibilities. Since the publishers of these novels, youthful or mature, were only in the business of selling joy and happiness, the stories might speak of mishaps and even misfortunes; but not tragedies. In these stories, everyone always lived, and lives, happily ever after! Yet we know this from family lore, national and international legends, in every single language on this earth, whether written, sung, danced, painted or in other ways recorded, that 'the course of true love stories is never smooth'! Meanwhile for the average, reading black female, young or adult, the reality was truly unspeakable. Since there were no black versions of even these romances, she was expected to identify with the white heroine! And homegrown African love stories? That definitely sounds like an anomaly. In fact, the controversial notion has gained ground that there are no love stories from Africa, classical or modern.

Yet, Africa, like all other regions of this earth, has been, and is, full of great love stories. Obviously, as in the judgement on all matters relating to Africa since the last five hundred years when the continent came into collision with Europe, and her world view got almost completely submerged under that of the West, this idea is predicated on some fairly controversial attitudes about Africa and African dynamics. One being that what we do not know about Africa does not exist. This notion covers all intellectual and cultural manifestations, as well as natural phenomena: including whole mountains and rivers. Nor does it stop there. There is a parallel belief to the effect that whatever exists in Africa does not count, if it does not conform to some known and accepted Euro/Western pattern, form or principle, and that such a thing should not be worth anyone's consideration. Even more tragically, 'anyone' here includes African academics/intellectuals and other opinion makers. Certainly, from the oral traditions, we know of great love stories which have lamentably stayed undocumented, or if documented, exist in forms that may be completely inaccessible. Meanwhile, if African writers are not writing love stories, then that must be due to a disconnection between contemporary African literature and its roots: oral and written.

'Achire's Heart'

Once upon a time, in a village in south central Ghana, there lived a beautiful . . . no, she was not a girl . . . and definitely not a virgin, since she was already the mother of about seven children. Yes . . . and no, she was not that old. So we shall describe her as a woman of a certain age. But she was still very, very pretty. In fact, she still had a lot of the beauty that had made her famous throughout the land when she was young. Her name was Achire, and she was the daughter of the former *Omanhene* of the state who had died not too long ago. One day, the entire state was thrown into commotion when people woke up to some very strange news. Achire had disappeared. Then it soon became clear that Achire and a man from another part of the state had fallen so hopelessly in love that they had planned that she would leave her husband and children and he would leave his wife and children, so that the two of them would set up house together. The man's name was Kwasa.

No one could understand it. Over a period of one year, everything was done to get them to get back to their senses. Successive emissaries were sent to bring her back home.

First her age-mates got together and sent three from among their group to her. When the three got to her place, Achire waited for them to talk, then proceeded to laugh in their faces. Then she cooked them a great meal. After they had all eaten, she sat around with them for the rest of the day singing their favourite songs and horsing around as if they were all still fourteen years old. Towards evening Achire's friends left to return home, and it was only when they approached their town that they began to feel foolish. Other messengers followed from her matrilineage and from her church. Nothing worked. Finally, her father, the new *Omanhene*, sent his messengers, bearing the special emissary's 'broom' of elephant hair bunched together with ropes of gold. These were the summons that must be absolutely obeyed. But Achire disregarded the broom, and no one could do a thing about it. After all, as the last king's daughter, she was the king's daughter. For a while, there was talk at meetings of the state council that her lover should be arrested and punished. However, some wise old men and women spoke against that. It would have been a crime to love the king's daughter if she had been young and a virgin, but she was neither. Besides, the woman had gone to the man of her own free will. The case for arresting Kwasa collapsed, and after that everyone left the lovers alone. Then, two years from the day the scandal first broke out, people woke up one morning to another strange kind of story. News had come to her father, the *Omanhene*, that while sweeping the courtyard where she and her lover lived, Achire had suddenly collapsed that morning and died. No, no one had heard of her illness. And no, she had not fainted first. She had just collapsed and died. They say that shortly after that Kwasa too died.
End of story.

No one has been able to understand why, given all the realities of her life, Achire did what she did; what had killed her so suddenly; and what had also ended her lover's life? What we know only, is that Achire and her lover did not live happily ever after. We also know that this story not only could have come from any region of the world, and got told in any language, but it also combines all the elements that make a great classic love story: beauty, power and wealth, the possibility of political and other intrigues, the false promise of farce, and of course, ultimate tragedy. However, it is very much an African love story, and a true story about Africans who lived (in the first half of the twentieth century).

Nor can the notion of contemporary African writers not writing love stories hold much water, except for those who never read novels like Ngũgĩ wa Thiong'o's *The River Between*, Mariama Bâ's *So Long a Letter*, Ama Ata Aidoo's *Changes*, Lewis Nkosi's *The Mating Birds*, or Buchi Emecheta's *The Joys of Motherhood*, in which, in the story of Ona and Agbadi, we encounter one of the most tender, heartbreakingly tragic and extremely short-lived love stories ever. There is also *Rain*, Grace Ogot's charming version of the classical love story motif from the oral traditions: all ingredients assured. It is not a short list. 'The only problem,' as one keen reader of African novels recently asserted in an informal conversation about the genre, 'is that in the modern African novel as a love story, the love story is *never* revealed as such. Because it is completely subsumed under "the more important social and political issues" which the modern African writer (thinks she/he) has to deal with: incompetent leadership and their betrayal of their peoples, the antics of "the lumpen militariat" (Ali Mazrui's formulation), complete economic collapse, racial tensions, outmoded traditional thought and practices . . . ' This list too is endless.

The twenty-one tales that make up this edition are some of the most complex love stories any reader may have come across in a long time. Many are at once heart breaking and at the same time heart warming. This is not only true of different stories, but also applies to individual stories. For instance, whereas 'heart breaking' is how we would want to describe Doreen Baingana's 'Tropical Fish', and a few others, we may have to admit that within the covers of this edition, many of the stories are both. Others like Monica Arac de Nyeko's 'Jambula Tree' are bold and even courageous. Meanwhile, how else can we describe Yaba Badoe's *The Rival* but hilarious? In it, we encounter a fourteen-year-old girl, who is determined to capture her uncle's heart, and not necessarily in a nice niecely way. 'She imagines she lived in her uncle's house, that she cooked for him and washed his clothes and in return he bought her *everything she wanted*: (emphasis mine) clothes and jewellery. And when she was older, he would buy her a car all to herself. The child, falling asleep, dreamt dreams in which she was queen of her uncle's household: on top of him, ruling his roost. His wife, she decided, would just have to go.' Mr. Mensah the uncle is all of sixty years old!

Quite often, the crafting of the story is so delightful, the excellence of the storyline is only an added bonus. 'He shouldn't have shown her his home, taking her through each room, pointing at the paintings on the walls, commenting on them. And he should definitely not have taken her to his bedroom. A bedroom is . . . the place where you hide your soul . . . and your vulnerability.' With this opening, you the reader feel immediately vulnerable. You sense that the writer is setting both you and the protagonist up in some big way. And Véronique Tadjo does not disappoint. Meanwhile, the nineteen-year-old Moriyike in Molara Ogundipe's *Give Us That Spade!* stuns everybody, including her mother, with an iron will and a determination to define herself against all odds, and according to her own perceptions. Then there is Nana of Promise Ogochukwu's *Needles of the Heart*, who reminds us, at the youthful age of eighty, that 'the heart is indeed a lonely hunter'.

It is generally accepted (in the world of writing) that the short story is not an abbreviated novel, but an autonomous genre that is far more tricky to handle, with one of its unwritten rules being that it cannot be cluttered with too many characters. So we know that we are dealing with a master story-teller when we meet a very minor character in Leila Aboulela's *Something Old, Something New*, who steals the entire show in four sketchy lines. After all, what did we expect of a 'Bill Cosby look-alike'? He even steps in at the end to tie things up neatly for everybody with his death!

With origins that span the length and breadth of Africa, the twenty-one wordsmiths have spun us tales that are as intriguing, diverse, yet strangely linked as the continent they represent. Examined closely, we would find that the dissimilarities are neither geographic nor ethnic, even when certain authors actually thought that their characters were exhibiting specific ethnic and cultural tendencies. This is not only because emotional naivety or pain and bewilderment are universal, but also because the collection exposes a general African landscape that is uniformly bewildering in every vital aspect: social, political and economic. Against such a background, it is almost impossible to characterise any of the protagonists' responses to their personal crises, or efforts to negotiate their environment, in specific ethnic or even sub-regional terms. Whereas, if we insist, as some of us do, that love is about the human condition, then there is hardly any aspect of women's lives which these stories do not touch. From labour pains to burials and funerals, from teenagers to octogenarians, and not to mention race-fraught and same-sex relationships – adult and pubescent, the human heart is all out there in these stories: beleaguered and bleeding, or bold and occasionally triumphant.

Since these are love stories, we are not surprised that a number of the protagonists get betrayed by those they love. What is really poignant to the point of being unbearable, is when, inevitably, some of the women manage to let motherhood betray them completely, as it happens to Uju in Chika Unigwe's 'Possessing the Secret of Joy'. Perhaps we should put 'modern' or even 'contemporary' somewhere in the title of this collection because, at their core, these stories are about the African woman today: struggling as her mother has done before her, coping as she must, but invariably with an independence won out of educational opportunities fully utilised, and career viability, with resulting economic security; all of which were denied her forebears. These African love stories are not only first-class yarns. The telling of them is often so good, you may catch yourself literally licking your lips with sheer delight and laughing out aloud. Meanwhile, sad, poignant or joyful, and there are not too many of the latter, some of the stories literally take your breath away with their lyrical openings and dazzling endings.

And then there is this one truly great fact about a collection of good short stories. It allows the most harried and time-challenged reader to participate in a learning experience, as well as have fun at their own leisure. So, not only should we not stress ourselves out if we cannot read all of them at a sitting. In fact, that is precisely what we should try not to do. Dear reader, it is highly recommended that you take these stories one at a time, so that you meet these African women properly and individually, and listen to them and their hearts: whether Sudanese, Kenyan, Ghanaian, Nigerian or Zimbabwean. As for the tales as a whole, you might find them eye-opening, perhaps even inspirational, but above all, you will be highly entertained by them. We welcome African Love Stories from Ayebia Publishing with pleasure.

Ama Ata Aidoo
May 2006
Accra, Ghana

Leila Aboulela

Something Old, Something New

Her country disturbed him. It reminded him of the first time he had held a human bone; the touching simplicity of it, the strength. Such was the landscape of Khartoum: bone-coloured sky, a purity in the desert air, bareness. A bit austere and therefore static. But he was driven by feelings, that was why he was here, that was why he had crossed boundaries and seas, and now walked through a blaze of hot air from the aeroplane steps to the terminal.

She was waiting for him outside the airport, wearing national dress; a pale orange robe that made her look even more slender than she was.

'I mustn't kiss you.'

'No,' shc laughed, 'you mustn't.'

He had forgotten how vibrant she was, how happy she made him feel. She talked, asked him questions. Did you have a good trip? Are you hungry? Did all your luggage arrive? Were they nice to you in the customs? I missed you too. There was a catch in her voice when she said that; in spite of her confidence, she was shy.

'Come, come and meet my brother.' They began to walk across a car park that was disorganised and dusty, the sun gleaming on the cars.

Her brother was leaning against a dilapidated Toyota. He was lanky with a hard-done-by expression. He looked irritated. Perhaps by the conflicting desire to get his sister off his hands and his misgivings about her marrying a foreigner. How did he see him now, through those narrow eyes, how did he judge him? A European coming to shake his hand, murmuring *salamu alleikum*, predictably wearing jeans, a white shirt, but somewhat subdued for a foreigner.

She sat in the front next to her brother. He sat in the back with the rucksack that wouldn't fit in the boot. The car seats were shabby, a thin film of dust covered everything. I will get used to the dust, he told himself, but not the heat. He could do with a breath of fresh air, that tang of rain he was accustomed to. He wanted her to be next to him. And it suddenly seemed to him, in a peevish sort of way, unfair that they should be separated like that. She turned her head back and looked at him, smiled as if she knew. He wanted to say, 'you have no idea how much I ache for you, you have no idea'. But he could not say that, not least because the brother understood English.

It was like a ride in a fun-fair. The windows wide open; voices, noises, car-horns, people crossing the road at random, pausing in the middle, touching the cars with their fingers as if the cars were benign cattle. Anyone of these passers-by could easily punch him through the window, yank off his watch, his sun-glasses, snatch his wallet from the pocket of his shirt. He tried to roll up the window but couldn't. She turned and said, 'It's broken, I'm sorry.' Her calmness made him feel that he needn't be so nervous. A group of school-boys walked on the pavement, one of them stared at him, grinned and waved. He became aware that everyone looked like her, shared her colour, the women were dressed like her and they walked with the same slowness which had seemed to him exotic when he had seen her walking in Edinburgh. 'Everything is new for you.' She turned and looked at him gently. The brother said something in Arabic.

The car moved away from the crowded market to a wide shady road.

'Look,' she said, 'take off your sun-glasses and look. There's the Nile.' And there was the Nile, a blue he had never seen before, a child's blue, a dream's blue.

'Do you like it?' she asked. She was proud of her Nile.

'Yes, it's beautiful,' he replied. But as he spoke he noticed that the river's flow was forceful, not innocent, not playful. Crocodiles no doubt lurked beneath the surface, hungry and ruthless. He could picture an accident; blood, death, bones.

'And here is your hotel,' she said. 'I booked you in the Hilton.' She was proud that her country had a Hilton.

The car swept up the drive. A porter in a gaudy green uniform and stiff turban opened the door for him before he could do it himself. The porter took his rucksack. There was a small fuss involving her brother in order to open the boot and get the suitcase. His luggage was mostly presents for her family. She had told him on the phone what to get and how much to get. They would be offended, she had explained, if you come empty handed, they would think you don't care for me enough.

The hotel lobby was impressive, the cool tingling blast of the air-conditioner, music playing, an expanse of marble. He felt soothed somehow, more in control, after the bumpy ride. With her brother away parking the car and a queue at the reception desk, they suddenly had time to talk.

'I need an exit visa,' she explained, 'to be able to leave and go back with you. To get the exit visa, I have to give a reason for leaving the country.'

'Because you're my wife,' he said and they smiled at the word. 'Will be my wife. Will be insha' Allah.'

'Insha' Allah.'

'That's it,' she said, 'we won't be able to get married and just leave. We'll have to stay a few days till the papers get sorted out. And the British Embassy... that's another story.'

'I don't understand what the problem is,' he said.

'Oh,' she sighed, 'people have a wedding and they go off on their honeymoon. But we won't be able to do that, we will have to hang around and run from the Ministry of Interior to the Passport Office to the British Embassy.'

'I see,' he said. 'I see. Do I need an exit visa?'

'No, you're a visitor. You can leave whenever you like. But I need a visa. I need a reason to leave.'

'Right.'

They looked at each other and then he said, 'I don't think your brother likes me.'

'No, no he doesn't mean to be unfriendly... you'll see.'

The first time he saw her was at the Sudanese restaurant near the new mosque in Edinburgh. His old Chemistry teacher had taken him there after Friday prayers. When she brought the menu, she told them that the peanut soup was good – a speciality – but his teacher wanted the humus salad and he ordered the lentil soup instead because it was familiar. He was cautious by nature, wanting new things but held back by a vague mistrust. It was enough for the time being that he had stepped into the Nile Café, he had no intention of experimenting with weird tastes.

He was conscious of her footsteps as she came from the kitchen, up the stairs. She was wearing trousers and a brown headscarf that was tied at the back of her neck. She had very black eyes that slanted. After that day he went to the Nile Café alone and often. It was convenient, close to the Department of Zoology where he worked as a lab technician. He wondered if, as she leaned to put the dish of couscous in front of him, she could smell the chemicals on him.

They got talking because there weren't many customers in the restaurant and she had time on her hands. The restaurant was new and word had not yet got round that it was good.

'We've started to get a few people coming in from the mosque,' she told him. 'Friday especially is a good day.'

'Yes, it was a Friday when I first came here and met you.'

She smiled in a friendly way. He told her that at one time he had not known that the big building next to the restaurant was a mosque. There was no sign that said so.

'I thought it was a church,' he said and she laughed and laughed. He left her an extra tip that day; it was not often that people laughed at his jokes.

Had it not been for his old Chemistry teacher he would never have gone to the mosque. At a bus stop, he had recognised a face he had not seen for a number of years; a face associated with a positive feeling, a time of encouragement – secondary school, the ease with which he had written lab reports. They recognised each other straight away. 'How are you? What are you doing now? You were my best student.'

In primary and secondary school, he had been the brightest in his class, the most able. He sat for the three sciences in his Standard Grades and got three As. It was the same when he did his Highers. There was no reason at all, his teachers said, why he should not sail through medical school. But he got to his third year in Medicine and failed, failed again and dropped out. He had counselling and his parents were supportive, but no one ever really understood what had gone wrong. He was as bewildered by his failure as everyone else was. His get-up-and-go had suddenly disappeared, as if amputated. 'What's it all for, what's the point?' he asked himself. He asked himself the taboo questions. And really, that was the worst of it; these were the questions that brought all the walls down.

Snap out of it, he was told, and snap out of it he eventually did. A girlfriend helped but then she found a job in London and drifted away. He was simply not up to medical school. It's a shame, everyone agreed. They were sympathetic but at the same time they labelled him now, they put him in a box, a student who had 'dropped-out', a 'giver-upper'.

One day when she brought him his plate of aubergine and mince meat he asked her, 'Would you like to go up to Arthur's Seat?' She had never been there before. It was windy, a summer wind that carried away the hats of tourists and messed up people's hair. Because her hair was covered, she looked neat, slightly apart from everyone else. It made the outing not as carefree as he imagined it would be. She told him she had recently got divorced after six months of marriage. She laughed when she said six months not six years, but he could tell she was sore – it was in her eyes.

'You have beautiful eyes,' he said.

'Everyone tells me that,' she replied. He flushed and looked away at the green and grey houses that made up Edinburgh. She had wanted to talk about her divorce; she had not wanted to hear compliments.

They talked a little about the castle. He told her about his girlfriend, not the nice one who had gone down south, but the previous one who had dumped him. He was able to laugh about it now. She said her husband had married her against his will. Not against her will, she stressed, but his will.

'He was in love with an English girl but his family disapproved and stopped sending the money he needed to continue his studies in Edinburgh. They thought a Sudanese girl like me would make him forget the girlfriend he had been living with. They were wrong. Everything went wrong from day one. It's a stupid story,' she said, her hands in her pockets.

'Did you love him?' he asked her. Yes, she had loved him, wanted to love him. She had not known about his English girlfriend. After the honeymoon, when he brought her to Edinburgh and started acting strange, she asked him and he told her everything.

'Would you believe it,' she said, 'his family now blames me for the divorce! They say I wasn't clever enough, I didn't try hard enough. They're going around Khartoum saying all these things about me. That's why I don't want to go back. But I'll have to eventually when my visa runs out.'

'I'm glad I'm not pregnant,' she went on. 'I thank Allah every day that I didn't become pregnant.'

After that they spoke about faith. He told her how he had become a Muslim. He spoke about his former Chemistry teacher – how, after meeting again, they had fallen back into the swing of their old teacher–student relationship. She listened, fascinated. She asked him questions.

'What was your religion before?'

'I was a Catholic.'

'Have you always believed in God?

'Yes.'

'Why on earth did you convert?'

She seemed almost surprised by his answers. She associated Islam with her dark skin, her African blood, her own weakness. She couldn't really understand why anyone like him would want to join the wretched of the world. But he spoke with warmth. It made her look at him properly, as if for the first time.

'Your parents probably don't like it,' she said, 'or your friends? They won't like you changing.' She was candid in that way. And she was right. He had lost one friend after a bitter, unnecessary argument; another withdrew. His parents struggled to hide their dismay. Ever since he had dropped out of medical school, they had feared for his well-being, fretted that he would get sucked up into unemployment, drugs, depression; the underworld that throbbed and dragged itself parallel to their active middle-class life. Only last week, their neighbour's son had hanged himself (drugs of course and days without showering). There was a secret plague that targeted young men.

Despite their misgivings about his conversion to Islam, his parents eventually had to admit that he looked well; he put on a bit of weight, got a raise at work. If only he would not talk about religion. They did not understand that side of him that was theoretical, intangible, belonging to the spiritual world. If only he would not mention religion then it would be easier to pretend that nothing had changed. He was confident enough to humour them. Elated that the questions he had once asked – what's it all for, what does it all mean, what's the point of going on – the questions that had tilted the walls around him and nearly smothered him, were now valid. They were questions that had answers, answers that provoked other questions, that opened new doors, that urged him to look at things in another way like holding a cube in his hand, turning it round and round, or like moving around a tall column and looking at it from the other side, how different it was and how the same.

When he took her to meet his parents, the afternoon was a

huge success. We're going to get married he said, and there a kind of relief in his mother's eyes. It was easier for his parents to accept that he was in love with a Muslim girl than it was to accept that he was in love with Islam.

From the balcony of his hotel room, he looked out at the Blue Nile. Sunshine so bright that he saw strands of shimmering light. Palm trees, boats, the river was so blue. Would the water be cool, he wondered, or tepid? He felt sleepy. The telephone rang and he went indoors again, sliding the tinted glass door behind him.

Her happy voice again. 'What were you doing, why aren't you asleep? Everyone sleeps this time in the afternoon, it's siesta time, you must be exhausted. Did you remember to bring dollar bills – not sterling, not traveller cheques? You mustn't eat at the hotel, it will be terribly expensive, you must eat only with us here at home. Yes, we'll pick you up later. You'll come for dinner, you'll meet my parents. Don't forget the gifts. Are you going to dream of me?'

He dreamt that he was still on the aeroplane. He woke up an hour later, thirsty, looked up and saw a small arrow painted on the ceiling of the room. What was the arrow for? Out on the balcony, the contrast startled him. Sunset had softened the sky, rimmed the west with pinks and soft orange. The Nile was benign, the sky already revealing a few stars, the air fresher. Birds swooped and zigzagged.

He heard the *azan*; the first time in his life to hear it outdoors. It was not as spectacular as he had thought it would be, not as sudden. It seemed to blend with the sound of the birds and the changing sky. He started to figure out the direction of Makkah using the setting sun as his guide. Straight east or even a little to the north-east it would be now, not south-east as it was from Scotland. He located the east and when he went back into the room, understood the purpose of the arrow that was painted on the ceiling. The arrow was to show the hotel guests which way to face Makkah. After he had prayed, he went downstairs and looked for the swimming pool. He swam in water that was warm and pungent with chlorine. Twilight was swift. In no time the sky turned a dark purple with sharp little stars. It was the first time he had swum under a night sky.

Her house was larger than he had imagined, shabbier. It was full of people – she had five brothers and sisters, several nephews and nieces, an uncle who looked like an older, smaller version of Bill Cosby and an aunt who was asleep on a string bed in the corner of the room. The television blared. Her mother smiled at him and offered him sweets. Her father talked to him in careful, broken English. Everyone stared at him, curious, pleased. Only the brother looking bored, stretched out on another string bed staring at the ceiling.

'So now you've seen my family,' she said, naming her sisters, her nieces and nephews. The names swam in his head. He smiled and smiled until he strained the muscles of his face.

'Now you've seen where I grew up,' she said, as if they had got over a hurdle. He realised, for the first time, the things she'd never had: a desk of her own, a room of her own, her own cupboard, her own dressing table, her own mug, her own packet of biscuits. She had always lived as part of a group, part of her family. What that was like, he didn't know. He did not know her well enough. He had yet to see her hair, he had yet to know what she looked like when she cried and what she looked like when she woke up in the morning.

'After we have had dinner,' she said, 'my uncle knows an English song.' She was laughing again, sitting on the arm of the sofa. 'He wants to sing it for you.'

Bill Cosby's look-a-like sat up straight in his armchair and sang, '*Cricket, lovely cricket at Lords where I saw it. Cricket, lovely cricket at Lords where I saw it.*'

Everyone laughed. After singing, the uncle was out of breath.

They went on outings which she organised. They went on a boat trip, a picnic in the forest, they visited the camel market. On each of these outings, they were accompanied by her brother, her sisters, her nephews and nieces, her girlfriends.

They were never alone. He remembered Michael in *The Godfather*, climbing the hills of Italy with his fiancée, surrounded by armed guards and her numerous relatives, backed by an unforgettable soundtrack. It was like that but without the guns. And instead of rolling hills, there was flat scrubland, the edges of a desert. He watched her, how she carried a nephew, how she smiled, how she peeled a grapefruit and gave him a piece to eat, how she giggled with her girlfriends. He took lots of photographs. She gave him strange fruit to eat. One was called *doum* and it was brown, large as an orange, almost hard as rock, with a woody taste and a straw-like texture. Only the thin outer layer was to be gnawed at and chewed, most of it was the stone. Another fruit was called *gongoleez*, sour, tangy, white chunks, chalky in texture to suck on and throw the black stones away. Tamarind to drink, *kerkadah* to drink, *turmus*, *kebkebeh*, *nabaq*. Peanut salad, stuffed aubergines, *moulah*, *kisra*, *waikah*, *mouloukhia*. Dishes he had eaten before in the Nile Café, dishes that were new. She never tired of saying to him, 'here, taste this, it's nice, try this!'

'Can't we be alone, just for a bit?' he appealed.

'My family is very strict, especially because I'm divorced; they're very strict,' she said but her eyes were smiling.

'Try and sort something out.'

'Next week after the wedding, you'll see me every day and get tired of me.'

'You know I can't ever get tired of you!' he exclaimed.

'How can I know that?' she smiled.

She could flirt for hours given the chance. Now there was no chance because it was not clear whether her uncle, Bill Cosby, eyes closed and head nodding forward, was dozing in his armchair or eavesdropping.

Mid-morning in Ghamhouriah Street, after they had bought ebony to take back to his parents, he felt a tug on his shoulder, turned and found his rucksack slashed open, his passport missing; his camera too. He started to shout.

'Calm down,' she said, but he could not calm down. It was not only anger – there was plenty of that – but the eruption of latent fears, the slap of a nightmare. Her brother had parked the car in a bit of shade in a side street. They reached it now, her brother tenser than ever, she downcast and he clutching his ravaged rucksack. He kicked the tyre of the car, f-this and f-that. Furious he was, and out to abuse the place, the time, the crime. The whole street stood still and watched a foreigner go berserk, as if they were watching a scene in an American movie. A car drove past and the driver craned his neck to get a better look, laughed.

'Please,' she said, 'stop it, you're embarrassing me.' He did not hear her. Her voice could not compete with the roar of anger in his ears.

'We'll have to go to the British Embassy and get him a new passport,' she said to her brother.

'No, we'll have to go the police station and report this first,' he replied, getting into the car, wiping the sweat on his forehead with his sleeves.

'Get in the car,' she said to him. 'We'll have to go to the police station and report your stolen passport.'

He got into the car, fuming.

The police station was surprisingly pleasant: a bungalow and several outbuildings. It was shady, cool. They were treated well, given cold water, tea. He refused to drink the tea, sat in a sulk.

'Do you know how much that camera cost?' he hissed. 'And it's not insured.'

She shrugged, less shocked by what had happened than he was. Soothed by the drink, she started to tease him.

'They'll chop off the hand of the thief who stole your camera. Really they will.' Her brother laughed with her.

'I really can't see what's so funny,' he was still brooding.

'Can't you take a joke?' she said and there was an edge to her voice. Afterwards they drove in silence to the British Embassy. There, they endured a long queue. The Embassy staff hemed and hawed. They did not like to hear of passports getting stolen. And as one question led to the other, they were not overjoyed either to hear of people getting married in a few days' time. They interrogated her and her brother, broad, flat questions but still she felt sullied and small. Coming out of the embassy, she was anything but calm.

'What did they think? What were they trying to insinuate? That I stole your passport! As if I am desperate to go back there... '

'What's that supposed to mean?' he asked.

'It's supposed to mean what it means! You think you're doing me a big favour by marrying me?'

'No, I don't think that, of course not...'

'They do! They do, the way they were talking. Sneering at me and you didn't even notice!'

'Okay, okay, calm down.'

A small boy touched his arm, begging. Gnarled fist, black skin turned grey from malnutrition, one eye clogged with thick mucous. He flinched at the unpleasant touch, felt guilty, fumbled in his pockets and started to take out a two-hundred dinar note.

'Are you out of your mind,' she said, 'giving him that amount? He'll get mugged for it.' She opened her bag and gave the boy instead some coins and an orange.

As she got in the car, she told her brother about the beggar and they both laughed in a mocking way – laughing at him in Arabic, the height of rudeness.

'Perhaps you can contribute to the petrol then,' the brother drawled, 'given you have so much cash to spare. I've burnt a lot of gas chauffeuring you and your fiancée around, you know.'

'Right, if this is what you want!' He yanked out the notes from his wallet and slammed them down near the handbrake.

'Thanks,' her brother said, but when he picked the wad of cash, he looked at it like it was not much, like he had expected more.

She sighed and looked out of the window. It was as if the

theft had brought out all the badness in them. He thought of asking to be dropped at the hotel. He thought of giving up and leaving for Scotland the next day. That would punish her for laughing at him; that would hurt her. But he did not ask to be dropped off. He did not give up. True he had no passport and would not be able to travel, but something else made him stay.

They walked into disarray – her house, almost unrecognisable for the sheer number of people who were distraught, in shock. A woman was pushing the furniture to one side; another dropped a mattress on the floor; everywhere weeping, weeping and a few hoarse voices shouting orders. Her uncle, Bill Cosby's look-alike, had died, dozing in his armchair.

For a moment, the three of them stood in the middle of the room, frozen in disbelief. The brother started to ask questions in a loud voice.

'That's it,' she hissed, 'we'll never have our wedding now, not in the middle of this mourning, never, never!' And she burst into tears.

Before he could respond, her brother led him away, saying 'the house will be for the women now, we have to go outside. Come on.'

The garden was hell that time of day, sun scorching the grass, reflecting on the concrete slabs of the garage. How precious shade was in this part of the world, how quickly a quarrel could be pushed aside, how quickly the dead were taken to their graves. Where was he now, the uncle who sang, '*Cricket, lovely cricket!*' Somewhere indoors being washed with soap, perfumed and then wrapped in white, that was the end then, without preliminaries. He could faint standing in the sun like that, without a passport, without her, without the reassurance that their wedding would go ahead. It couldn't be true. But it was and minute after minute passed with him standing in the garden. Where was her brother now, who had previously watched his every move while she had circled him with attention, advice, plans? She was indoors sucked up in rituals of grief he knew nothing about. Well he could leave now, slip away unnoticed. He could walk to the main road and hail a taxi – something he had not done before because she and her brother had picked him up and dropped him back at the hotel every single day. Death, the destroyer of pleasures.

The body was being taken away. There it was shrouded in white and the shock of seeing that Bill Cosby face again, asleep, fast asleep. The folds of nostrils and lips, the pleasing contrast of white hair against dark skin. He found himself following her brother into the car, getting into what now had become his seat at the back, two men crammed in next to him, an elderly man sat in front. The short drive to the mosque, rows of men. He had prayed that special prayer for the dead once before in Edinburgh, for a still-born baby. It did not involve any kneeling, was brief, cool. Here it was also raw, the fans whirling down from the ceiling, the smell of sweat and haste.

They drove out of town to the cemetery. He no longer asked himself why he was accompanying them; it seemed the right thing to do. In the car, there was a new ease between them, a kind of bonding because they had prayed together. They began to talk of the funeral announcement that went out on the radio after the news, the obituaries that would be published in the newspaper the next day. He half-listened to the Arabic he could not understand, to the summary in English which one of them would suddenly give, remembering his presence.

Sandy wind blowing, a home that was flat ground, a home that had no walls, no doors. My family's cemetery, her brother said suddenly addressing him. Once he married her and took her back with him to Edinburgh, would he be expected to bring her back here if she, God-forbid, died? Why think these miserable thoughts? A hole was eventually made in the ground; you would think they were enjoying the scooping out of dirt, so whole-heartedly were they digging. With the sleeve of his shirt, he wiped the sweat off his brow – he was beginning to act like them – since when did he wipe his face with his shirtsleeves in Edinburgh? He wanted a glass of cold water but they were lowering the uncle in the grave now. They put him in a niche, wedged him in so that when they filled the grave, the soil they poured in did not fall on him.

For the next three days, he sat in the tent that had been set up in the garden for the men. A kind of normality prevailed, people pouring in to pay their condolences, the women going indoors, the men to the tent. A flow of water glasses, coffee, tea, the buzz of flies. Rows of metal chairs became loose circles and knots, as old friends caught up with each other, a laugh here and there could be heard. 'What's going to happen to your wedding now?' he was asked. He shrugged, he did not want to talk about it, was numbed by what had happened, dulled by the separation from her that the mourning customs seemed to impose. In the tent, the men agreed that the deceased had had a good death, no hospital, no pain, no intensive care and he was in his eighties, for God's sake, what more do you expect? A strange comfort in that tent. He fell into this new routine. After breakfast in the hotel, he would walk along the Nile, and after passing the Presidential Palace, hail down a taxi, go to her house. He never met her and she never phoned him. After spending the day in the tent and having lunch with her brother and his friends, one of them would offer him a lift back to the Hilton.

Late in the evening or the early morning, he would go swimming. Every day he could hold his breath longer under water. When he went for a walk, he saw army trucks carrying young soldiers in green uniforms. The civil war in the south had gone on for years and wasn't drawing to an end – on the local television station there were patriotic songs, marches. He had thought, from the books he'd read and the particular British Islam he had been exposed to, that in a Muslim country he would find elegance and reason. Instead he found melancholy, a sensuous place, life stripped to the bare bones.

On the third evening after the funeral, the tent was pulled down, the official mourning period was over.

'I want to talk to you,' he said to her brother, 'perhaps we could go for a walk?'

They walked in a street calmed by the impending sunset. Only a few cars passed. He said, 'I can't stay here for long. I have to go back to my work in Scotland.'

'I'm sorry,' the brother said, 'we could not have your wedding. But you understand...'

'It's going to be difficult for me to come again. I think we should go ahead with our plans...'

'We can't celebrate at a time like this.'

'It doesn't have to be a big celebration.'

'You know, she had a big wedding party last time?'

'No, I didn't know. She didn't tell me.'

'I blame myself,' her brother suddenly blurted out, 'that son of a dog and what he did to her! I knew, you see. I heard rumours that he was going with that girl but I didn't think much of it, I thought it was just a fling he was having and he'd put his girlfriend away once he got married.'

They walked in silence after that, the sound of their footsteps on crumbling asphalt. There was movement and voices in the houses around them, the rustle and barks of stray dogs. Finally her brother said, 'I suppose we could have the marriage ceremony at my flat. But just the ceremony, no party...'

'No no, there's no need for a party...'

'I'll talk to my father and my mother, see if they approve the idea.'

'Yes please, and after the ceremony...'

'After the ceremony you can take her back with you to your hotel...'

'Right.'

'Her father has to agree first.'

'Yes, of course.' He walked lighter now, but there was still another hitch.

'You know,' her brother said, 'we lost a lot of money marrying her off to that son of a dog. A lot of money. And now again this time...even just for a simple ceremony at my place, I will have to buy drinks, sweets, pay for this and that.'

On a street corner, money was exchanged between them. He handed her brother one fifty dollar bill after the other, not stopping until he sensed a saturation.

'Thanks, better not tell her about this, okay? My sister's always been sensitive and she doesn't realise how much things cost.'

His hand trembled a little as he put his wallet away. He had previously paid a dowry (a modest one, the amount decided by her) and he had brought the gifts in good faith. Now he felt humiliated, as if he had been hoodwinked or as if he had been so insensitive as to underestimate his share in the costs. Or as if he had paid for her.

On the night before the wedding, he slept lightly, on and off, so the night seemed to him elongated, obtuse. At one time he dreamt of a vivid but unclear sadness and when he woke he wished that his parents were with him, wished that he was not alone, getting married all alone. Where were the stag night, the church wedding, invitation cards, a reception and speeches? His older brother had got married in church wearing the family kilt. It had been a sunny day and his mother had worn a blue hat. He remembered the unexpected sunshine, the photos. He had turned his back on these customs, returned them as if they were borrowed, not his. He had no regrets, but he had passed the stage of rejection now, burnt out the zeal of the new convert, was less proud, more ready to admit to himself what he missed. No, his parents could not have accompanied him. They were not hardy enough to cope with the heat, the mosquitoes, the maimed beggars in the street, all the harshness that even a good hotel could not shield. Leave them be, thank them now humbly in the dark for the generous cheque they had given him.

He dreamt he was being chased by the man who had ripped his rucksack, stolen his passport and camera. He woke up sweaty and thirsty. It was three in the morning, not yet dawn. He prayed, willing himself to concentrate, to focus on what he was saying, who he was saying it to. In this early hour of the morning, before the stir of dawn, all was still – even his mind which usually buzzed with activity, even his feelings which tumbled young. Just a precious stillness, patience, patience for the door to open, for the contact to be made, for the comforting closeness. He had heard a talk once at the mosque, that there are certain times of the day and the year when Allah answers prayers indiscriminately, fully, immediately – certain times – so who knows, you might one moment pray and be spot on, you might ask and straight away be given.

After dawn he slept and felt warm as if he had a fever. But he felt better when he woke late with the telephone ringing and her clear voice saying, 'I'm so excited I'm going to be coming to the Hilton to stay with you. I've never stayed in a Hilton before, I can't wait.' It was a matter of hours now.

Her brother's flat was in a newly built area, a little deserted, out of the way. One of her cousins had picked him up from the hotel and now they both shuffled up the stairs. The staircase was in sand, not yet laid out in tiles or concrete, there was a sharp smell of paint and bareness. The flat itself was neat and simple; a few potted plants, a large photograph of the *Ka'ba*. The men – her brother, father, various relations and neighbours whom he recognized from the days in the mourning tent – occupied the front room, the one near the door. The women were at the back of the flat. He couldn't see them, couldn't see her.

Shaking hands, the hum of a general conversation in another language. The Imam wore a white *jellabiya*, a brown cloak, a large turban. He led them for the *maghrib* prayer and after that the ceremony began. Only it was not much of a ceremony, but a signing of a contract between the groom and the bride's father. The Imam pushed away the dish of dates that was on the coffee table and started to fill out a form. The date in the Western calendar, the date in the Islamic calendar. The amount of dowry (the original figure she had named and not the additional dollars her brother had taken on the street corner). The name of the bride. The name of her father who was representing her. The name of the groom who was representing himself.

'But that is not a Muslim name.' The Imam put the pen down, sat back in his chair.

'Show him your certificate from the mosque in Edinburgh,' urged her brother, 'the one you showed me when you first arrived.'

'I can't,' he said, 'it was stolen or it fell out when the things in my bag were stolen.'

'No matter,' the brother sighed and turned to speak to the Imam. 'He's a Muslim for sure. He prayed with us. Didn't you see him praying just now behind you?'

'Did they tell you I have eyes at the back of my head?' enquired the Iman.

Laughter... that didn't last long.

'Come on, sheikh,' one of the guests said, 'we're all gathered here for this marriage to take place *insha' Allah*. We've all seen this foreigner praying, not just now but also on the days of the funeral. Let's not start to make problems.'

'Look, he will recite for you the *Fatiha*,' the brother said, 'won't you?' He put his hand on his shoulder as a way of encouragement.

'Come on, sheikh,' another guest said, 'these people aren't even celebrating or having a party. They're in difficult circumstances, don't make things more difficult. The bride's brother said he saw an official certificate; that should be enough.'

'*Insha' Allah* there won't be any difficulties,' someone ventured.

'Let him recite,' the Imam said, looking away.

He was sweating now. No, not everyone's eyes were on him, some were looking away, hiding their amusement or feeling embarrassed on his behalf. He sat forward, his elbows on his knees.

'In the Name of Allah, the Compassionate, the Merciful,' her brother whispered helpfully.

'In the Name of Allah, the Compassionate, the Merciful,' he repeated, his voice hoarse but loud enough. 'All praise to Allah, Lord of the Worlds,' and the rest followed, one stammered letter after the other, one hesitant word after the other.

Silence. The scratch of a pen. His hand in her father's hand. The *Fatiha* again, everyone saying it to themselves, mumbling it fast, raising their palms, 'Ameen,' wiping their faces.

'Congratulations, we've given her to you now.'

'She's all yours now.'

When he saw her, when he walked down the corridor to where the women were gathered, when the door opened for him and he saw her, all he could say was, 'Oh my God, I can't believe it!' It was as if it were her and not her at the same time – her familiar voice saying his name, those dark slanting eye smiling at him. But her hair long and falling on her shoulders (she had had it chemically relaxed), make-up that made her glow, a secret glamour. Her dress in soft red, sleeveless, she was not thin…

'God, I can't believe it,' he said, and the few people around them laughed.

A haze in the room, smoke from the incense they were burning, the perfume making him light-headed, tilting his mind, a dreaminess in the material of her dress, how altered she was, how so much more of her there was. He coughed.

'Is the incense bothering you?' she asked him.

A blur as someone suggested that the two of them sit out on the balcony. It would be cooler there, just for a while, until they could get a lift to the hotel. He followed her out into a sultry darkness, a privacy granted without doors or curtains, the classical African sky dwarfing the city below.

She did not chat like she usually did. He could not stop looking at her and she became shy, overcome. He wanted to tell her she was beautiful, he wanted to tell her about the ceremony, about the last few days and how he had missed her, but the words, any words wouldn't come. He was stilled, choked by a kind of brightness.

At last she said, 'Can you see the henna pattern on my palms? It's light enough.' He could trace, in the grey light of the stars, delicate leaves and swirls.

'I'll wear gloves,' she said, 'when we go back to Scotland, I'll wear gloves, so as not to shock everyone.'

'No, you needn't do that,' he said, 'it's lovely.'

It was his voice that made her ask. 'Are you all right, you're not well?' She put her hand on his cheek, on his forehead. So that was how soft she was, so that was how she smelt, that was her secret. He said without thinking, 'It's been rough for me, these past days, please, feel sorry for me.'

'I do,' she whispered, 'I do.'

Tomi Adeaga

Marriage and Other Impediments

My friend Veronica told me some years ago about a friend of hers who was in love with a German guy and wanted to get married to him, but his parents categorically refused to accept her as their future daughter-in-law. In fact, his mother almost went mad at the thought of her son giving her '*kleine Neger Enkelkinder*'. But, I never knew I would find myself in the same situation later. Paradoxically, even my parents vehemently refused to give their consent to the union. They could not bear the thought of their daughter getting married to a German guy. Looking back at the whole incident now, I do not fail to see the disparities born not only out of differences in language but also in cultures and mentalities. This is my story...

Indeed, the thought of getting married at twenty-seven years ought to be a source of joy for me, but instead, it is a source of worry. *Ach du je!* How am I going to tell my dad that the guy I've chosen is not a Nigerian, but a German? What am I going to do, I asked myself? Just then, the phone rang and my dad was on the line. Blood rushed into my head and I almost choked.

'Tola, my dear child, how are you?' he asked me.

'Fine, Dad, and you, have you missed me?' I said breathlessly.

'Yes, honey bunch, I've missed you. It's been such a long time since you last came home on a visit. I know you're busy, but we also want to see more of you.'

'How are Mom and my siblings?'

'They're all doing fine. Even little Dola is now a big girl.

You'll hardly recognise her because she was still a baby at the time you left for Germany.'

'Dad, I do want to visit you soon. I've got some wonderful news for you.'

'Really, what is it, a boyfriend or promotion at work?'

'Dad, I'm engaged.'

'*_l_run seun o!!* Praise God. My child, this is the most wonderful news you've given me since you went to study in that country. When are you going to introduce him to us?'

'Soon, Dad, soon,' I said.

'Are you bringing him home with you, to introduce him to the rest of the family?'

'Not yet, but I'm coming home next week and he'll come later,' I said evasively.

'Whose child is he? Do we know his family? Anyway, we will discuss all that later. I will tell your mother the good news as soon as she wakes up. I'm sure she'll call you later. We have to start making preparations for the wedding.'

'Dad, you're going too fast, it's not like we want to get married tomorrow,' I said.

'I know my child, but I'm excited because it's not every day you tell me you want to get married,' he said with a joyful voice.

'Dad, please have Titi make arrangements for me to be picked up at the airport by next week Saturday,' I said.

'Okay, sleep well dearest. We love you.'

'Love you too, Dad.'

He hung up and I sank to the floor, wondering why I had let him assume that Till is a Nigerian and not German. What am I going to do now? I have to tell my dad the truth and give him time to get used to the idea. When I agreed to get married to Till, we both knew what problems it was likely to bring. The first hurdle we had to jump was with his family. Looking back at what happened then, I can't help but marvel at the way Till handled the situation and made his family give their consent to our impending marriage. His parents, Margit and Klaus

Sutherer, and his paternal grandmother, Ursula, live in the posh part of Olpe in Sauerland, North-Rhine Westphalia. They were not euphoric when we told them of our decision to get married. In fact his Omi Ursula angrily exclaimed in their Sauerländer Platt dialect '*Wat is? Biste von allen juten Geistern verlassen? Du glaubst ja woll nit, dat die in der Lage sind zu lieben. Se heiraten doch alle wegen de Papiere. Neuerlich sprach iek met meiner Freundin Jerda und se erzählte mir dat dai Frau ihres Enkels, Jürgen wegjelaufen sei und zwar nachdem se ihre Papiere hatte. Es kann nix Jutes drauskommen. Klaus sprich met deinem Sohn, iek glaube er is verhext worden. Dies is de einzije Erklärung für sein Verhalten.*' (What? Are you mad? You most certainly do not believe that they can fall in love. They all get married to get their papers. I recently spoke with my friend, Jerda, and she told me that her grandson, Jürgen's wife, left him after she got her papers. Nothing good can come out of it. Klaus, talk to your son; I think he's been bewitched. This is the only explanation for his behaviour.)

Till's father, a medical doctor, also tried to talk him out of it without success. He then threatened to disown him if he went ahead with the wedding to the '*Negerin*'. His mother was also very much against her only son getting married to a '*Negerin*'. She said, 'How can someone whose family lives in a jungle somewhere in Africa think she's good enough for my son? What will the neighbours say when they suddenly see *kleine Negerlein* running around in our garden? I'm not going to have anything to do with the marriage. I will not have you bring shame into our family by tainting our blood with this woman.'

Till asked his family how they could simply draw such conclusions without even taking the trouble to get to know me and my family. His mother said, 'We don't have to do so because Africa is a poor and uncivilised continent where the inhabitants depend on aid from hard-working German taxpayers. Once you get married, you'll have all those hungry looking villagers asking you and your family for aid. Is this the kind of life you want to lead?' But he was undaunted and told them he had no intention of marrying someone else. They would just have to get used to me becoming a part of their family. These discussions went back and forth for a while and when his parents saw that they were getting nowhere, they started tolerating me but didn't take to me.

A week later, Till came to help pack my bags and stayed with me to assuage my fears before I boarded the plane. While holding on tight to him, I realised that a lot depended on my family giving me their consent, because no matter how long I may have lived away from home, I still cannot do away with my traditions. It has been the most important part of my education.

With these thoughts I disembarked from the plane and walked absentmindedly out of the Muritala Muhammed International Airport in Lagos.

'Tola! Tola! Tola!' a familiar voice broke into my reverie.

'Hey, Titi!' I said, jumping on my sister.

We held on to each other for some time before breaking away and walking outside to the parking lot, where Titi's chauffeur was waiting for us. After getting into the car, Titi turned to me and asked how my journey had been.

'Fine,' I said.

'Congratulations! Dad told me you intend to get married soon, is it true?' she enquired.

'Yes it is,' I responded.

'But why are you looking so sad, as if someone just died?' she pressed me. 'Shouldn't you be bubbling with joy at the thought of your impending nuptials?'

'Titi, he's German,' I said.

'Sho,' she said in pidgin English, 'wetin happen? Of all the men wey dey for yonder, you no fit get yourself a Nigerian man?'

'Wetin dey do you, Titi?' I replied in the same format. 'You done come visit me before and you done see the kind people wey dey for there. Abi, you see one black face wey ah fit take home with me?'

'How you go come tell the family? Abi, you go paint him face black?'

'I guess I will have to talk to Mom and Dad,' I rejoined.

'Well, good luck. I can see we're home and they all seem to be waiting eagerly for you. Wait till evening before you drop the bomb on them, okay?' she advised.

'Have I got any choice? I can't spoil their joy at seeing me now.'

Just then, the car stopped in front of my parents' house in Victoria Island Extension. 'Hmmm,' I inhaled the salty, beach air I had missed so much.

Dola, my little sister, suddenly came running out of the house and threw herself on me. 'Big sis, sis, sis, welcome! Welcome! Welcome!'

'Hi, little one, or should I say big lady. How you've grown; you're now twice my size. What have you been eating?'

'Hehehe, nothing much. Come in, everyone is waiting for you in the family lounge. Hope you brought something nice for me?'

'Of course I did.'

'Mom, Dad, I'm home,' I said and walked right into their open arms and knelt down to greet them. My mom was overjoyed to see me and my dad was beaming from ear to ear.

My mom started reciting my oriki as a sign of her happiness.

'Welcome home my daughter,' my dad said.

Titi came in, closely followed by my brother, Bayo.

'Hi, Tola!' said Bayo and gave me a bear hug.

I was totally overwhelmed by the warm welcome I received, which made my news all the harder for me to tell. What am I going to do? I kept asking myself.

After having settled down, my dad and mom called me to their sitting room upstairs, away from the rest of the family.

'How was your journey, my child?' my dad asked.

'Fine, it went smoothly,' I responded.

'How is your fiancé?' my mom asked in an excited voice.

'Oh, he's fine,' I replied, a bit hesitant.

'What is wrong with you, my child? Aren't you happy that you've finally found a man of your kind? I thank God that you have not brought one of those Germans back home with you,' my dad added quietly.

'Dad, Mom, please sit down, I've got something to tell you,' I said.

They both sat down on the settee and waited expectantly for me to say something.

'My fiancé's name is Tillmann Sutherer and he's German,' I said quietly. I waited and waited, but no sound came from my parents. My mom jumped up and put her hands on her head. She started screaming in Yoruba.

'*_k_ mi*, you want to kill me! Where is all this nonsense coming from? Can you show me a member of the family who went to study abroad and came back with an *oyinbo* and a German for that matter?'

After a long time, my dad stood up and walked away and my mom followed him. My mom's tirades were painful but they did not hurt me as much as my father's silence.

Although they both refused to come out of their bedroom for the rest of the evening, we could still hear them arguing until late into the night. My mom was doing most of the talking. She was worried about what the other members of the family were most certainly going to say. How will I show my face in public, she screamed. Everybody will say that after spending all that money to send her abroad, she had to repay us by choosing to get married to one of those *oyinbos* and a German for that matter. They don't even have a compound. Who will we talk to if there are family issues to discuss? How can they understand us when they don't even speak our language? My mom went on and on and on and my dad said little.

I went into my old room and looked round. Nothing had changed because it had been kept intact. I suddenly remembered those good old days when I was growing up, when my friends and I used to spend a lot of time in my room listening to music and talking about boys and parties, like most teenagers did at that time. After much deliberation, I settled down for the night and tried to sleep. I kept tossing in bed and but couldn't sleep.

'Tola, Tola, my daughter,' my father said and he shook my shoulders.

'Dad, what is wrong?' I asked in a startled voice.

'Nothing, I just need to talk to you and since you're also unable to get some sleep, I feel this is just the suitable time to discuss the problem at hand. There is a proverb in our culture which says that a child whose parents bless her first thing in the morning, when she wakes up, she will come to no harm. This is what we want for you. Although we know that you're of age, we are still responsible for you. Remember that, in our culture, when you marry someone, you also marry the whole family. If this man marries you, he should know that he is also marrying the whole family.'

'But Dad,' I protested.

'No, my child, hear me out,' my dad responded. 'I know that parents are supposed to lead their children up to the stage where they can walk the streets of life on their own. But we still need to express our views on important things like this. How did you meet this man?'

'I met him through a friend in Bonn and to be honest with you, I didn't want to have anything to do with him. But he didn't let my reaction deter him from coming after me and after some time, I found I liked him and gave in. It took a long time for me to get used to the idea, because living in Germany has made me aware of the problems mixed relationships face. But since love is one thing we cannot control, I am prepared to deal with the problems when they come.'

'Hmm, but what about your future, have you given it a thought? It is one thing for you to live there as a foreigner, it's another thing for you to be married to one of them. They will never accept you. Look around you, do you think he will also be accepted in this family? It is not just enough to speak a language; you also have to understand a person's culture. Quite frankly, we will never understand his culture, and ours will be strange to him as well.'

'Dad, I've thought of it a lot and I know the path we've chosen is a rough one. But I can only get married to him with your blessings because without your moral support, I will not survive it. Things are changing today and the world I move in is a multi-cultural one. Sorry Dad, I'm deviating again. No, I know it is supposed to be a marriage between the two families, and not just the two of us, and I've also prepared Till as much as possible for it. Please do say you agree!'

'I only want the best for you and if you insist on going on with this relationship, then you'll have to live with whatever comes out of it. Are you prepared to do so?'

'Yes, Dad, I am,' I replied. 'I'm prepared to face the consequences.'

'Okay, let me talk to the rest of the family and we'll see how it goes.'

'Dad, there is one question that has been burning in my mind,' I said. I paused a bit and chose my words carefully.

'Why is it that when a male child brings a white girl back home as wife, she is accepted as our wife, our *iyawo*, but if a female child introduces an *oyinbo* as her future husband or husband, a lot of fuss is made over it?'

My dad paused for a minute before responding. 'My child,' he said, 'it's easier for a white woman to adapt to our culture because she is marrying into our culture and is considered part of it. But the female experience is different because she is marrying into a white family which, in most cases, already has a preconceived notion of what blacks look like. Those *oyinbos* generally feel that we are uncivilised and that we still live in the Stone Age. They don't know that, just as things are changing in the rest of the world, so are they changing for better or for worse in parts of Africa. My child, I don't want to see you hurt or treated like a second- or even third-class citizen by your husband's family, who probably feel they're better than you based on your skin colour. I know you have to get married, but I don't want you to lower your standards by settling for the second best.'

'Dad, his family is well off. His dad is a medical doctor and his mom is a housewife,' I responded.

'So, are they willing to accept you wholeheartedly into their family?' he enquired.

'We're still working at it,' I answered.

'Sleep now and we'll talk more about it tomorrow morning.'

The next morning, my mom came to my room, just as I was getting ready to take a shower.

'Tola,' she said, 'I refuse to give my consent to this marriage. It is not done that a child of mine whom I carried in my womb for nine months could take it upon herself to get married to an *oyinbo* man. What is wrong with you? Do you want to bring shame to our family? As if the world we live in today is not hard enough. Look at those mixed race kids at the Ikoyi club, their parents may be rich, but they still cannot dictate how society should accept them. They're neither here nor there. This is not the future I have in mind for my grandchildren. I don't want them to be strangers in their mother's country because of their skin colour! Moreover, what guarantee do you have that you will grow old with this man? No, no, let me finish what I'm saying! What if his family decides to give him a girl who will bear children whose skin colour will be like theirs? Has this thought never crossed your mind? Yes, I know he is standing by you today but will he always do so? I do not want you to get married to him because they will alienate you from your family!'

'Mom, I am very much aware of the problems you just talked about, but we cannot always choose who to fall in love with. I know we will work them out when the time comes. There is no guarantee that a marriage will work out. It is up to us to make it work. Apart from that, I have no one else to marry. You're not losing your daughter – instead you're gaining a son.'

'Tola, I refuse to carry on with this discussion because it is getting us nowhere.' She then walked out and shortly afterwards she left the house.

Later that evening, my mom's brother, Uncle Bade, came round to see us and he didn't waste time with pleasantries. He said that my mom had told him of my intention to get married to a German man. 'What is wrong with you?' he asked. 'Do you want to kill your parents? If you couldn't find a Nigerian to marry there, why didn't you come back home to choose a husband? Must you bring such shame to us?'

'No, uncle, it is not my intention to make you all unhappy. I cannot know if it is going to succeed without giving it a try. Tillmann is the only man I want to marry. I have tried to explain to Mom and Dad that I am interested only in him but they feel I'm making a mistake. I know their fears are grounded but what should I do, call off the wedding because of the culture clash?'

Uncle Bade stood up to leave and said he was going to talk to my parents later. The next day, a family meeting took place in our house and my parents' siblings as well as others from the extended family were present. They all raised their views on the situation. My dad spoke for the family and my mom looked on. After the arguments had gone on for a few hours, the head of my dad's family, my great uncle whom everyone calls Papa, raised his cane and told everyone to keep quiet. He paused for a moment before he started talking. He said that no one should blame me for choosing a white man.

'Athough I am old,' he said, 'I know that once we send our children abroad to study, there is no way we can stop them from making such choices. By coming home to tell her parents and family of her intention to marry a white man, it means that Tola has not forgotten her traditions and when the white man's family sees that we do not sell our children, that our children are precious to us, they will treat her well. They will know that we're keeping an eye on them and will not hesitate to take action if things should go wrong. Akin and Bunmi, as her parents, you have to let her go. Give your consent to this wedding!'

My dad thanked him and said both he and my mom would give their consent under the condition that both the engagement and wedding ceremonies take place in Lagos. They then called me in and Papa told me what the family had decided upon. I knelt down, as the tradition demands, and thanked all of them.

'I'm happy that you have given your consent to the wedding because without it, I wouldn't have gone ahead.'

Later I called Till and told him the family had given their consent to our wedding. He was euphoric with joy. After my two week stay at home, I had to fly back. Bayo and Dola took me to the airport and I tearfully boarded the plane. Till picked me up at the Köln-Bonn airport. We were both glad to see each other after the longest time we had ever spent apart. He wanted to know how my discussion with my family had gone so I told him what happened. We were really relieved that we could now look forward to the wedding.

Till went to visit his parents and related what I had told him. They were quite astonished because they failed to comprehend my family's aversion to the wedding. Until then, they had felt that my family would be happy that their child was getting married to a civilised man. They felt that they should be the ones to be against it, if anyone. Did this mean that they were unwanted?

'This is unbelievable!' his dad exclaimed. When they heard that it was going to take place in Lagos, they didn't put up much fuss because they were curious and wanted to meet my family. Shortly afterwards, the initial contact between both families was made on the phone as Till's dad called my parents and spoke with them. They then wrote a formal letter asking for my hand in marriage.

Afterwards, all the necessary arrangements were made and I flew home ahead of Till for the wedding. My prospective parents-in-law accompanied their son to the wedding and met with the members of my family who took care of all their needs. They were put up at the Federal Palace Hotel in Victoria Island and all their bills were paid. The engagement ceremony was modified for their sake and the wedding and reception were impressive. My parents-in-law enjoyed themselves so much that they decided to extend their visit for a few days.

On getting back to Germany, they could not stop telling stories and showing pictures of the wedding and my family to their family members and friends. Even Till's *Omi* Ursula had to concede that we are not the savages she thought we were. This is how I became Frau Sutherer and now live with my beloved husband, Till, and our two lovely kids in Bonn.

Chimamanda Ngozi Adichie

Transition to Glory

Her clothes smell of spices. It is the middle of the rainy season and as she cooks jollof rice, the ceiling fan is off, the rain slaps against the closed windows and the aroma from her pot rises in heady wafts and soaks into the living room curtains, into her clothes, into the bedcover in her tiny room. Later, she pulls her blouse over her head before getting into the bath and stops to breathe in curry and maggi and thyme. And doing that, she catches her breath, catches a sob in her throat. Yet, she didn't even cook much for Agha. Only once, in fact, the Saturday he came by from his tennis club. But it is the act of trying to catch something, or recapture something, that causes her pain, that causes the choking sounds to come from her. When she lies in bed and waits for sleep, when she tosses and clutches her pillow, she smells on it the scent of spices gone stale; and she gets up and rips off her pillowcase and her bed covers.

She rolled her car windows up as she approached the traffic jam at Oshodi. The last time, a hand had snaked into her car and yanked her left earring and necklace off, so swift and slick that she may have doubted it even happened but for her torn, bleeding ear. It happened last week, the jewellery snatching, and now she wondered if that young man whose hand had snaked into her car would have thought twice if he knew who she was. What if she had shouted, 'I'm Ozioma, from Ray Power FM.'? Would he have stared blankly at her before going on to snatch the necklace anyway? She liked to think not; she liked to think that both the 'big men' sitting behind their monster cars in the traffic jams of Victoria Island, and the alaye boys loitering on these market streets of Oshodi, listened to her show. Sometimes she wasn't so sure. Her producer said her audience was more of the former – but then her producer said a lot of things that made her wish she could slap his face.

It was hot in the car, her air conditioner was long broken, and her throat was starting to itch from the stuffiness. The traffic jam was chaos: a bus edged so close she thought it would scratch her, a hawker pressed a Celine Dion CD to her window, horns blared, drivers stuck out their heads and cursed. The sweat felt heavy on her neck and she lifted her braids and held them up in a ponytail with an elastic band. She would let them loose when she got to Surulere, to the hotel, because Agha liked them that way. Agha. She didn't want to think about him just yet, in the breathless heat of the car. She liked to keep thoughts of him special – aside – for when there was nothing else in her mind to taint them, to get in the way. Just as she liked to eat chocomilo sweets before she ate anything else so that the bittersweet cocoa taste would melt in her mouth, pure and unspoiled.

She finally drove out of the car mêlée of Oshodi and rolled her windows down, letting in a breeze that smelled like the flooded roadside gutter. Just before she turned into the hotel compound with purple bougainvillea climbing on its white walls, she pulled the elastic band from her hair and felt the tiny braids graze her neck. She parked and dabbed perfume behind her ears, blended her lipstick, arranged her breasts in her bra.

Agha was in the room, their room, watching CNN. His white T-shirt clung to the slight swell of his belly, as well as to the bulge of his arms kept youthful with tennis. She looked at him and felt the same thrill as the first day she met him, and she wondered, again, just what it was about this smallish man who walked with his back straight.

'How are you, eh?' he said. She liked it when he said that, the lazy way he spoke, and before she could say anything he

was touching her braids, pulling her to him.

He had just led her to the bed when his GSM phone rang. He got up and picked it up from the sofa, where he'd thrown down his tennis bag and racket. He looked at the number, hesitated, then placed the phone on the nightstand and let it ring.

'I should have switched it off,' he said, and when she asked, 'Was it your wife?' he didn't answer, he just he went on kissing her and she tasted the spring roll he had been eating.

She turns the TV on and a newscaster on NTA 10 is saying that it is the fourth straight day of rain in Lagos. There is footage of cars submerged in brown floods. During the commercial break, a pastor announces a special fellowship on the theme of Noah's Ark, a Bible pressed to his chest. She turns the TV off. The rain thumping on the roof is relentless, it pounds inside her head, and she wishes she had the flat downstairs. Agha had said he would get her a new flat, a ground floor flat in Abebe Court. 'How will I explain affording a place in Abebe Court?' she had asked him, teasing, and he said nothing, he only smiled in that quietly knowing way. She remembers that smile now, that moment in the hotel room, so clearly that she closes her eyes, shakes her head.

She feels faint. She is not sure when she last ate the bread on top of the fridge. Yesterday night? It couldn't have been, because when she picks up the bread, there are ringlets of purple mould all over it. She admires the pretty colours for a while, then opens the pot on the stove, full of jollof rice that feels sticky when she stirs it with a ladle. Her GSM phone starts ringing, and she wonders how that is possible – she switched it off, didn't she?

She looks around her small living room, not sure where the phone is, even though she is not prepared to answer it. The *Guardian* on the table is crumpled, almost into a ball, and she doesn't remember crumpling it; she never crumples newspapers anyway, she saves them and gives them to the mallam on the next street, the one with the tiny kiosk where she buys matches and sugar. He probably sells the newspapers to the akara hawkers, who use them to wrap akara. But she is not sure; she only knows that the mallam thanks her warmly whenever she gives the newspapers to him. Maybe it is also why he offers to find her a Water Boy during water scarcities, those lean boys who take her one hundred naira and come back with her jerry cans mysteriously full, even when the scarcity is all over the whole of Lagos mainland.

She slowly starts to straighten the *Guardian*; the mallam won't like it crumpled. She lays it on the table and is running her hand over it when she sees the face, Agha's face, the obituary announcement. And now she remembers crumpling the paper, she remembers seeing his face fill an entire page, below the words 'Transition to Glory', and she remembers the rain hitting her closed windows and she remembers thinking how stupid that sounded – Transition to Glory.

Her phone rang and a strange number appeared and, for a moment, she peered at it and wanted to ignore it, thinking that maybe some stranger who listened to Ray Power FM had gotten hold of her number. Finally, she picked it up. It was Agha.

'Are you using somebody's phone?' she asked.

He told her it was his; he had just bought a new phone to call her. Just her. From the way he said it, the timbre of his voice, she knew she was supposed to be pleased. But she wasn't. Instead, she felt irritation run over her like a cold shiver. He had bought the phone especially for her, a phone he could easily switch off when his wife was there.

'Can I see you, please?' he asked. They were not supposed to see each other today; he said he would be busy with meetings. Besides, her producer had just annoyed her. She was reading some of the letters that listeners sent in when he called her into his wood-panelled office and told her to ease off on the philosophy and keep it simple. Her listeners didn't much care that she thought God was a human construct, or else why did happy people serve a happy God and surly

people serve a mean God? Her listeners wanted, instead, to hear her poke fun at Obasanjo and all his sycophants, at the farce called democracy. They liked it the most – the phone lines were clogged – when she did her 'man-woman specials', like the one she did today when she poked fun at the women who stood on roadsides all over Lagos, as if they were waiting for taxis when they were really waiting for men to give them rides – men who were stupid enough not to realise that the women wanted to save transport money and were not interested in them.

She didn't agree with her producer, of course, she felt her audience, felt that they liked her questioning the deeper things in life in addition to mocking the shallower. So she said to him, 'You think everybody is a dunce like you, eh?' And he laughed and asked her to smile, to have a coke, because they both knew she would ease off on the philosophy: many people would give anything for her job. She walked out of the office with her lower lip clenched between her teeth, and now she was even more annoyed that Agha had gotten a phone just for her calls and she wanted to say 'no, I can't see you today and go to hell at that'. But she said 'yes'.

He smelled of sweat and 'Eternity for Men' when he hugged her at the door of the hotel room. She thought he would grab her and push her to the bed, but he ordered them shredded chicken with rice and after they had eaten, they sat up in bed and drank orange juice and he asked how her day had been. He said her producer was probably right; she had to keep the show simpler. Not many people can handle that first-class brain, he teased.

She knew he never missed listening to her show – and she wondered now if his wife listened to it, too, since it was on at the time when he would be at breakfast. His youngest child, Emeka, might be there as well as his daughter Nnennaya, the one who had just finished secondary school, whose chirpy photo was on his office desk. And perhaps the first daughter, Adamma, would drive by from her flat, on her way to work, and join the family for breakfast and they would all listen to her show.

At this thought, she moved away from his embrace, lay face-up on the bed. He didn't ask her what was wrong, and she wondered if he knew that she felt as though she had tripped and was now lunging, head first, into a deep hole; a deep hole full of cold water.

'Did you know it's three months into our affair,' she said. In her better moods, she liked that word – affair – liked the decadent affectation that clung to it. But now she said it in a tone that taunted him, that taunted everything.

'Did you know it's three months since I found happiness,' he said, in that slow, careful way. And she wanted to kick him, because he sounded so predictable. But it made a giddy, sneaky warmth course through her, nonetheless, hearing him say that.

'I have to be in London this weekend,' he said, after a while. 'I would like you to come with me.'

She didn't say anything, just kept looking at the ceiling. He reached out to touch her braids, she moved away and all of a sudden she wanted to shout – crazed loud shouting. She wanted to ask where his wife would be at the weekend. She wanted to ask if he ever was consumed with the same thoughts as she was; thoughts about right and need.

'Come to London with me, please,' he said. 'We'll stay the weekend and you'll be back in time for your show.'

He always spoke to her like that, quietly, courteously. Yet sometimes she wished he would raise his voice, do something, so that it would all seem more real.

She sits on the toilet seat and stares at the newspaper, at the slope of the print. Lovingly remembered by Didi and the children. Didi. She is sure Didi has done all the proper things a wife should do, followed all the traditions. Heaven knows, she would not have. She would not even have tolerated a funeral, or joined in the Igbo songs that would ask God to have mercy on him as though he had done something wrong, as though it was not he who needed to have mercy on God. She would not have sat with the visitors who would come in shaking solemn heads and muttering *ndo* in an irritating drone. She would not have worn all-black or all-white for a year. Is Didi wearing white or black she wonders.

Didi. Her name is Ndidiamaka but Agha called her Didi on the few occasions that he slipped and did not say 'my wife'. Didi. It is a name Ozioma dislikes, a name she would dislike even if it were not his wife's. It makes her think of a supercilious cat, or a furry white dog, or a rabbit. It reminds her of the Ikejianis who lived next door when she was growing up in Nsukka, and the green-eyed German Mrs Ikejiani raising rabbits with names like Didi and Fifi in wire-mesh cages in the garage. Mrs Ikejiani talked to the rabbits in German and stroked their fur on the days her husband staggered home late from the staff club, and then on Sundays Mrs Ikejiani selected the fattest of the rabbits for her stew.

Ozioma does not know where to get a rabbit in Lagos, does not even know who to ask about one. She finds her GSM phone under a chair (she does not remember flinging it there) and calls her producer. When she asks him if he knows where she can get a rabbit, he cackles and asks if she is now too big to eat beef and chicken like everyone else. Rabbit *kwa*?

She puts the phone down. There must be rabbits in Nsukka. Mrs Ikejiani went back to Germany years ago, even before she entered the University, but she is sure somebody will have rabbits in Nsukka.

She calls her producer to tell him she is going to Nsukka and he wants to know when she will be back because they start the new season in two weeks. She tells him she will be back in time for the show.

They were on the roof of the London tour bus, red and rickety, and when the rain started, he held her tight and kissed her. The guide was dashing down into the bus, the two couples behind them as well. But he kept kissing her, and the rain was warm on her head and it was so unlike him, this public display, and the breath mint she tasted on his tongue was sharp and sweet. Finally, when the rain slowed, he unwrapped her from his arms and helped her up. They got off at the next stop, Trafalgar Square.

A wizened man, Indian-looking, with folded skin the color of cinnamon, came up to Agha and asked, 'You want pigeon on your wife's head?'

He had a crumpled bag in his hand, pigeon food, and he offered to pour it on her head so the pigeons would land on her. Nice photos, he said, they make nice photos; for only one pound. Agha laughed and gave the man five pounds, waved him away. 'There must be more dignity in farming a piece of land in Bangladesh, abi?' he asked her.

'You don't know he's from Bangladesh,' she said and laughed, a laugh that did not need something funny, really, like a drunken laugh.

He sat down on the pavement and pulled her down on his lap, and they sat there, tangled and silly, and he said he had never done this in all his other times in London. He had never come to Trafalgar Square or been on a tour bus; never had the time to talk to a pigeon man; to do the touristy things. He said nothing about the man calling her his wife. She wished he had and so, as they got up and walked along with their hands locked, she asked if his wife would have wanted pigeons on her head.

'I don't know,' he said and then he changed the subject and asked what she thought of a statue nearby and she wanted to cry. The tears felt so close. She started to run across the wet ground; she hoped that the air would rush past her ears and clear her head, take the tears back. He was chasing her, she heard his heavy breathing behind, and when he caught her wet coat, he held her to him and pressed his lips to her neck.

'You want to give an old man a heart attack, eh?' he said. He held her for a while and then finally they walked to the road and took a cab to an Italian restaurant in Piccadilly. He pretended to speak poor English to the cab driver, and then

gave him a huge tip afterwards. He laughed with the hostess at the restaurant. He reached out and took her hand as they were seated, then came over and kissed her. He seemed a different person, as if something that had fit just right back in Lagos was now a little loose.

A Ghanaian couple on the way out came up and introduced themselves: Abena and Djangmah from Accra. They were slightly drunk. 'We knew right away that you were real West Africans,' they said, with generous laughter. 'We all know how those Londonised West Africans look, and of course those Kenyans and Tanzanians are different from us, talk less of the Jamaicans!'

They assumed she was his wife, and it didn't help when Agha said, 'Ozioma and I live in Lagos.' As though they came together, two making one.

After the Ghanaian couple left, she asked him, 'Is that how you would have introduced your wife?' And because she knew he would shrug and change the subject again, she added, 'Tell me about your wife.'

'Don't do this,' he said, taking her hand. But it annoyed her, the way he said that, as if he were acting a film, as if he were saying what he thought he was supposed to say.

'Tell me,' she said. 'Tell me about her.'

'What is there to tell?'

'Anything, just anything,' she said. So he told her about the marriage rites, before the white wedding, when they first did the Door Knocking and then the Bride Price and finally the Wine Carrying. How her uncles had complained that the cow was small, that the yams were not that big, that the kegs of palm wine were not that many. She didn't ask him to stop, she should have, but she didn't. She should have told him she was only bringing his wife up to remind them both that a wife existed, somewhere, rather than to talk about his wife. She should have asked him, didn't he realise that her bringing his wife up was because she was afraid to bring other things up. But she didn't. Instead she imagined that it was to her father's

house that he and his people had brought the palm wine and the yams. And when he told her that, during the Wine Carrying ceremony, the children in the neighbourhood had stolen a lot of meat, fried beef wrapped in banana leaves and hidden in pans, she even laughed.

Later, as they lay in bed in the Kensington hotel room, she said, almost in a whisper, 'I don't know what is happening to me.' And he held her close and stroked her braids and she wished he would say something but he didn't. Finally, she asked, 'Do you know your name means war? It's a bad sign, being with a man called War.'

And he said, with humour, 'And do you know yours means gospel? It's a good sign being with a woman called Gospel.'

The house in Nsukka looks the same; it has the same smells from her childhood, the smells of cleaning detergent and spices. The dining room curtains are different, though, they are a brighter yellow. Her mother likes cheerful colours: the living room curtains are pink. She thinks she remembers her mother mentioning the new curtains the last time they talked, but she is not sure. Talking to her mother is a monotony of 'I know you have a good job but you need to find a nice young man,' and so sometimes she puts the phone on the table as her mother talks, so she can fold her clothes or stir her stew.

She hugs her mother, says nothing is wrong; she just wanted to come visit for a few days. Her mother's friends are in the living room, fat women, all members of the Legion of Mary, with black scarves tied across their foreheads. They hug her one after another. They say she has lost so much weight and ask if she is all right, if she recently had malaria. She tells them that somebody died.

'*Onye*?' they ask. 'Who died?'

She tells them it is the man she was engaged to and she keeps her face blank because she knows her mother is looking at her in bewilderment.

'Ewooooo,' the women moan, 'your mother did not even tell us you were engaged.' She knows her mother has offered endless masses for her to find a husband and she knows her mother's friends have given up on her. Now for her to have come so close to being married – she has their sympathy and more now.

The house help brings her rice and plantains on a plate and she sits at the dining table and stares at the food and listens to her mother's friends talking in the living room. She is sitting on the seat she sat on as a teenager, looking at the same painting of a serene woman – Tutu by Ben Enwonwu – that has hung there forever. She is leaning on the same wood table that she leaned on when she was a seven-year-old with a runny nose, long before she knew that Agha existed, that she would fall for a man with a quiet smile and a careful voice who would die before she had a chance to sort her feelings out, to sort anything out. She wonders if it was all predestined. When she was that child climbing the mango tree right outside this dining room, was Agha already pencilled into her life?

She shakes her head, shakes the tears back, and asks her mother's friends if they know where she can get a rabbit and they say, of course, a man in Orba sells them, and they look at her strangely because they are wondering what she wants with, of all things, a rabbit.

The rabbit she gets is grey and its puff of a tail is white. Very meaty, the man in Orba says, feeling the rabbit's thighs. Very meaty.

She doesn't bargain, she only asks that the man get her a leash and even though he looks at her oddly – how crazy these young people from Lagos behave nowadays – he gets her a dog leash and she puts it round the rabbit's neck before leaving.

She mostly ignores her mother, watches the days slide past and walks barefoot under the rains. The rains are different here, more fragrant, less angry. The mud stains her feet red and sometimes she stops to make a careful imprint of the rabbit's feet on the path or to pluck a wild grass or to touch an anthill. They take slightly different paths to Odim Hill every day, she and the rabbit, and at the top of the hill they drink from a plastic water bottle, she first and then the rabbit, sometimes from the cap of the bottle, other times from the cup of her palm.

'Look,' she says to the rabbit. 'Look how the hills are laid all around us; I can see God's hand doing it.' It is what her mother used to tell her when she was a child, and she would see God's brown hands with clipped nails, laying out the green-covered hills of Nsukka. But that was when God still had some sense, she thinks now, when he laid out those hills.

She lets the rabbit play in the backyard, after the walks. The leash is long, as much freedom as possible, but she holds on to it anyway because anything can happen – the frangipani trees can fall and squash the rabbit, the lean guava trees can rain hard unripe fruit down. She sits under the mango tree, swats at the flies following the fallen mangoes, and watches carefully for an accident, ready to pull at the leash. Somebody should have put a leash on Agha; somebody should have pulled his car back before the drunken trailer driver ran into it on Ibadan road.

But then, if what her mother says is right – that it was God's will – then the leash would have broken or that car would have careened into Agha somehow, anyhow. (She had told her mother a sketchy story, and let her assume that Agha had been single and Catholic and a nice young man.) God's will. It really is the same thing as God's fault. Blame God. But she doesn't blame God for doing it, she blames Him for not preventing it. It is a healthier way to think, a more reasonable way, and then she realises that Agha would have liked her thinking that way. She gets up, picks the rabbit up and goes to her room. She lies in bed and remembers how Agha slept with his hands tucked under the pillow, how easy it was for him to fall asleep after he came. She wonders if Didi saved the last pillowcase he slept on, if it still bears the indentation of his head – she would have saved it. She wonders what his bedroom at home looks like, if he used to leave chewed toothpicks on his nightstand like he did those nights in their London hotel room.

She gets up, beginning to cry, and starts to pick up the dark balls of rabbit shit from her bedroom floor.

Ozioma watched him sleep. She was sated, tired, but she could not sleep because it was his first visit to her flat and he would leave soon – he was supposed to be at the tennis club – and she wanted to remember every minute. His snoring was raspy. She reached out and touched his lips, which were slightly parted. Then she moved closer and placed her cheek next to his. He stirred, mumbled something, and she thought she heard her name. She smelled the spices on his breath, the thyme and curry from the jollof rice she'd cooked; the rice he'd eaten with the same attentiveness that he paid her body. He was so very gentle. She liked that he took his time, that he looked in her eyes for long, eloquent moments, that he had a spreading waist. Did it make sense? She wished she could ask somebody, but there was nobody to ask. She couldn't even imagine asking Chikwere. Chikwere was her only friend who knew about Agha. But she didn't like to talk too much about Agha with Chikwere, because she was scared that somehow it would slip out that she could not imagine dating any young man, that she practised her first name and Agha's last name in front of her bathroom mirror. Chikwere would laugh, she knew, but worse, Chikwere would not understand. And Chikwere might even tease her and say in Igbo 'Nekwanum anya biko,' – is he not almost fifty? 'Haven't you heard that if you must eat a frog, then eat a bull frog so that when they call you a frog-eater you can answer? If you want to get serious with a man, then, my dear, find a real man!'

She was gently stroking the hair on his arm when he opened his eyes. She said she was sorry she had woken him and he said no, it was fine, and he had a strange expression as he looked around her tiny room, at her dressing table crowded with creams, her mirror plastered with photos, her shelf lined with books.

'What are you thinking?' she asked.

'I shouldn't have come,' he said. 'Being here, where you live, makes me want something more. It makes me want more than I should.'

There was something to the way he said 'live,' the way he stressed it; he had never said anything like that before. At first she was happy that he said that because it meant that his mind was not always as careful as his smile. Then she was angry that he said that because it meant he did not think he should want more.

'I'm driving to Ibadan tomorrow. I would ask you to come with me but it's just for a meeting and then I'll be back in the evening. Can I see you when I come back?' he asked.

'No.'

He looked at her for a while then got up and started to get dressed. And she wondered why he never asked her to snap out of it, why he was never insistent.

'I'll call you when I get back,' he said.

'What if your wife goes to the tennis club one of these days?' she asked.

He said nothing. He placed a small wrapped box on the table before he left, one of the many politely quiet things he did, leaving her presents – and they were always wrapped – this one a necklace and matching earrings.

The people she walks past on Odim Street, before she gets to the hill, no longer try to grasp her hand, not after she sank her teeth into the shoulder of the woman who forced her into an embrace. Now they focus their sympathetic glances on the leash around the rabbit's neck. It is the same look Doctor Nwoye has; her mother brings him often, begs her to talk to him.

The day before she leaves Nsukka, she asks the house help to kill the rabbit and she cooks it herself, makes a stew with tomatoes and onions. She adds no spices, not even salt, and the meat is bland and tough and she suffers indigestion through the night.

When her bus stops in Lagos the next day, she takes a taxi but she does not tell the driver to go to Yaba, where she lives. Instead she tells him to go to Victoria Island, where Agha lives, where Agha lived. At the compound gate, a simple gate, not the ostentatious structures lining the rest of the street, the gateman asks her what she wants, eyeing her travelling bag. She tells him to tell madam that Ozioma from Ray Power FM is here. The gateman lights up, clutches her hand, asks her to come in and before he goes to the front door to announce her presence, he points at the black transistor radio in his booth and tells her he never misses her show.

A maid lets her into a living room with wide spaces and elegant, uncomfortable-looking chairs. Is this what is called Queen Anne furniture, she wonders. She knows the huge photo on the wall is Agha but she avoids looking right at it as she sits on the tip of a sofa.

Didi appears. She is everything Ozioma imagined, light-skinned and manicured, wearing a black *bou-bou* with exquisite embroidery down its front. Didi is looking at her and it is clear – by the sudden moist tension in the air – that Didi knows who she is, what she is, what she was.

'Will you drink orange juice?' Didi asks.

Ozioma stares at her, startled, because it is the last thing she expects. Didi is the kind of woman that she would poke fun at in her show, the kind of woman who goes to the Nail Studio twice a week, who receives calls from boutique owners when they get a new shipment from Italy and Dubai.

'Or would you prefer a coke? Malt?' Didi's face is expressionless.

'No,' Ozioma finally says when she finds her voice. 'No, thank you.'

Didi sits down. 'How dare you come here? How dare you?'

The question does not surprise Ozioma, but Didi's calmness does. And she realises how like Agha Didi is, the same calm smile, the same civil coating over their body movements. The same incredible control. They are both cultured, worldly people, Agha and Didi. Ozioma feels a strange helplessness, a weightlessness; she is sure she would float away if she jumped up now, if her feet left the ground. 'Did he tell you about me?' she asks.

Didi is silent for a while. 'He was perfect, my husband. He was perfect at lying, he was perfect at everything.' A pause, and for the first time, there is a sneer on Didi's face, or maybe the sneer has always been there and lets itself out now. 'No, my dear, of course he didn't tell me about you.'

'Then how did you know?'

'I assume you expect me to answer your question.' Didi shifts on her seat and slowly crosses her legs. 'What I find interesting is that my daughter Adamma is a year older than you.' Didi is smiling, and even though it is that familiar civil smile, Ozioma sees the rage in it, in the stretch of lip over teeth. Suddenly she too is angry, she too feels full of a frothy rage that bubbles up in her, that buoys her up and she shouts, 'How do you know how old I am, eh?'

Didi says nothing. Ozioma feels a churning in her stomach, a mish mash of emotions. There is a long stretch of silence, like a taut string tied from Didi's sofa to hers, and then Didi starts to cry. She has her head in her hands and she is sobbing and her shoulders are moving and for a moment Ozioma wonders if Didi is playing a joke, this woman who offered her orange juice instead of calling the gateman to throw her out.

But she knows the tears are real when she hears the familiar choking sounds – the same sounds that have come out of her, the sounds of angry grief, of grieving anger. She wants to go over and touch Didi, sooth her, say '*ebezi na*', but she decides not to, because she does not trust herself and she does not trust Didi.

She gets up and quietly lets herself out.

Sefi Atta

The Lawless

We were third year theatre arts students due to graduate in the summer of 1994 when the Abacha regime closed down our university, just two weeks before our convocation ceremony. They announced the closure was for public safety, but who didn't know they were punishing our students' union? That hapless body of enthusiasts, still hoarse from screaming 'no' to the IMF, had organised a peaceful protest in support of the National Democratic Coalition. All they succeeded in rallying were a few area boys, who marched to our Chancellor's office, threw petrol bombs through his window, set a couple of lecturers' cars on fire, assaulted the cooks in the canteen, while chanting, 'Sufferin' rights for de masses.'

This was just after our President Elect was detained, way before his wife was assassinated. Anyone who dared to disagree with the regime's constitutional conference was being spirited off by State Security for questioning. Those who could, and would, had fled overseas to claim political asylum. Lagos was not exactly a peaceful paradise when the Lawless was formed. We were not a band of armed robbers, or some student cult. We certainly had no intention of adding to the bloodshed around. I, for one, feared barbarism and guns more than I did the student unionists with their placards and self-righteousness.

The founding members of the group were Crazehead, Professor, Fineboy, Shango and I, Ogun. They were out-of-town friends who asked if they could stay with me until our university reopened, and I said yes. It was the middle of the rainy season, no time to be looking for a place to bunk.

Fineboy was from the Niger Delta, thick-chested, and he had all that Norwegian ancestry working for him. He'd slept with girls from all faculties. The rich ones wouldn't speak to him after they'd used him. They said he was a bushman: he couldn't use a fork and knife properly.

Professor was another who had good reasons to begrudge women: his small hands, small feet. Add to that, his back was crooked from scoliosis, so he panicked when he got undressed and couldn't successfully get laid. To save himself, he wrote poetry. His tributes to Biafra were so masterful they drove a literature lecturer to accuse him of plagiarism. I told the Professor I wasn't taking any of that tribal bullshit from him. The Civil War ended decades ago and Nigeria was one nation now, united in its mess. He said, 'But you don't know what I witnessed as a boy. My father got shot in the head. My family almost starved. My whole town was razed . . . ' He went on and on until I apologized for my insensitivity and stupidity. The little liar! His family were in France throughout the war. True, true, he was a poet.

Crazchcad, now, hc had spcnt morc timc in Fcla Kuti's nightclub, Shrine, than he had on campus. IIe mixed up his 'II's like a typical Yoruba, had these crowded teeth covered in plaque, and his eyes were perpetually red and swollen. At one point he said he was giving up theatre arts to be in an afro juju band. 'Doing what?' I asked him. 'Shaking the *shekere*?' Crazehead had no musical talent whatsoever, except for singing off-key after he'd smoked a joint. He said the purity of his falsetto intimidated the other band members, so they were jealous and they dropped him. Perhaps it was Crazehead's belches that overpowered that band. 'What the hell did you eat, man?' I once asked when he let out a combination of fried fish, boiled eggs and mango. He rubbed his belly and explained that hactually, 'emp made him 'ungry, and he had inherited a susceptibility to food allergies, 'ence he experienced occasional bloating. I asked him to clean himself up, from all orifices. The guy was a bloody mess. He was the one who asked me to consider using real guns on our opening night as the Lawless. 'That's the trouble with you,' I said. 'Too many drugs in your blood. Too many *Rambo* movies in your head.'

Shango was my right hand man. We named him after the god of thunder and lightning whom he played in the one-act, written by him and me, though I did most of the creative work because Shango wasn't exactly what you call 'that bright'. The Goethe Institute in Lagos agreed to sponsor us. Shango received a standing ovation for his suicide scene, during which he pretended to hang himself. He was over six foot tall with deep dimples, the darling of our drama association in university. Women trusted him. He and I were room-mates in our first year and, I swear, he had lace curtains hanging from our barred windows, a jar of hibiscus on the floor next to his mattress with semen stains. For a while there he was a Buddhist, and then a Seventh-Day Adventist. Shango was just big for nothing, really. He couldn't swipe a mosquito without feeling guilty. He wouldn't even squash the cockroaches that sauntered into our kitchen, snatched bits of bread, and strutted out. Crazehead chased them around and tried to pound them to pulp with his heels. 'Leave them alone,' Shango always pleaded. Cockroaches were just trying to survive, like us, he said.

We lived in the two-storey house my father had designed in Shapati Town, his hometown. Our plot had no street number and the street had no telephone lines. My father had had a brick wall built so high that armed robbers would need pole vaults to catapult themselves into the grounds. He must have envisaged them trying despite the odds; on top of his wall were broken bottle pieces, like jewels on the crest of his architectural crown. In our garden was his one concession to my mother, a now empty swimming pool, shaded by her favorite jacaranda and flame-of-the-forest trees. The pool was four feet at its deepest. My father, God rest his soul, could not swim. He had nightmares of dying by drowning, not by the bullet. That fate, he never expected in the fortress that was our home.

The garden all but blossomed into a bush after my family was killed. That happened one night while I was accepting my runner-up award for Mr Caveman on campus. I was also in the process of failing my first year in engineering. I came home the next morning with my inscribed Mr Caveman club and found them dead in the dining room. I broke all the windows in the house so that the whole of Shapati Town could hear me crying for them to come back to life, then crawled into the garden and sniffed the grass and earth until I wet myself. Shango found me out there and almost developed a hernia from trying to pull me away. I was clutching the grass and would not let go. Strangely, the blades did not break; they came out by their roots and I believe that was when I kind of lost my mind.

From then on, as a tribute to my family, I placed candles on the pool steps whenever the Lawless performed in the shallow end of the swimming pool. They also served as stage lights in the evenings, unless the rain unleashed on us. Our stage, of course, was missing tiles, and our backstage was a thatched gazebo. Our audience sat on the veranda of the house. They clapped during scenes, oftentimes jeered and shouted out warnings like, 'He's after you,' or 'He's plotting your demise.' One deaf man, who had a wandering eye, sounded a broken gong at the point of Shango's suicide. A more hilarious death knell I'd not heard. Some audience members, who couldn't help themselves, ran into the swimming pool and yanked off Professor's wig, or snatched his wrapper to see what he was wearing underneath. He played the goddess Oya, Shango's beloved wife, complete with red lipstick and thick Charlie Chaplin-like eyebrows.

Our audiences were people from the neighbourhood. They doubled as extras, stagehands, sound technicians. They improvised. They wanted us to ad lib. There was no dividing line between them and us, but this wasn't Wole Soyinka's intellectual mythology or street-level guerrilla theatre. This was theatre of the basest kind, theatre as it was performed in the villages of old, theatre as it was meant to be performed, or so we thought after enough bottles of Star Beer. The point was, who said theatre was dead in Nigeria?

Toyosi joined the group when we were tired of getting constipated from the roasted plantains and groundnuts we bought from local food hawkers. I was becoming more and more sluggish, particularly doing the acrobatic scenes in which I wrestled with Shango. One night, I tumbled on stage and couldn't get up again, and there I was, playing Ogun, the god of ore and war.

Toyosi was an actress in a soap opera. Her part had been discontinued due to 'lack of funding' – she refused to sleep with the producer. She came to see us after a show, with her plump daughter clamped to her hip.

'I'll cook for you,' she said, 'if you let me stay.'

'No space for you,' Professor said, shooing her away. 'I play the women here.'

'Did I say I was looking for a part?' she asked.

'What did you come here for then?' he said, removing his glasses to eye her up and down, as if she was sent to poison us.

Fineboy stepped forward, sticking out his massive chest. 'Beautiful lady, we go by aliases in this place. What shall we call you? Nerfetiti? Queen Amina of Zaria?'

I couldn't believe what the *bubbuh* was saying.

'Call me whatever you want,' Toyosi said. 'Just give me a place to stay.'

'I thought we were friends here,' I said. 'I thought we treated people with respect.'

I wanted her to like me more than the rest, even though I was about to let her down. We had no room for one more, let alone a woman with a child. She had cropped natural hair, bleached gold. It made her skin look darker. Her legs were a little bandy, and her expression was, well, sort of bored. I winked at her daughter.

'Hey,' I said.

The little so-and-so began to howl. She bucked and threw

her head back. Toyosi tried to hush her. The more she did, the louder the child cried. Then Toyosi unbuttoned her blouse and released the tiniest breasts I'd ever seen on a woman. None of us knew where to look, except Crazehead.

She eased her nipple into her daughter's mouth. 'You guys should really consider taking me in, you know. I'm writing a play and from what I've seen, you need better material.'

'Are you also a Broadway critic?' Professor snapped.

Toyosi smiled. She could have been teasing him.

'I've seen what *you* do,' she said.

Professor's voice became shrill. 'So say thanks then! Isn't it for free you entered?'

'Enough,' I said.

Sometimes I wondered about him. Why was he so effeminate? Toyosi shifted her daughter higher up her hip. She might as well have yawned. Her daughter was sucking away. She was such a pretty child.

'Em, what do you mean better material?' I asked, trying to focus on Toyosi's face.

'Come on,' she said. 'A play about warring Yoruba deities? It's like drama society in secondary school, not even original. Haven't you just copied Duro Ladipo's *Oba Koso*?'

'*Oba Koso* is based on the story of Shango. The story of Shango belongs to everyone.'

'Yeah, an old folktale.'

'Not a folktale. Shango is part of the Yoruba religion, like Adam and Eve in the Bible. You see? That is the problem with we Africans. We disrespect ourselves . . . '

She rolled her eyes. 'Oh, here we go again. Who cares? The story is so parochial and not relevant today. Then you wonder why no one will sponsor you and you have to end up performing in an empty swimming pool.'

'We had the Goethe.'

'They must have pitied you.'

'The British Council is considering.'

'You won't be lucky twice.'

'The Americans . . . '

'Who?' She clapped and doubled over as if I'd cracked a joke.

'Listen,' I said. 'Don't come here and insult us. It's bad enough everyone thinks our years of studying drama was a waste of time. Anyone who produces relevant plays in Nigeria of today will be locked up. You of all people should understand.'

She hissed. 'You're not acting. You're messing around over here, and you might impress a few expats, who are always suckers for an authentic cultural display, so steeped in native metaphor that the average Nigerian can't digest it, or thrill a few locals who can't tell the difference between a drama performance and a wrestling match, but don't expect me to be singing your praises after I leave this place.'

'At least we have formal training,' I said. 'At least we didn't get our training in a dubious local soap.'

'Theatre arts grads?' she said. 'You're right there at the bottom of the manure heap, next to the agriculture students. Tell me something, with no bio to speak of, who will employ you when you finally graduate?'

That led to fake coughs and covering of crotches.

'Excuse me,' I said. 'I have to talk to my friends.'

'No,' Professor said. 'I don't want her here. You heard how she insulted us. She'll come here and ruin everything.'

Everything. We were in what my mother would have called the parlour. I was on my father's faded reclining chair, the rest were sitting on sofas with pockmarks. The white paint on the wall was peeling, the carpet had missing patches, and the windows had wooden bars. I'd nailed the bars in myself after I'd smashed the panes. So many mornings, after overnight rains, we'd wake up to find puddles all over the floor.

'She didn't go for my line,' Fineboy murmured. 'Nerfetiti, Queen Amina of Zaria. Why didn't she go for my line?'

'Crazehead?' I asked, ignoring him.

Crazehead was scratching his head again. Did he have ringworm?

'Shango,' I said, hoping he might have something useful to add.

'You're the owner of the house,' he said, shrugging. 'It's your decision. Although, I don't know why she needs a place to stay. The way she speaks and behaves, she's an elite, definitely a pepperless chick. She even sounds like an away Nigerian. She probably went to school in England, probably has an old man somewhere with a house twice as big as this ... '

I'd almost forgotten his inability to stick to issues, any issue at hand. There was agreement all around; Toyosi was definitely an away Nigerian, a pepperless Nigerian, an assorted chick, an *aje* butter.

'So why is she an actress?' Professor asked. 'Aren't they working in a bank or in Daddy's law firm or medical practice?'

'Perhaps she's been thrown out of home,' I said. 'She has the baby girl and no ring on her finger. You know the elite: their children must carry on their shenanigans within wedlock, or else ... '

'Or else it's instant disownment,' Fineboy said, as though I'd reminded him of an incident in his past.

I had to ask Toyosi, since she had so many answers. 'I don't understand, a woman like you, why do you want to cook for a group of guys?'

She frowned. 'I beg your pardon?'

'Aren't you for the liberation of women?'

Her daughter was sleeping face up on the mattress that was my sister's. I couldn't confirm the mattress was free of bugs. My sister's photograph was in a square-shaped frame on her dresser. Sweet troublemaker, she had been fourteen at the time, and was always harassing me for fifty naira to buy fruit-flavoured lip gloss.

Toyosi shrugged. 'Why should I be for women's liberation? The person who chased my father and broke up my family is a woman. My mother herself, who threw me out of home, is a woman. Plus, what other skills do I have to offer a group of hungry guys?'

Her lips were so thin I could gobble them up with one parting of my mouth, or at least nibble on her lower one, I thought.

I sat on the mattress. 'Em, what about this play you're writing?'

'What about it?'

'Title?'

'The Lawless.'

'Premise?'

'The breakdown of society.'

That was huge. 'How many players?'

'I haven't written it yet. Don't keep hounding me.'

'Who's hounding you?'

She wagged her forefinger. 'Yes, you were. Yes, you were, just now. Stop it, you hear?'

Why did I still want her to like me? I kept trying: 'I suppose you must be fed up with the kind of material for women, em, actors . . . '

I'd read that in a magazine passed around the Theatre Arts department for so long that it had more palm oil stains than print. It came from a Hollywood actress with skin as delicate as crepe. She was half starved, and yet she wanted to be taken seriously. We looked to America for slang and elements of craft, and to our budding local Nollywood video and stage productions – not to the British; they were inaccessible, like their Queen's English.

'Poor parts for women,' Toyosi said, stroking her daughter's legs. 'That's a good reason to quit acting, not to pick up a pen.'

'I can never give up acting, *sha*.'

'You probably can't do anything else.'

'Not since I caught the bug.'

'It's more like a terminal disease to me. Me, I'm through with it.'

'How come you're so cold?' I asked.

She tucked her chin in. 'How come you're trying to sleep with me?'

If she didn't work miracles with beans and palm oil, I would have asked her to leave. Immediately. I would have told her, 'Look here, you're harsh, snobbish and not that attractive.'

I never once saw her write, but she could cook, and she had our scenes moving again. That, and the other good reason for having her around was that every girlfriend I'd ever had had looked endearing, even the campus sluts and sugar daddy types I ended up with. Whatever their conduct in private, they were the sort of women my mother would have approved of, because they had the same wash-and-set hairdo that was popular in Lagos, and they slept with pink foam rollers to maintain that look.

'How can we ever have decent sex with rollers?' I'd asked my last girlfriend. 'I mean, can't I ruffle up your hair once in a while?' She said, as an African woman, she didn't appreciate her hair being ruffled up. I complained and complained until she agreed, 'Okay, I'll take them out, but after sex, I'm rolling my hair up again.'

For that alone I broke up with her, so Toyosi was right, and I was surprised she knew me that well from the start. Whenever I saw a woman who was different from the norm, all I wanted, all I'd ever wanted, was to sleep with her.

Toyosi occupied my sister's room. Sometimes, I'd see her snoring with her mouth open and her daughter's head in her armpit, and I suppose that was when I loved her, or perhaps it was later. Who knows? I let her share my parents' bathroom, scrubbed the tub daily so she could wash her daughter in the evenings. She never once said thank you.

I noticed how she spent more time with Professor than any of us. She smiled at him and let him bounce her daughter on his knee. One morning, I heard him singing a special anthem he'd made for her: 'Pretty girl, pretty girl, who is your daddy? I'm your daddy.' I could have kicked the door down.

'He's trying to chase you,' I whispered in Toyosi's ear. 'He's even using your daughter. How come you treat him better than me?'

'Prof?' she said. 'He likes women?'

Prof. 'Of course he does.'

'*Na wa*. I could have sworn he wasn't that way inclined. He told me he lost his father in the Civil War.'

'He's a poet and a liar.'

Professor and his sisters were raised by their mother. Their father was so devastated when Biafra lost the war, he stayed in France.

As soon as I had the opportunity, I made sure I tripped him up. He was coming out of her room with a soiled nappy. The nappy went flying, followed by his glasses.

'Ah-ah, see what you made me do?' he whined, picking himself off the floor.

'*Ehen*,' I said. 'So what are you going to do about it?'

The water shortage in Shapati Town changed our friendship in that house. Every tap in the town centre dried up after the rainy season, right through the beginning of the harmattan season, so we had the usual dusty winds in the mornings and evenings. During the hot afternoons, the town's people disappeared into their cement brick bungalows, under the shelter of their corrugated-iron roofs, just waiting.

Our local council couldn't tell us when they would 'recutify de problem'. A water tanker came round every other day. We had to be on the look out for the driver, because two honks and that man was off. When he arrived, we ran outside with our aluminum buckets, shouting, 'We're here, oh. We're here, oh.' Then he'd grab his big hose between his legs and drench us until he'd filled our buckets, then we'd hobble back into the house.

We boiled some of the water to drink and brush our teeth. The rest was for bathing, flushing and Toyosi's cooking. After about three weeks of this, we were exhausted in the evenings, and not prepared for our performances. People in our audience, who couldn't afford tanker water, were fetching polluted water from Lagos Lagoon and Five Cowry Creek. When they showed up, they crossed their arms and expected us to bring not just entertainment, but some frigging joy into their lives. Shango did his usual fire-breathing trick, spitting kerosene from his mouth onto the flame of a hidden lighter. They hissed and called us useless; our story about Yoruba gods was no longer relevant.

We stopped putting on our free show. I went to the British Council to see how far our script had gone there. They said they were still considering us. Shango went to the Americans. Some asshole there told him they only sponsored talented people. Back at the house, my friends were beginning to smell as guys do when they stay together too long, of rivalry and unsatisfied desires, and sheer bad manners.

One evening, Crazehead let out one of his belches. Normally, I would hold my nose until the mist subsided, but I was too tired. I was lying on a sofa. We were in the parlour again. We'd had a power cut and there were shadows dancing on the ceiling from the light of our kerosene lanterns. Shango was studying a journey of ants to and from a bit of bread. 'Can't you even say excuse me?' he said.

'Hexcuse,' Crazehead said.

Professor hissed. 'You this boy, you have no manners.'

Toyosi was in the kitchen, boiling water to make her daughter a bottle of milk. She was trying to wean her – not that this was the right time to introduce any child to Lagos water, but the girl was almost one year old and biting hard.

'No consid'ration,' Fineboy said.

'Ah-ah?' Crazehead said, smiling as if he were made popular by our criticisms. 'Why is everyone picking on me tonight?' He shuffled across the room and dived by my feet, then he let out another belch. I smelled it first: bush meat and orange peel.

'What the hell did you eat, man?' I asked.

The parlour already stunk of mosquito repellent.

'Shit,' Fineboy said, burying his face in a cushion.

'One more coming up,' Crazehead said.

Fineboy sprang from his chair. 'I swear to God if you . . .' He reached for Crazehead's feet. Crazehead sat up: 'It's not my fault! It's not my fault!'

'Out of this place,' Fineboy ordered. 'Are you an animal or what?'

Fineboy, and I suppose this tallied with his good looks, was particular about personal hygiene. He insisted on shaving despite the water shortage. I'd caught him, numerous times, glaring at Crazehead who walked around with patches of beard on his chin and dried up sleep in his eyes.

I heard Toyosi's daughter crying. Toyosi was checking her boiling water. I turned around again and Fineboy and Crazehead were on the floor, writhing. Crazehead was on top.

'Wetin you dey fight for?' I asked.

Toyosi hurried into the parlour with her daughter on her hip. Shango dragged Crazehead and Fineboy apart. They were breathing through their mouths. Shango grabbed Crazehead's shoulders and lifted him. I thought he was about to throw Crazehead across the room. Crazehead kicked his shins. He looked like a puppet with entangled strings.

'Shangooo!'

Toyosi's shriek so reminded me of my mother's that I sat up straight. Shango lowered Crazehead to the floor and went back to studying ants, as if he'd never moved from there.

Crazehead was grinning. 'What's wrong with 'im?'

I walked over to Shango as he crouched by the wall. 'Hope nothing,' I said. He was watching the ants crawl up and down. 'Everyone thinks I'm soft. I'm not that soft.'

'Why did you do that to Crazehead? You know his head is not correct.'

'Are we really useless and untalented?'

'We're extremely talented, in fact.'

'Then why will no one sponsor us?'

'Because theatre is dead, art is . . .'

I had to stop myself; I was sounding like the students'

unionists, specialists in screaming about how they were voiceless victims. But who were we to feel sorry for ourselves because a few foreign embassies wouldn't give us attention? And why did we have to depend on their charity anyway? Not one stinking rich Nigerian was willing to support us?

I slapped Shango's back. 'What do you expect, *jo*?'

After all, if I allowed myself to address the issue at hand – the real issue: what was the state of art under a dictatorship? Where was the state of art under a dictatorship?

My house was one state. Here, we were so free we deserved to fly our own flag. For this, we had to be grateful, at least. Shango let an ant crawl on the tip of his forefinger. 'You know the people I feel sorry for most in the whole wide world?'

'Who?' I asked.

'Ants,' he said. 'Because all they ever do is live for their work and see how we trample on them.'

I placed my hand on his shoulder. Shango wasn't soft; he was as thick as a tree trunk.

'Why are your friends such morons?' Toyosi asked, as she bathed her daughter that evening. Her hair was tied up in a turban and she carried the girl in the crook of her arm.

'They're not so bad,' I said, meaning it.

'Why can't they just go home to their parents?'

'They don't have homes they can "go" to.'

On campus, I'd dreaded being on my own in the house. The thought had had me sitting up at nights with a dry throat. Now, I wondered if I should brave it. Toyosi wiped her daughter's cheeks with a washcloth.

'Are they orphans or what?' she asked.

'Their families can't afford them.'

'Can you?'

I was broke from paying for water, food and baby milk. What little funds I had left would cover my electricity bills. I remembered the smartest statement Shango ever made. 'You'll spend your inheritance,' he said, 'until pain is all you have to live on.'

'What happened to your parents?' Toyosi asked.

'Killed.'

'Eh? How?'

'Armed robbers.'

'*Kai*. Where?'

'Here. Gateman took a bribe and let them in.'

She looked around the bathroom as if she could feel their ghosts watching us. The window pane over the bathtub was smashed; I could hear crickets outside.

'My sister too,' I said.

'When?'

'Remember when there were so many raids?'

There were riots after the Abacha regime announced their constitutional conference. They were promptly quashed by the mobile police squad. Armed robbers took over Lagos streets at night. They attacked homes with machetes and guns. People swore some of them were university students – they spoke so well. The raids were a social revolution, I'd bragged at the time, not knowing I would be personally affected. Meanwhile, the Abacha regime was passing decrees to muzzle dissidents. Lagos State set up a special squad to combat armed robberies, and the rumour was that the squad was selling arms to the robbers.

Toyosi pulled her wrapper up her thigh and trickled water over her daughter's belly. 'What's Shango's own story?'

'His parents had twelve kids. They gave him away. My parents were his guardians. He got me involved in drama, saved me from insanity.'

'Crazehead?'

'*Ogogoro* and hemp. His father is a trumpeter, drinks *ogogoro* like water. Crazehead himself started smoking hemp at the age of ten.'

'Professor?'

'Premature ejaculation.'

'Fineboy?'

'He made a pass at you. How come you don't shun him?'

She shook her head. 'I don't understand. You're not from the same background as any of your friends.'

'What do you mean?'

'You're... you know.'

'You know, what?'

'Posh,' she said, but I was the son of an architect who'd inherited an estate, and the middle-class were as non-existent as theatre was dead.

Her daughter took ill with malaria, or bad water; we were not sure. At first she was refusing to take her bottle, then her temperature spiked in the evenings, and her little eyeballs sunk. At night we could hear her gibbering in baby language. Toyosi got up every hour to sponge her. I gave up asking if I could help. She wouldn't even let Professor near the child, only during the day, when her temperature subsided. Then we would take turns to place her on our chests and feel her tiny heart pumping and her fingers grasping at our sleeves. She scratched us with her fingernails, wet us with the sweat from her head, and left us smelling of milk and medicine. Professor, Fineboy, Shango, Crazehead, we were all involved in administering her chloroquine and antibiotic drops that Toyosi bought from Hausa street hawkers, knowing they could well be fake.

After a week, she was not getting better, so, regardless of my fatherly feelings, I told Toyosi, 'You have to take her to a doctor.'

We were in my sister's room. Toyosi smoothed the mattress with such diligence I knew she was scared. The child kicked weakly. I'd never seen a baby with cheek bones before.

'I can't afford to,' Toyosi said.

'A pharmacist then,' I said.

'I can't afford that either.'

'This child will dehydrate. You want her to? *Abi* is that it?'

She didn't answer.

'Toyosi,' I said.

'What?' she said wagging her forefinger at me. 'You can

nag somebody like an old woman. Leave me alone.'

'At least get her a proper diagnosis.'

'How?'

'You know what I mean. Go home. Apologise to your people if necessary. Lagos without family? You're not that rugged. It's over now. This is our reality not yours. You can't romanticise slumming.'

She hissed. 'Who is romanticising? You think living in a dilapidated mansion is slumming?'

'Go home.'

'No. I'm not going back. They suffered me: "Toyosi, don't say such things. Toyosi, Uncle would never do that to you."'

'Who is Uncle?'

'My mother's I-don't-know-what.'

'What did he do to you?'

'This is his daughter. Is that not enough?'

Her own story was as Byzantine as our national politics, the stuff of Lagos suburban life, as debauched as it was hidden. I understood that her mother, having divorced her philandering father, was now the outside woman in a polygamous union with this Uncle, and this Uncle thought he'd help himself to Toyosi.

'He denied it. My mother tells everyone I slept with the houseboy. My father says I'm unnatural for sleeping with a houseboy, worse than unnatural. I'm dead to him. Now, I'm kicked out of home. That's fine, but nobody should tell me about violation of rights, or censorship, or persecution in this country. These things have been going on in homes for years and I don't see anyone fighting for freedom in that realm.'

'But what can we actually do for you here?' I asked, hoping she would find practical ways for us to support her. So we were both without families, slightly unbalanced, and far removed from the struggle for democracy, but I was going back to university. She couldn't stay in the house forever.

'Steal,' she said.

I thought she was joking.

'We're not thieves,' I said.

The last I stole was from Duro Ladipo's *Oba Koso* and I didn't even do that properly.

'You've played gods,' she said. 'Can't you play thieves for a night?'

I stood up. 'You're the one playing here.'

She carried her daughter. 'I know someone. Someone with money. Someone you can get money from. Easily.'

'Didn't I just tell you what armed robbers did to my family?'

'What will I do? My child is sick. You're running out of money. We're your family. Me, you, her and the village idiots downstairs. You're lord of the mansion. You want to be with me? Save us, instead of sniffing around me like a dog on heat.'

She beckoned with one hand, as if she was looking for a fight rather than love. I was done for, I thought, and warped. How could I still be attracted to her?

'Who is this someone?'

Yes, that was the moment I loved Toyosi.

'My sister. She's a banker. She won't speak to me now I've been disowned. Just because she is my father's favourite. Just because she doesn't want to fall out of favour. She goes around calling me a liar, the selfish, spoiled . . . '

'Toyosi, the men in your life have some responsibility to bear.'

'It's the women I trusted.'

'Okay,' I said.

'Speak to your friends,' she said. 'I beg you.'

'What if she's setting us up?' Professor asked. 'I don't know. I just don't.'

He was hugging himself and rocking. The rest had said yes. I was waiting for one more voice.

'Shango?' I asked.

He pursed his lips. 'Well . . . at least it's a real gig.'

'She lives on Victoria Island. She works for a merchant bank there. She makes stupid money doing foreign exchange deals.'

'Which kin'?' Crazehead asked.

'It's too complex to explain.'

'Fraud?' Professor asked.

'Probably,' I said.

'I don't pity her then,' Fineboy said. 'Let's do it. I'm in.'

'All right?' I asked.

The rest nodded; they were in. We'd taken greater risks in life anyway: pursuing careers in theatre arts for a start, condoms we should have used for another.

We set off at night in my mother's Volkswagen Beetle, because the gear stick of my father's Peugeot got stuck. I was driving, Shango was by my side, Crazehead and Fineboy were behind with the Professor between them. We backed out of the gates and Crazehead said, 'Alt!'

'What for?' I asked.

'Let us pray,' he said.

I pleaded with my palms pressed together. 'I know your head is not normally correct, but please, let it be correct tonight, okay?'

We'd bathed, shaved, washed and pressed our clothes. Crazehead was carrying two blunt daggers.

The road to Victoria Island was an expressway that ran through market towns and fishing villages. We passed hamlets which had red flags to show the incumbents were Cherubim and Seraphim worshippers, Lekki and Eleko beaches, oil palm clusters and bushes. There was a plot for Lagos Business School, a satellite centre for the University of Calabar, Victoria Court Cemetery where I'd buried my family. The sky was indigo and the air smelled of dust and salt. Billboards advertised the usual cigarettes, beer, medicine, Born-Again churches and toothpaste. Towards the island were villas with terracotta roofs and balconies. Victoria Island was meant to be a residential district; it was a commercial one now, bright with the neon lights of banks and finance houses. It was also a red light district; prostitutes flagged us down near the diplomatic section, at the junction of a street named after Louis Farrakhan, to spite the Americans.

The block of flats Toyosi's sister lived in was one of those built to capitalise on the commercial growth on the island. It was converted from someone's knocked-down home, had no corporate security, mirrors for windows and a cemented yard. Expatriates wouldn't rent a flat here. The gateman, a Fulani man in a black tunic and embroidered skull cap, let us in. He took a bribe, as Toyosi said he would, holding his prayer beads in his other hand. Fineboy, Crazehead and I came out of the Beetle. Shango and Professor waited as our look out and back up.

I knocked on the door: no bell, no peep hole.

'Ye-es?' I heard her say.

I breathed in. 'Daddy says you should come downstairs.'

She hesitated. 'My father?'

'Yes. Daddy is downstairs and he says you should come down right now.'

She muttered, 'Again? For goodness sake.'

My heart scrambled around my chest. I glanced at Fineboy who was bowing his head, preparing himself to waylay her. Crazehead was behind me. We heard footsteps then clicks in her keyhole. Security was generally tight in Lagos. How did robberies happen? Because, sometimes, robbers had inside information.

Toyosi's father had forbidden her sister to leave home and move into a flat of her own. She was an unmarried woman and it was not done in society, but she was also making enough money to disobey him. It was Toyosi's mother, feeling bitter about the divorce, who had given her daughter permission to leave home, and her father paid unexpected visits, on his way from Island Club, or from his girlfriend's, to check that his own daughter wasn't entertaining men. He was a lawyer for an oil company, too fat and important to get out of his car. His chauffeurs called him Daddy. Everyone who worked for him called him Daddy.

Toyosi's sister opened her door with a wig on her head and one brow raised.

'So how many of you does it take to drive my father's Merc?' she asked.

Fineboy ushered her back into her flat.

'Inside,' he said. 'And don't make a sound.'

'Yeah,' Crazehead said. 'Or else we'll fug you hup.'

I raised my eyes. Was this what we agreed on? No one forced me, though. I walked in with my own two legs.

Her eyes puffed up from crying. She was sweating in her black skirt suit. Her wig was askew and her mouth was shaped like a chicken bone was wedged in sideways. Her flat was done up in matching purple tie-and-dye sofas and chairs with ruffles. Toyosi had said a well-known Lagos interior decorator was responsible for the mess. Her sister was a smoker, stunk of tobacco and perfume, and in her living room was a crystal ashtray of lipstick-stained cigarette butts. Crazehead and I searched the wardrobe in her bedroom where she said her money would be. Bruno Magli and Ferragamo were the shoes she favoured. Her bags were Louis Vuitton and Fendi.

The money was in a mesh bag of dirty underwear. I handed it to Crazehead, who dug his hand inside and pulled out a bra.

'La Perla,' he said. 'Dis one be African Jackie Onassis. Are Ferragamo and Fendi your mother and father?'

He rolled the bra into a ball and sniffed it, then cast it on the floor and pulled out a thong. I winced. He sniffed that too.

'The money,' I said, feeling nauseous, and yet strangely intrigued.

Toyosi's sister was crying again. Crazehead found the wad of dollars.

'Is this all?' he asked.

She nodded. Mucus trailed from her nostrils into her mouth.

'Let's fade,' I said, overwhelmed with shame.

'No,' Fineboy said. 'Let her do one more thing for us.'

I frowned. 'Like what?'

'Call Daddy,' he said.

The woman herself looked bemused. She had to know we were fakes now. No armed robbers could be this stupid.

'Call Daddy for what?' I asked.

'Let her call him and you'll see,' he said.

'Now!' Crazehead barked so loud I jumped.

I promised myself that I would one day have to think about why my friends were such morons. Toyosi's sister dropped her mobile phone three times, she was trembling so much as she called her father.

'H-hello? D-daddy?'

'Tell him you like sex,' Fineboy whispered. 'Don't start crying wah-wah.'

She clutched the phone. 'It's me, Daddy. I like . . . sex.'

'Tell him,' Fineboy said, 'you have a boyfriend who is not from a good family.'

She shut her eyes. 'Daddy, my boyfriend is not from a good family.'

'But,' Fineboy said, 'he gives it to you hard.'

She shook her head. Crazehead was giggling. He raised his dagger and bit the edge. 'Real 'ard,' he whispered.

Toyosi's sister placed her hand on her chest. She was gasping for air. Her skin was fair, probably from chemical bleaching.

'Daddy,' she said. 'My boyfriend . . . gives it to me . . . hard.'

As soon as my shoes touched the ground outside, I smacked Fineboy's big chest.

'You're a bastard,' I said.

'*Yei*,' he said and ducked.

'And you,' I said pointing at Crazehead. 'Your head is not correct. Why did you do that to her? Was that our plan?'

They were throwing fists. Shango and Professor were leaning on the bonnet of the Beetle. I tossed the mobile phone on the driver's seat, unable to bear what had passed between father and daughter. Wasn't our population over a hundred million when last I checked, give or take ten million for census fudging? And less than ten people in Nigeria, I was sure, would admit to their parents that they'd had sex, let alone enjoyed it. We didn't even have to lock her up in her bedroom; she collapsed on the floor after her phone call to Daddy.

'Let's go,' I said.

'What happened?' Shango asked.

I pointed at Crazehead and Fineboy. 'Ask them.'

Crazehead was calling the gateman, '*Tss, Mallam,* you get kolanut?'

The gateman was standing at attention by the cement column of the gates with his wife by his side. She was a street hawker. They were nomadic people, sort of permanently stuck in the city. They'd come from the north, with robes as colourful as petals and feet as filthy as roots. The woman had a pink chiffon scarf covering her head. Her husband shoved her and she immediately squatted over her tray of Bicycle cigarettes, Trebor Mints and Bazooka Joe chewing gum.

Professor hissed. 'Why did he push her like that?'

'Blame Crazehead,' I said. 'Is it now he's asking for kolanuts?

I yanked the door of the Beetle open. Shango went round to the other side. Fineboy was coming toward us. I noticed Professor waddling over to the gateman.

'Prof,' I called. 'What happuns? I said, we're leaving.'

Professor placed his hand on his crooked back like someone's grandmother and began to berate the gateman: 'Why did you push her? Did you have to push her? Isn't she your wife? Couldn't you say common please?'

The gateman backed away, gabbling in his language.

'Ignorant northerners,' Professor said. 'All of you are the same.'

I shook my head. He was being a tribalist at this late hour?

'Misogynist,' he said. 'You have no respect for women.'

No, he was being a feminist. I knocked my head against the Beetle.

'Prof,' I whispered. 'Why?'

He waved his arms like a traffic warden: '*Alla Wakuba.* That's all you know. *Alla Wakuba.*'

The gateman, who couldn't understand a word of English, understood Professor's attempt at Arabic. He was warbling like a turkey now. I was sure he was calling Professor an infidel. He snatched Professor's arm and twisted so hard that Professor was off balance and flat on the gravel in one second. His glasses went flying, followed by his confidence.

'*Chineke*, hellep me oh,' he yelped.

The gateman reached into his robe and pulled out a scabbard longer than Crazehead's puny daggers placed together.

'Shango,' I said. 'Save the *bubbuh*.'

Shango ran across the gravel. He grabbed the gateman's shoulders, lifted him, and threw him against the cement column. The gateman slumped at the foot of the column. His wife screamed, '*Barawo! Barawo!*' Thieves.

I sped out of the gates. My mother's Beetle protested with a screech. I tried to straighten the wheel, but my hands were shaking too much.

'D-did we kill him?' Professor was asking. He was squinting. We'd left his glasses on the gravel when we fled.

'We injured 'im,' Crazehead said. 'There was blood everywhere.'

His voice was loaded with an accusation. Shango stared out of the window. Fineboy leaned forward and squeezed my shoulder. 'Steady on, o-boy. At least let's get home. Drive safely and all that, eh?'

'I'm trying,' I said.

I was so ashamed: I had a hard on.

When we reached The Mansion, I snatched the wad of dollars from Crazehead and delivered it to the real Lord – Toyosi.

'Here,' I said. 'Are you satisfied?'

She glanced at the notes in her usual manner, as if they were inevitable circumstances in her life, but she wouldn't move, so I threw the notes on my sister's bed where her daughter was sleeping. I didn't even care if she hated me. I was fed up with her lack of gratitude.

'Thank you,' she mumbled.

'We almost killed a man for this.'

'Thank you. You've been so kind to me.'

'Make sure you get her to a doctor and buy her the right medicines.'

She reached for me and I pushed her away. What if Shango had killed the gateman?

'Did you hurt my sister?' she asked.

I rolled my fist against my mouth. 'I can't say.'

'Ogun, answer me.'

'I cannot.'

'Ogun, tell me. Did you hurt my sister?'

Ogun had several translations depending on how it was pronounced. It could mean sweat, poison, medicine, inheritance, an army, a battle, the number twenty, or the god of ore and war. With Toyosi's appalling Yoruba intonation, Ogun was a basket for catching shrimps, but she gripped my wrist and her eyes watered, so I told her about Fineboy's inferiority complex, Shango's hidden rage, Professor's over-identification with women and my desperation to avenge my family. I also told her about her sister's forced confession, and she smirked.

'Serves her right.'

'We were not acting. We were just being ourselves and yet . . .'

Was that redemption I felt? That rush of potency and sense of possibilities? I leaned against Toyosi. Who was I to think theatre could save us? Who was I to think art could save anyone in Lagos?

She stroked my forehead. 'See? See why I had to give up? There's enough drama in our lives. We must be supernatural to survive here. Why bother with any myth about gods?'

We heard a giggle as heartening as rainbow-coloured bubbles popping. It was her daughter. She'd woken up and found the dollar bills.

'Hrscht,' she said. 'Hrsch-tup.'

Her first words. Shut up, she was trying to say, and she was absolutely justified. There was no need for her mother to pontificate, not at that stage.

At first we were a little shy of ourselves in that house. We were not sure how to regard each other, as actors or armed robbers. Then, the haze of harmattan lifted and it became clear that we were brothers.

The Abacha regime announced they were reopening our university. We knew we would not be returning to graduate. We heard from the British Council and I asked them to save their patronage for a more deserving theatre group.

One surprise, as we prepared for our next night as the Lawless, it was Crazehead who became the most solemn in our group, Crazehead who made us promise to stick to our plans and vow never to spill blood again.

As for Toyosi, and this was way before she christened me Lord of the Lawless, way before we became lovers, her daughter got better, plumper than the day she arrived, and Toyosi began to write her play. Just like that. She didn't know how the story would end, but I had a clue how it began. She claimed that she'd unblocked us and now we were unblocking her. I told her she'd invented a new form of plagiarism. As we went out to perform in homes throughout Lagos, the woman just wrote and wrote, and wrote.

Yaba Badoe

The Rival

The night Mrs Mensah dreamt of fruit bats in her garden, she knew that she was in for trouble. Forcing herself awake, she whispered a prayer for guidance, for protection from the evils of the world, the machinations of her enemies. 'Thy will be done, O Lord,' she murmured in affirmation, folding her body against the frame of her husband. 'Let thy will be done, Amen.'

Closing her eyes, Mrs Mensah tried to retrieve her dream. She relaxed her body, allowing her mind to drift once again. This time she was in control, her hand on a rudder she steered towards sleep. She believed that if she could return to what she had seen, she could undo it, repelling the bats from her trees, protecting herself and her husband.

For the rest of the night she tossed and turned, assailed by dark-winged moths. These she struck with a broom. But when she hit them, the moths became crows circling her garden. So Mrs Mensah flung stones at them and once again they became bats. Bats with sharp teeth that devoured everything as they rampaged through the garden: mangoes, sour-sop, guava, ripening avocado. They ravaged Mrs Mensah's trees until there was no fruit left. Defeated, in tears, the woman awoke.

'Well at least I've been warned,' she said valiantly, preparing herself for the day.

She chose her clothes carefully, putting on a faded *bou-bou* in pale blue and grey; colours selected to dispel envy, to show the world that, although still attractive at fifty-five, her appearance was not uppermost in her mind. Her attention was on higher things. Sitting on the veranda, a well-thumbed Bible on her lap, Mrs Mensah spent the day preparing for her dream to take human form.

They arrived before dusk when the sun, slipping away from the garden, glanced at it one last time. The sun's goodbye, Mrs Mensah called it, for the golden iridescence of waning light on her plants was her favourite time of day. The bougainvillea glowed, the hibiscus shimmered and the leaves of the cassia tree, dipping through the bars of the veranda, were glazed with the sun's fading smile.

'Of course! They would choose now to arrive, wouldn't they?' Mrs Mensah murmured as she saw them approaching. 'People of night bring darkness with them. Along with bats and moths and crows.'

There were two of them this time, a woman and her daughter, dishevelled and tired at the end of a long journey.

'Albert! Visitors!' Mrs Mensah cried, calling up to her husband. She heard him moving upstairs, the bedroom door opening and shutting, heavy footsteps coming down.

'And if he wasn't tired already,' she sniffed, 'he soon will be.'

Her husband's face hardened when he saw their visitors. 'Sister,' he sighed, 'what a surprise.' The visitor got up, and holding out a hand she lowered her head, dipping her body in a show of respect to her older brother. Her daughter, a slim, dark girl of about fourteen, followed her example. But before she curtseyed, she gave her uncle a dazzling smile. Mrs Mensah, noticing her husband's face softening, thought, 'Aha! It's beginning.'

That night, Mrs Mensah didn't sleep at all. She lay awake praying, delving into the past, while in the spare bedroom, the visitors slept soundly.

'I won't let them do it to us this time,' she promised herself. 'I won't let them take advantage of us again. Just because Albert has a kind heart doesn't mean he's a money tree for them to shake whenever they want something. And though I'm a Christian, I refuse to be a sleeping mat for them to spread themselves over. She's not going to use me again.'

Throughout the night Mrs Mensah remembered. She remembered the first time she had seen Albert's sister, the only girl in a family of four. Straight away she'd noticed the woman's self-satisfied demeanour, the air of the spoilt child about her, which came from being the only receptacle through which the family's lineage could continue. The family's survival depended on the fruit of her womb and, an Ashanti to the core, Esi manipulated her power brilliantly.

Before they were married, her brothers had pampered her, showering her with gifts; and after marriage they'd slipped her money whenever she needed it. Regardless of the extravagance of her lifestyle and the number of men she dusted from her hair, Esi's brothers always gave in to her. Though, to begin with, she had tried to accommodate her, Mrs Mensah disapproved of her sister-in-law. She disapproved of women who, after conceiving children with an assortment of men, farm them out to other people to look after – especially when 'other people' included herself.

Turning her back to her husband in case her growing indignation should rouse him, Mrs Mensah remembered the children she had raised: four of her own and two of Esi's – a girl and a boy. 'Who do they think I am?' She gritted her teeth thinking of her husband and his relatives. 'Do they think I'm their slave? Do they think I was born so that whenever Esi Mensah has children, I look after them? Who the hell do they think I am?'

By morning, Mrs Mensah's indignation had hardened into resolve. Albert could see by the firm line on her mouth and the determined expression with which she tied her head wrap that she was spoiling for a fight. He avoided one by taking her to church. Afterwards, picking her up again and dropping off one of her friends, he kept out of her way. He settled down to a cold bottle of beer while he waited patiently for lunch. An amiable man, Albert Mensah had long ago realised that the wisest thing to do in a tense situation was to relax into it. If you relaxed for long enough, he believed, the situation would usually go away.

Taking a sip of beer, he closed his eyes and began concentrating on his lungs filling with air. In. Out. In. Out. In the kitchen a saucepan clattered to the ground. He sat up. He heard a crescendo of voices followed by a piercing scream. Albert took another deep breath. By the time his lungs had expanded to capacity, the kitchen door had been flung open and his sister, in tears, was standing in front of him.

'Brother,' she sobbed, 'why do you allow her to treat me like this?'

The years had dealt harshly with Esi Mensah. She had never been beautiful, but in her youth her exuberance for life had exaggerated her attributes, giving her an aura of glossy well-being. But her appetite for men had not been matched by a willingness to manage her affairs sensibly. Since the men she gave herself to gave little in return, she was forced to rely on her brothers for almost everything. Nonetheless she refused to question her inability to make a path for herself, preferring to see what was given her as her due. After all, thanks to her fecundity, the family line would continue. She'd had six children, all girls except one; so because of her dalliances, the family tree was flourishing. Soon her daughters would start having children as well.

'Answer me, Brother,' she pouted. 'Why do you allow her to behave like this?'

Albert's bemusement forced her to explain herself. 'I was only trying to help. I was going to make you pancakes. I know how much you like pancakes, Brother.'

Her brother sighed, and Esi, anxious to maintain his goodwill, gave a mischievous smile, unaware that her teeth weren't what they used to be, and that a pout from a woman of almost fifty rarely achieves the miracles that a similar expression on a woman half her age can.

And yet something inside her brother stirred. The ridiculous woman standing before him was his younger sister; the child he'd played with and cherished after their mother's death. The child who, at four, had wanted to marry him and, at six, had hated him for sending her to school. At fourteen, she had begged him for a brand-new Singer machine and he had provided it gladly. And at eighteen, leaving her first child in his care, she had declared, 'Brother, you are my everything. Please care for my child with the same tenderness that you've cared for me.' How could Albert deny her?

'Esi, remember this is my wife's house as well as mine. Remember, you're a guest in her kitchen.'

'But aren't you the head of the house, Brother? Aren't you the one who bought the stove and the fridge and just about everything in this your wife's kitchen?'

'You know as well as I do, my wife controls her kitchen.'

'But I'm your sister! Don't I have rights there as well?'

'No,' Albert replied. 'So far as the kitchen's concerned, Beatrice is in control.'

Esi pouted, peeved. 'She seems to control everything in this house. I suppose she controls you as well.'

If he had been a day younger than his sixty years and a man of less maturity, Albert Mensah might have risen to the bait. Instead he smiled at his sister, shaking his head sadly. 'It's not going to work this time, Esi. You're not going to cause dissension in my house again.'

'Aaah, so she's got you by the balls, has she?'

Albert shifted uncomfortably. 'In household matters, I give Beatrice all the support she needs.'

'Admit it Brother, she's got you by the balls.'

Her face twisting in a contemptuous scowl, Esi scurried upstairs into the spare bedroom, slamming the door and locking it. A moment later, Albert heard furniture moving. His sister was dragging a bed against the door. She was barring everyone from entering.

That afternoon, the Mensahs ate Sunday lunch in silence. If she said anything, Mrs Mensah believed, it would be in anger, and this wasn't a time to speak in anger. She intended to protect the fruit of her labour – her marriage and the good will of her husband – with every fibre of her being. So, gathering her strength, she kept her own counsel.

Outside, Esi's daughter, sitting on the kitchen steps, wept into her food. Albert, hearing the mewling of a lost kitten in her whimpering, felt inclined to protect her; to stroke her until she started purring again. He stared mournfully at his wife. Beatrice shook her head.

When night came, Esi was still locked in the spare room. The child, abandoned in her uncle's house, spread her sleeping mat in the corridor outside his door. She slept in a dark corner below a window, the night breeze wafting over her face. Before she slept, her uncle came out of the master bedroom to wish her good night. Brushing aside her shyness as she would a startled moth, she gave him the full radiance of her smile; and when the door closed, she allowed herself to feel the quickening of her desire. She imagined she lived in her uncle's house, that she cooked for him and washed his clothes and in return he bought her everything she wanted: clothes and jewellery. And when she was older, he would buy her a car all to herself; a big car. The child, falling asleep, dreamt dreams in which she was queen of her uncle's household: on top of him, ruling his roost. His wife, she decided, would just have to go.

Next door, Mrs Mensah kept vigil over her husband, taking note of every gesture of tenderness between Albert and his niece. They had argued over the child many times in the past. From the beginning, Albert had wanted to raise her as his own, using the fecklessness of his sister as an excuse to have his way. But Beatrice was implacable. She had raised two of Esi's children already. Enough was enough, she said. It was time Esi took care of her own children. The force of his wife's resistance astonished Mr Mensah, for she was usually compliant and always understanding.

'Is this what you think of me?' she asked. 'Am I here to be used whenever you feel like it? Did you marry me to finish off whatever your sister starts? Albert, we're getting old. Let's enjoy the time left without your sister's interference, I beg you.'

'I was thinking of the child's future. If we leave her in Esi's care, what will become of her?'

'Well, Esi should have thought of that before she opened her legs.'

'Beatrice! I'm surprised at you.'

Early the next morning, Mr Mensah knocked on the locked door of the guest room. He heard a shuffling of feet followed by silence. He knocked again. The door opened. Esi, already in her travelling clothes, gestured him inside with a conspiratorial smile.

'I'm leaving today and I'm leaving the child with you,' she announced.

'But Beatrice hasn't . . . she doesn't . . .'

'Brother, I know you want to look after my daughter. You want to care for her and teach her a skill. You want to accomplish with her what you found impossible with me.'

The expression on his face made her add quickly, 'I'm not blaming you, Brother. I know the sort of person that I am.'

For a moment Albert Mensah wondered if this was the petulant woman who'd locked herself in the day before. Self-knowledge was not a trait he usually attributed to his little sister, and the possibility that there might be more to her than he imagined, stopped him short.

'My dear brother Albert,' she continued with a smile, 'I'm not a fool. I know what I'm doing and even if you can't admit it because of that woman you call your wife, I know that leaving my child with you is what you want as well.'

'But it's not what Beatrice wants.'

'And what do I care about your wife?'

Esi's indifference to the enormity of the task ahead of him, the repercussions it might have on his marriage, was typical. His sister invariably did as she pleased, leaving it to others to smooth out the kinks in her life. It was as if some part of her had never quite matured, clinging to a child-like need for gratification, irrespective of the consequences. What have I done to her, Albert wondered. Where did I go wrong?

He was trying to ease the burden of his responsibility for his sister as a prelude to explaining that he couldn't take on her child as well because Beatrice refused to, when Esi ignited the silence between them. She looked at him with their mother's eyes: chocolate coloured, the light of adoration shining through.

'Brother Albert, you are my everything,' she crooned. 'You are my mother, my father, my husband. Please care for my child as you've cared for me. Who knows, maybe this time, yes this time, everything will come right. Do it for my sake, please, Brother.'

And so it was that Albert Mensah's determination to be firm, upholding his wife's decision, yielded to the softness within him. The child stayed, sleeping in a dark corner of the corridor, outside the master bedroom. She would stay for the holidays, he explained to Beatrice, though they both knew that the 'holiday' was likely to last for years.

At night, the bitterness in her heart turning her blood to bile, Mrs Mensah dreamt of fruit bats, while the child in the corridor, imagining that she was ruler of the house, delighted in having her uncle at her beck and call. Though she kept her few possessions in the spare room and was told repeatedly to sleep there, she preferred to dream outside her uncle's door. She needed his warmth for shelter, his proximity for entry to his soul. Ever watchful, Mrs Mensah felt the chord running between her husband and niece thickening, growing plump as a maggot; she felt the fruit of her labour withering as the child's teeth, becoming sharp and strong, revealed the strength of her desire. Beatrice Mensah watched. She saw the child's grace, the nubile ease with which she teased money from her husband, believing the mistress' back was turned.

'Is there nothing new beneath the sun? First the mother, then her children. But this one, Lord, this one is the worst of them all. If I let her in, her hatred will lacerate my soul.' Watching carefully, Mrs Mensah sensed the steel jaws behind the sweetness of the child's smile tightening as her husband succumbed to her charms. She watched and examined the minutiae of their interaction, the dimpled sighs, the stain of money changing hands; she pushed aside her pride.

One evening, the daily ritual of Albert's goodnight to the child over, Beatrice Mensah got out of bed. Flinging the bedroom door open, she demanded in a voice loud enough for her husband to hear, 'So you want to share my bed, do you? So you want to sleep with my husband? Well come in! Come in, child. You can have him if you want. Get up and come in!'

Pretending to be asleep, the child rolled over, turning her back to her aunt. Beatrice, furious, grabbed her by the throat, forcing her to her feet. 'Go to him,' she commanded. 'Take him! Take him! But if you haven't the courage to do so, go and lie in your own bed. For while this man is my husband, you will never sleep outside my door again. Do you understand? You will never disturb my dreams.'

Crying softly, the child gathered her cover cloth and, rolling up her sleeping mat, she slipped into the spare room, while Mrs Mensah, released at last from silence, began scolding her husband.

Doreen Baingana

Tropical Fish

Peter always plopped down heavily on top of me after he came, breathing short and fast, as if he had just swum across Lake Victoria. My worry that he was dying was quickly dispelled by his deep snores, moments after he rolled off me. I was left wondering exactly what I was doing there, in the middle of the night, next to a snoring white man. And why was it that men fell asleep so easily, so deeply, after huffing and puffing over you? There I was, awake, alone with my thoughts, loud in my head and never ending, like a ghost train. Sex was like school, something I just did. I mean, of course I wanted to; I took myself there, no one forced me.

Peter was pink, actually, not white, except for his hair, what was left of it. It had suddenly turned colour from the stress of his first rough years in Uganda trying to start his fish exporting business. He was only thirty-five but to me, at twenty-five, that was ancient. When naked, though, he looked more like fourteen. He had an adolescent plumpness, a soft body, almost effeminate, with pale saggy legs. His skin felt just like mine. We met though Zac, a campus friend who also worked for Peter's company. Peter exported tropical fish bought from all over the country – Lake Victoria, Lake Albert, Lake Kyoga and the River Nile. He paid next to nothing to the local fishermen, then sent the fish by tank load to Britain for pet shops – very good profits.

Zac and I were both at Makerere University, which used to be called 'the Harvard of Africa' south of the Sahara, not counting South Africa, which didn't leave much else. But that was back in the sixties before Big Daddy, Idi Amin, tried to kill off as many professors as he could. Most ran into exile, and the 'economic war' did the rest of the damage. But we didn't complain; we were lucky to be there.

I was drinking *waragi* in Zac's room when Peter came in one evening. I liked Zac because he knew he wasn't going to become some big shot in life and so didn't even try. Apparently, he supplied Peter with *ganja*. Because of my lifelong training to catch a suitable mate, I found myself immediately turning on the sweet, simpering self I reserve for men when Peter walked in. I recede into myself, behind an automatic plastic-doll smile. Peter seemed amused by the shabby room. He looked around like a wide-eyed tourist at the cracked and peeling paint, the single bare bulb, an old tattered poster of Bob Marley on the wall, the long line of dog-eared Penguin Classics leaning sideways on Zac's desk, the untidy piles of handwritten class notes – Zac was finishing his BA in literature.

Zac got off his chair quickly and offered it to Peter. 'Hey man!' Zac had convinced himself he was black American. We laughed at the nasal way he talked, the slang culled from videos, his crippled-leopard swagger – incongruous, especially for someone so short. I kept telling him, 'Give up, Zac, no one's impressed,' but that was his way.

Peter refused the chair and gingerly settled onto Zac's single bed, which was covered with a thin brown blanket. The *mzungu* wanted to do the slumming right. I was sitting at the other end of the bed. Its tired springs creaked and created a deep hole in the middle as he sat down. I felt myself leaning over as if to fall into the hole, too close to Peter, into his warm personal space. I shifted away and sat up on the pillow, pulling my legs up under me. Did he think I didn't want to sit too close to him, a white man? There was a short uncomfortable silence. But with the two men there, I didn't have to start the conversation.

Zac said, 'How about a drink, man? Peter, meet Christine, the beautifullest chick on campus.' He was trying to be suave, but it sounded more like mockery. I smiled like a fool.

Peter turned and smiled back at me. 'Nice to meet you, Christine.' No teeth showed, only the small, grey shadow of his mouth. I put a limp hand into his outstretched one. He squeezed it hard, like a punishment. His skin was hot. I murmured something in return, still smiling about nothing, then took a large swallow from my drink, keeping my face in the glass.

Zac reached into a small dark cupboard. Inside were two oily-looking red plastic plates, a green plastic mug, a dusty glass with two or three spoons and forks in it, a tin of salt, and another of Kimbo cooking fat. He took out the glass, removed the spoons and blew into it. With his finger, he rubbed off a dead insect's wing stuck to the inside. 'I've got to wash this. I'll be right back,' and he left me alone in the tiny, shadowless room with Peter. It was my first time along with a white person. There was a nervous bare-bulbed silence.

Peter returned to looking around the plain one-desk, one-chair, one-bed room with an obvious smirk. I wished I could open the window and let in the coolness of the night outside. But I didn't want to move, and besides mosquitoes would quickly drone in. It was raining lightly outside, pitter-patter on the glass, which made the small square lights of the next hall shimmer like a black and yellow curtain, far away and inaccessible. Wisps of white hair at the back of Peter's heard stuck out unevenly over his collar. The light's shine moved over the bare pink hilltop of his head as he turned to me.

'So, you are a student here too?"

'Yes.' Soft and shallow.

'Yes? And what do you study, Christine?' Like a kind uncle to a five-year-old.

'Sociology.'

'Sociooo-logy?' He stretched out the word, and couldn't hide his amusement. 'That's quite impressive. You must be a very intelligent girl.' His smile was kind in an evilish, shadowed-mouth way. I smiled back, showing him that I, at least, had big bright teeth. There. I don't think he noticed.

Luckily Zac came back at that moment. I quickly swallowed the rest of my drink and left. In the warm, just-rained night, the wet grass and soaked ground smelt fertile. I dodged the puddles in the cracked pavement, which twinkled with reflected street-lamp. Not that I really noticed, I was too busy beating myself inside. You smiling fool, why didn't you say something clever? Almost walking past my hall, I wondered why I was so unsettled, even intrigued.

That weekend, Zac told me Peter wanted us to visit him at his house on Tank Hill.

'Me? Why?"

'The *mzungu* likes you.' He chuckled shortly, drily.

'Don't be silly. I'm not going.'

'Come on, we'll have fun. There'll be lots to drink, eat – videos too. Bring Miriam if you want.'

We went in the end, of course. Peter lived on top of Tank Hill, one of Kampala's seven hills – like Rome, as we were always told in class. Up there, diplomats' huge mansions hide behind high cement walls, lined across the top with shards of sharp glass. Rent is paid in dollars only. Swimming pools, security guards – and he wanted me. Nothing would happen if I went with Zac and Miriam, my tall Tutsi friend, who Peter would prefer anyway, I told myself. She had the kind of looks whites like: very thin, with high angular cheekbones and jaw, and large slanting eyes. And she was so daring, did whatever she wanted with a bold stare and brash laugh. No simpering for her. She even smoked in public. I was safe.

It was fun – sort of. Peter was overly attentive, serving drinks, plumping pillows, asking questions. We ate in courses brought in by his houseboy, Deogracias, an old man with crooked spindly legs attached to big, bare, boat-like feet. Black on bright pink. Deo spoke to us in *Luganda*, as if we were at his houseboy level, but not to Peter, of course. I told Zac and Miriam I found Deo's familiarity vaguely offensive, as if he was saying, 'I've seen your kind pass through this house before'. They both laughed it off. 'Christine, you're too much. What's wrong with being friendly?'

Peter chose *Karate Kids* for us to watch, saying it was our kind of movie. How would he know? I concentrated on gin and tonics. This was a whole world away from home, from school. The brightly painted, big-windowed house smelt of mosquito repellent from emerald rings smoking discreetly in every room. Bright batiks on clean white walls, shiny glass cupboards full of drinks and china. Everything worked: the phone, the hot water taps, a dustbin you clicked open with your foot. No need to touch. As soon as the power went off, a generator switched itself on automatically, with a reassuring low hum.

We turned off the lights to watch the movie, and Peter somehow snuggled up close to me. I pretended not to notice as I sank into the comfort of having all my needs satisfied. There was nothing to worry about. The drinks eased me. When the movie was over, the lights stayed off. Peter prepared a joint and we all became giggly. Everything slowed down pleasantly. He moved back close to me and stroked my trousered thigh up and down, up and down, gently, absentmindedly. It was soothing. I sat still. I didn't have to do anything.

Zac talked in a monotonous drone about the hidden treasures of Egypt: the esoteric wisdom that Aristotle stole – or was it Plato – which the Egyptians forgot. Peter asked, 'Why didn't they write it down?' and we all laughed for a very long time. Miriam got up and weaved around the room, holding her head, saying, 'I feel mellow, very, very mellow.' Over and over, giggling. Peter led her to his spare bedroom that was always ready, with clean sheets, soft lamps, and its own multi-mirrored bathroom. He brought Zac a bedcover for the soft sofa, then took me to his room as though it was the practical, natural thing to do. It felt sort of like a privilege – the Master Bedroom.

In the bathroom he got me a new toothbrush from a packet of about twenty, already opened. 'You have many visitors?' I wondered out loud. He laughed and kissed me on the mouth. 'Women,' I mumbled, as he ate up my lips. I thought about the wrapping: coloured blue plastic over the cardboard box, each toothbrush wrapped again in its own plastic, and lying in its own little cardboard coffin. I wanted to keep the box, but didn't dare ask; he would have laughed at me again.

I lay on the bed in my clothes. Peter took off his clothes and draped them neatly folded over a chair, pointing two small pale buttocks towards me as he leaned over. Then he took my blouse and pants off methodically, gently, like it was the best thing to do, as if I was sick and he was a nurse, and I just lay there. In the same practical way he lay down and stroked me for a few appropriate minutes, put on a condom, opened my legs, and stuck his penis in. I couldn't bring myself to hold him in any convincing way. I thought I should moan and groan and act feverish, overcome by a wild rage of some sort, like white people in movies. But I was feeling well fed and well taken care of; a child full of warm milk. One thought was constant in my head like a newspaper headline: I am having sex with a white man. It was strange because it wasn't strange. He was done in a few minutes. He tucked me under his arm like an old habit, and we sank into sleep.

Peter became my comfortable habit. On Friday evenings I escaped from the usual round of campus parties to go to my old white man; my snug, private life. No one scrutinized, questioned my motives, or made any judgements, up on Tank Hill, except Deo. He was a silent, knowing, irritating reminder of the real, ordinary world and my place in it. But when Deo had cleared up the supper things and left to go scrub his huge bare boat-feet with a stone, I was free to walk around the large, airy house naked, a gin and tonic melting in my hand. This made me feel floaty, a clean open hanky wandering in the wind. I didn't have to squash myself into clothes, pull in my stomach, tie my breasts up in a bra, worry about anything, be anything. Who cared what Peter thought? He said nonsensical things like, 'You're so many colours all over, how come?'

'What about your red neck?'

'That's coz I'm a redneck, luv.'

'I thought so.'

'Come here, you!' Our tussle ended up in bed.

My eldest sister, Patti, might have heard about Peter from someone. She was a born-again Christian, like I was once – 'saved' with too clear and rigid a sense of right and wrong. But she wouldn't say, 'Stop seeing that white man.' Instead, she told me of a dream she'd had: that I was given drugs by some whites. 'They only want to use you,' she said. I didn't answer. What could I say? That it actually was okay? Her self-righteousness made me want to go right back to Peter's.

For some reason I told him about Patti's dream. He laughed at me. I heard 'superstitious, ignorant blacks!' in his laugh. Maybe not, but like most things between us, I wasn't going to try and explain it, what one can see or read in dreams. I don't mean they're not true. But we couldn't climb over that laugh to some sort of understanding. Or didn't want to try.

One weekend, Zac told me they had gone to the Entebbe Sailing Club with another girl, some young ignorant waitress or something. 'Why are you telling me?' I scoffed. Didn't he think I knew Peter? I didn't like the Sailing Club anyway; it was practically white only because of the high membership fees and selective sponsorship rules. I felt very black over there. Zac was surprised I didn't seem to care about the other girls. Why squander feelings, I told myself. What was more annoying to me was Peter's choice of those waitress types.

Deogracias called him Mr Peter. I asked him, after two months or more, what his last name was. He said, 'Call me Mr Peter,' and chuckled. He enjoyed the lavishing of respect I knew he didn't get from anyone back home. Mr Smithson, I read a letter of his. How ordinary. Whenever he whined about the insects everywhere, the terrible ice cream, and only one Chinese restaurant, I wanted to tell him I knew he was lower class, Cockney, and doing much better here – practically stealing our fish – than he ever would in Britain. So he should just shut up. But of course I didn't: Our Lady of Smiles and Open Body.

When Peter called one Friday evening, I was having my period. I felt I shouldn't go – what for? But I couldn't tell him that, not so bluntly. How could we openly admit that he wanted me for sex, and I knew it, and agreed? Over the phone, moreover? It was easier for me to say nothing, as usual. I took a taxi to his house, and he paid for it. Peter had already started on the evening's drinks with *muchomo*, roasted meat, on his veranda. A Danish man was visiting, one of the usual aid types, who Peter had just met. These expats quickly made friends with one another; being white was enough. They grouped together at half-London, a collection of little shops lined along a dusty road at the bottom of Tank Hill. At each storefront, melting in the hazy heat, plastic chairs sat under gaudy red and white umbrellas advertising Coca-Cola and Sportsman cigarettes with the loud slogan, *Ye, Ssebo*! With all the beer-drinking and prostitute-hunting going on, it was a let's-pretend-we're-local hangout I avoided.

I put off telling Peter about my period, but felt guilty for some reason. Finally, in bed with the lights off, he reached for me as usual, but I moved away. 'I'm having my period.'

'What?' I had never said no to him.

'You know... my period. I'm bleed—'

'Oh, I see. Well...' He lay back on the bed, a little put out. But he fell asleep pretty soon all the same. Instead of relief, I felt empty, a box of air.

That Christmas, Peter went off to Nairobi. He left very cheerfully, wearing a brightly flowered shirt, the sun glinting off his sparse white hair and pint baldness. The perfect picture of a retiree set for a cruise. He was off to enjoy the relative comforts of Kenya, the movie theatres, safari lodges, maybe Mombasa's beach resorts. He had sent off a good number of rare fish; it was time for a holiday.

In town, as Peter dropped me off, he kissed me on the mouth, in the middle of Luwum Street, in front of the crowds, before breezing away. I was left in the bustling, dusty street, feeling the people's stares like the sun burning. Who was this girl being kissed in broad daylight by some *mzungu*? Aa-haa, these *malayas* are becoming too bold. Couldn't she find a younger one at the Sheraton? One man shouted to Peter, for the crowd, in Luganda, 'She's going to give you AIDS, look how thin she is!' Everyone laughed. Another one answered, 'It's their fault, these *bazungu*, they like their women thin. Let them fall sick.' General laughter.

I walked down to the taxi part, ignoring them. A girl like me didn't spend her time in the streets arguing with *bayaye*. I had better things to do. Not over Christmas, but he would come back; call me when he needed me, and I would escape to the big white house, the gin-and-tonic life, my holiday. Well, campus too was a kind of holiday before real life ahead of me: work, if I could get it, a government job that didn't pay, in a dusty old colonial-style office, wearing shoes in desperate need of repair, eating roasted maize for lunch, getting debts and kids, becoming my parents. One option was marriage to someone from the right family, the right tribe, right pocket-book and potbelly, and have him pay the bills. With my degree I would be worth exotic cows, Friesians or Jerseys, not the common long-horned Ankole cattle. But I didn't have to think about that for two more years. For now, I had my game: being someone else, or no one, for a few hours.

Peter brought me a bubble-bath soap from Nairobi because I said I'd never used it before. He prepared the bath for me. Water gushed out of both taps forever; abundance, the luxury of wasting. If you've never fetched water, known how heavy the jerrycans can be, how each drop is precious, you can't really enjoy a bubble bath. To luxuriate in a whole bathtub of water, just for you. The lovely warm green froth was a caress all over.

Peter undressed and joined me, his penis curled up shyly in his red pubic hair. He spread my thighs gently and played with my lips. I closed my eyes, shutting out everything but his careful, practised touch. Sank, sank, into the pleasure of it.

The warm water flopped around, splashing out onto the white bathmat and shiny mirrors. Peter crept up over me and entered slowly, and I thought, maybe I do care for him, maybe this is all that love is. A tender, comfortable easing into me.

I found out I was pregnant. We used condoms most of the time. I didn't say anything when we didn't. My breasts started to swell, and my heart grew suspicious, as though my belly had secretly passed on the message. When my period was more than twelve days late, I told Miriam. I couldn't tell Peter. It didn't seem to be his problem; not a part of our silent sex pact. This was personal. Miriam's sister, Margaret, a nurse, worked at a private clinic in the city. Nobody stopped me; they all knew it had to be done. I tried not to think about it. At the clinic, the anaesthetist droned at me in a deep, kind voice as he injected me. I was going to remain conscious but wouldn't feel anything, he said. Just like real life. The doctor was cream-gloved, efficient, and kind, like Peter. I fell into pleasant dreaminess. Why did I always seem to have my legs spread open before kind men poking things into me? I let them.

At the clinic, I read an article about all the species of fish that are disappearing from Uganda's freshwater lakes and rivers because of the Nile perch. It was introduced by the colonial government Fisheries Development Department in the fifties. The Nile perch is ugly and tasteless, but it is huge, and provides a lot more food for the populace. But it was eating up all the smaller, rarer, gloriously coloured tropical fish. Many of these rare species were not named, let alone discovered, before they disappeared. Every day, somewhere deep and dark, it was too late.

Margaret gave me antibiotics and about two years' supply of the pill, saying curtly, 'I hope we don't see you here again.' I was rather worried, though, because the doctor said I should not have sex for at least two weeks. What would I tell Peter when he called? Maybe I should explain what happened. Now that I had dealt with the problem, I wasn't bothering him with it. I just wanted to tell him.

I went to Peter's office without calling, not knowing what to say. It was on Barclay Street, where all the major airline and cargo offices are, convenient for his business. It was surprising how different Peter was at work: his serious twin, totally sober, a rare sight for me. He got authority from somewhere and turned into the boss, no longer the drunken lover. Once, at night, he told me how worried he was because all the workers depended on him – what if he failed? This talk, the concern, made me uncomfortable. This wasn't my picture of him.

The first time Peter took me to his office, on my way back to school, an Indian businessman came in to see him. The Asians were coming back, fifteen years after Amin gave them seventy-two hours to pack up and leave the country. They were tentatively re-establishing themselves, which didn't please the Ugandan business class too much.

Peter let the short, bustling black-turbaned man into his back office, where I was sitting. The Indian glanced my way and back at Peter, summing up the situation. After a curt 'How are you?' he dismissed me and turned to business. Jagjit had come to sell Peter dollars, which was illegal except through the Bank of Uganda, but everyone did it anyway, by *magendo*, the black market. He produced a thick envelope and drew out old, tattered green notes. Peter checked each one carefully, rubbed it between his palms, held it up under the light, turned it over, and scrutinised it until he was satisfied. He put aside one note, then went back to it after checking them all. He said, 'Sorry, Jagjit, this one's no good.' It was a one-hundred-dollar bill. That was about one million shillings.

'No, no, that can't be. I got this from Sunjab Patel – you know him – over in the industrial area.' Very fast, impatient.

'Yeah, but I'm telling you it's not worth anything. Look here' and they compared it to another, straining their necks and heads from note to note. Finally, Peter picked up the false note and, with his usual smirk, slowly tore it into two, steadily watching Jagjit's face. He was too shocked to protest, his large brown eyes fixed on the half-notes in each of Peter's raised hands. Peter held the torn pieces over the dustbin and let them float down slowly into it, all of us watching. 'You've got to be careful; anyone can cheat you around here,' he said, and shrugged. Peter turned to his safe, snug in a corner, and pulled out a canvas bag, which he emptied onto the table. Jagjit counted the many bundles of weary-looking Ugandan notes. He was flustered, whether with embarrassment or annoyance, I couldn't tell. He packed them up and out he rushed, after one last look at the torn note, as if he wanted to grab it out of the rubbish bin and run. Poor him I thought, but then again, he deserved it for giving me the once-over and deciding I didn't count.

Peter shook his head slowly. 'The bastard.'

'I don't think he knew.'

Peter reached over and took the half-notes from the dustbin, patted them off, and laid them together on the table.

'Peter!'

He smiled to himself, then looked up. 'What if I gave it to you?'

'What!? What would I do with it?'

'My little Christian Christine,' and he chuckled.

This time, Peter was busy with a group of men who were loading a pickup parked on the street. I was startled again by the way he was at work: stern and controlling, giving directions in a loud voice, striding up and down. Then he saw me.

'What are you doing here?' Brusque and impatient.

'I was just passing by.' I felt horribly in the way.

'I'm busy.'

'But – I – I have something to tell you.'

'Okay, okay, wait.'

He waved me on into his back office. After a short while he followed. But, somehow, I couldn't say it, so I asked him for a piece of paper and biro, which made him even more exasperated. I wrote down, 'I have just had an abortion.'

Peter took the paper, smiling impatiently, thinking I was

playing a childish game. His usual smile got stuck for an instant. A hint of what looked like anger flickered across his boyish face. He didn't look up at me. He took his biro from me, wrote something down, and passed the note back across the table. It read, 'Do you want some money?'

I read it, glanced up at him quickly, then away, embarrassed. Back to his five little words. I shook my head, no, my face lowered away from his . . . no, not money. I had nothing to say, and he said nothing back. After a bleak silence, like the silence while we made love, far away from each other, I got up to leave.

'I'll call you, okay?' Always kind.

'Okay.' Always agreeing. Yes, okay, yes.

As I walked out, Peter's men moved aside in that over-respectful way they treat whites, but with a mocking exaggeration acted out for their black women. As usual, I ignored them, but shrank inside as Peter kissed me drily on the lips, in front of them all, before I left.

The street was hard and hot; filled with people walking through their lives so purposefully, up and down the street, so in control. But they seemed to be backing away from me. Did I look strange? Was there blood on my dress? The hot, dusty air blown up by the noisy, rushing traffic filled my head like thunder.

Did I want money? What did I want? Bubble baths, gin and tonics, *ganga* sex, the clean, airy white house where I could forget the hot dust outside, school, my all too ordinary life, the bleak future? A few hours free from myself? Was that so bad? Had I wanted him to care, of all people? He was trying to help, I suppose. I'm sure the only Africans he knew needed money. Six months of sex, and did I want money? What did we want from each other? Not a baby. What a joke. I discarded my baby like I did my body, down a pit latrine crawling with cockroaches.

I waded through the taxi-park bedlam into a *matatu*, and was squashed up on all sides by strangely comforting fat hips, warm arms, moist breath. The old engine roared to a start, blocking out the radio's loud wail of *soukous*. The driver revved the engine repeatedly to get passengers to come running, as if we were leaving right away, only to sit for another fifteen minutes. The conductor screamed for more, for more people, ordering us to move over, squash up, we all wanted to get home, didn't we? Hawkers pushed cheap plastic through the windows into our faces, their spit landing on our cheeks. The voice of one of them pierced through the noise, pleading insistently for me to buy some Orbit chewing gum for my young children at home. 'Auntie, remember the children; be nice to the children!'

We finally moved away, swaying and bumping up and down together with each dive in and out of potholes, each swerve to avoid the oncoming cars that headed straight towards us like life. I closed my eyes, willing the noise and heat and sweat to recede to the very back of my mind. The glaring sun hit us all.

Mildred Kiconco Barya

Scars of Earth

The journey found us. Long after it was over, I returned to the place of first love.

My mother was the first person to hug me when I reached home. She felt my flesh, my bones, my heart.

'You've lost so much weight, dear child!'

'It's been a hectic life, Mama.' That's normal justification when you live in the city.

Dad appeared from the farm gate just across the compound, carrying a large cabbage that weighed about 10 kilograms. He was wearing his usual calf-length black books, being the farmer he's always been. A surge of fondness welled up in me. He held me for over five minutes, until his red cotton shirt was warm and wet with my tears.

'Welcome home,' he said. But I know he did not have to say those words, for they were carried on his hands as he smoothed and flattened my back. They were said in the way he hugged me, his eyes searching for the soul in me, his heart bleeding for me.

Mama whistled and sung at the same time. She stroked my dreadlocks like I had not stormed out of the house threatening no return, tired of a country life.

Wind blows in the eucalyptus trees. I stand still in the compound, consciously smelling the honeysuckle that's grown wildly on our fence. I inhale the sweet nectar and stretch out my arms to gather and hold as much sweetness as I can contain. I want to cuddle earth and holler that this is where I belong. I want to clasp time in the cold palms of my hands and not look back to wonder where my years have gone.

Mama disappears into the kitchen and shortly returns with a pot of coffee.

'I have mixed all the spices you used to love.'

'Yes, I smell the cinnamon, especially.'

'We shall sit here, outside.'

The sun is setting behind the hills. The sky wraps around herself a beautiful purple hue; it makes me want to weep. In our dreams, that's the colour we had chosen for the wedding clothes.

I hold the coffee cup and it warms my hands. I want it to reach the ice on the outside but it does not, cannot. Mama is across the table, silent. I could sit here forever in the quiet.

'Whenever I watch the golden sunset, your face breaks right through,' she says.

'You used to threaten me that Lakelekele, the green monster, would kidnap me if I did not move into the house.'

'You didn't even fear the mosquitoes. You were so loyal to that sunset you had no life indoors.'

I fight the desperate urge to cry. Just like me, sunsets were his favourite.

Sanyu, the kid who lost both her parents and ended up staying home, is laying the table for dinner. Dish after dish, she puts food on the tablemats and invites us to eat. Dad has completed his evening tasks, checking the paddocks and making sure all the farm gates are closed. He hangs his long coat on the nail in the dining room and joins us at the table.

'Lord God we thank you for your provisions that never run out, and we thank you for Nama who is with us tonight. Sanctify this food that it may nourish us, in Jesus' name we pray.' Dad's prayers were always brief and to the point.

'God has the whole universe crying to him, he doesn't need an essay to answer us,' he would say, when we told him, that the reverend would call his requests 'popcorn prayers bursting out so fast.'

'Nama, here's your favourite dodo,' he says, giving me the vegetables I've long missed.

'And here, groundnuts in mushroom sauce.'

'Here, your roast pumpkin, you used to love that, remember!'

'Oh yeah, thanks.' My voice can hardly manage to audibly pass through the maze of food in my mouth.

'And this is smoked beef in simsim paste; there's your chicken breast; the mashed Irish potatoes you liked as a child; here's the eggplant mixed with bitter tomatoes; sliced carrot in tender bean-pods; rice sprinkled with newly-picked peas and cardamoms, and your favourite millet bread . . .' Dad keeps passing round more of this and more of that.

The feast melts my heart. Then jugs of sweet porridge, sour porridge, fermented pineapple juice, sour milk, hot African tea flavoured with ginger, and every type of tropical fruit to be found in Kigezi. Sanyu has taken care to cut the water melon in triangular shapes, papaya in rectangular blocks, mangoes and avocados in oval shapes, oranges and guavas in crescent shapes, the berries retaining their round shapes . . . they dance before my eyes, and I pray to the Lord to make me brave so I do not make a mess of myself.

The conversation is punctuated with lightness, laughter and talking spoons. Even when we discuss sad issues that are the village's concern we connect like I haven't been away too long, like I just slept yesterday and woke up today with no estrangement between us. We discuss the sand and bricks business that's a trademark of our village; the neighbour's son who drowned; the couple who are going blind with age; heavy rains that flood our gardens from time to time; the village kids who have died of AIDS . . . we talk long into the night. When I finally retire to my room, I stretch out on the bed and listen to the once familiar songs of frogs croaking in the swamp nearby. The cockroaches stir the night with their melodies; the crickets make known their high stereo pitches.

Through my curtain-less window, the night is seductive. I

summon the verdant green trees to be my shade. I see the moon peep to greet me with her smile. I smile back. The stars shine brilliantly and I marvel how they are held up there, without falling, while we who walk the earth where we are supposed to be from, are always in a fall.

She walks into my room unannounced. I am watching the sun rise to the sorghum fields in the horizon. She puts her hands flat on my shoulders and works out a soothing massage. Because I cannot laugh or cry, I heave a pregnant sigh of relief. Gently she caresses my neck, my face and my tangled hair.

'You love my locks?'

She ignores the question. Her hands magically snake through the locks and squeeze my scalp. Energy flows back into me through her hands. This woman that is mother is a God. With her restorative touch my walls come down in total release.

'His name was Selestino,' I say. 'We did not set out on a trip, yet a few months later we embraced the future and talked wedding plans.'

Mama knows how near the surface my buried hurts are. She works her way from the surface to the deep, slowly moving down my back, circling rings of spine softly but firmly. I close my eyes and relax.

'He was an economist, he loved reading my dark poetry. All is gone and a wound grows festering inch by inch.'

The hands touch parts I'd never known to feel the kind of sensation I was getting. The kind of weightlessness that comes with being a leaf floating on a wave. The kind of lightness known only when you're touched by love.

'I remember mostly how he made me feel. With Tino, love was not the fiery passion of a bush in flames, but a calm fire kindled from beneath and brought out in soft whispers.'

Her hands remove the ache from my body, heart and mind.

'His love was not the loud hammer that shatters rocks, but the gentle falling drop of water that melts the stone.'

'Are you still clutching the past like gold nuggets that cannot be put away?' Those are Mama's first words since the confession. I had thought she would chide me for never telling her about the relationship while it was soaring high.

'I have moved on, but I do not forget. Sometimes I call out to him like deep calls to deep. I see him in rays of the sun breaking through dawn to my day.'

'You're throwing away the present.'

'The past was beautiful.'

'Learn to face the future.'

'I can only learn to survive the transition, to accept the interval. Years have gone with the locusts. I still seek his brown eyes to look for the soul that gave me wings.'

'I feel your pain.' Mama speaks from the depth of her kindness.

'I think love and pain have a symbiotic kind of relationship. They are intertwined like twigs in a crown of thorns. You cannot have one without the other. This I never knew.'

'There are many things we do not know,' she calmly responds.

'You and Dad have always loved each other, how do you do it?'

'We have many lifetimes in a lifetime. Like seasons, we do not take any for granted.'

So we talk about winter, summer, fall and spring. Each has a beautiful purpose for which it was created. Each sheds a different life on mother earth. Earth does not complain when spring leaves and there's winter. Neither does she grumble when summer ends and fall sets in.

I recall how I groaned within when Tino left me. When he told me he had prayed and God advised him to cancel our relationship. It was God's doing, not Tino's decision per se. He always took cover in spiritualizing everything.

'What else did God say in your prayer?' I had the nerve to ask.

'He showed me another woman.'

For a whole week I was a bundle of nerves and only a thin sheet of mercy held me from losing myself. Half the time, I was dizzy and suicidal, the other half of the time I was truly mad.

'I am glad you've come home. I am glad you're sharing with me what happened to you.' Her hands are now making repeated performances, playing in my locks and running to and from my spine.

That day I chose to become earth. To embrace each season, each love, each friendship in its lifetime. To release each season when it goes without questioning why or when it would happen again. On nights when I look up, the sky is full of a million stars. Clouds and all, I rejoice to be part of that heavenly orbit. On days when it rains, I open up to the softness and touch of rain and drink to my fill. When the sun comes out, I welcome the warmth, the heat. When the wind blows falling leaves over me, I receive them. I have found the joys of being mellow in spite of the scars. I have been earth since talking with Mama.

Rounke Coker

Ojo and theArmed Robbers

Rich, deep, honeyed, totally native, not self-conscious, it gently, but persistently, penetrated my dream. Gradually, I became aware of it, and the dream began to slip reluctantly away. My eyes stayed closed, as I tried desperately to cling to the healing nothingness of sleep. I needed to be healed. The stress of investigating economic policy, while avoiding the sexual predators who implemented it, had made life unpleasant of late. This provincial university town was the location of my refuge, Tunde and Felicity's home. My bed was in the spare room right at the back of a 1950s bungalow, off a laterite track that meandered into the bush from the main road. It was the quietest room in the house. Yet, this sound kept intruding, refusing to go away and becoming more pronounced. I held on for as long as possible but, in the end, my consciousness finally tuned in. It was so rich, so deep, so honeyed, so totally native; no sign of 'been to' with this one; comfortable in his own skin; confident in his own expressions. I had to investigate.

There was still sleep in my eyes, yet I could see immediately that the sound belonged to an interesting-looking man. His skin was not dark chocolate in colour. It was a deep, velvety, moist black – the kind that does not need to be oiled after bathing. His hair was jet black with a light grey streak to one side. His body was, not to put too fine a point on it, enchanting. He was chatting to Felicity as she picked up Dotun's toys. His legs were long and clad in much-washed greyish jeans, through which I could make out the firm shapes of the muscles of his thighs and calves. His shoulders were square and wide, and his arms suggested a gentle strength. He was sprawled, half sitting and half lying, across the entire length of the sofa, like he owned it. Why was this gorgeous specimen of manhood feeling so at home in this house, chatting to Felicity like they were old friends? How come she hadn't even mentioned him to me before? Who was he?

My hostess said, 'Oh, hello, sleepy-head! Did we wake you?' Frowning with the effort, I dragged my eyes away from the gorgeousness, towards Felicity, grunting in the affirmative. The rich voice said, 'Oops! Sorry-o! I didn't realise there was someone asleep in the house! Well, I'd better be going then!'

I hastily opened my eyes, and croaked a protest. 'Stay,' I begged, 'tell me who you are'. At least, that's what my heart and loins said. I hope my mouth said something less obvious. Truth to tell, I can't remember what actually transpired after that. Tunde and little Dotun came home. We must have eaten. Our hosts must have bathed and gone to bed. We, Ojo and I, were found still talking at breakfast time the next day. He was still sprawled across the sofa, and I sat with my legs tucked up on an adjacent armchair. Goodness knows what we spoke of during the night, but I remember that my heart and soul were filled with an indescribable happiness, a feeling that I had, at last, found my own personal, living, breathing port in the storm of life. This was a man interested in my mind, not just in my body.

He left after breakfast to deliver lectures to his class of undergraduates. I retired to bed. The affair began in earnest the next day, once we'd each had a chance to catch up on sleep. We were totally wrapped up in each other; in each other's likes and dislikes, hopes and dreams, fears and worries, knowledge and experience. He was steeped in the practices and folklore of the Yorubas of his poor rural upbringing, recounting proud stories of survival against the forces of unfair world trade and unpredictable nature. I learnt that if one had to relieve one's self out in the open – as one was often forced to do in a country where public toilets are rare and usually inhabited by thieves and drug addicts – to spit on the urine afterwards. Ojo stressed that I must do this in order to deter the use of my bodily fluids in witchcraft. The spit made the urine unusable. As a child of the city, I'd never come across these fears and practices before, though they made sense when he explained the context to me. This kind of learning made me feel somehow closer to the real pulse of my people and culture. In return, I made him laugh till he cried by recounting my attempts at foregoing the luxuries of middle-class Lagos – in solidarity with the people, you understand – by using the mass transport system. On one occasion at a bus stop, I managed to bring a rugby scrum of commuters to a complete halt by screaming from somewhere in their tangled midst, 'Mind my glasses! MIND MY GLASSES!' The hardened men and women had been so shocked by this little voice bellowing out for mercy, that they silently made way and allowed me to board first – which of course, left me wandering if this was all a set up by armed robbers…

It became impossible for us to do things separately. In fact, the only things he did without me were give lectures and mark his students' written assignments. The only things I did without him were interview fat economists and prepare reports for my department from which I was on secondment. We did everything else together, often with a delighted – not to say rejuvenated – Tunde and Felicity in tow. There did seem to be some mutterings of disquiet which, as they were not made to my face, I ignored. As long as Tunde said Ojo was all right, then all was well. We discovered that we both liked really soft plantain, fried and eaten with anything – though our favourite accompaniment was fried chips of yam and an 'Ojo Special' made with cheap smoked fish, oil, tomato puree, chillies and chopped onions. This was generally our breakfast, with large mugs of tea. At that time of the day, when the sun still had some distance to rise and the dew was therefore still capable of drenching your feet as you walked over fields to school or work, I often heard this bird song. It sounded exactly as if the bird was saying, 'Ojo-o-o-o! Ojo-o-o-o!' The world just seemed very interesting and new, now. It was like we were in an unbreakable capsule, insulating us – certainly me – from the vicissitudes of life and all other suddenly extraneous activities.

I should have been listening harder; listening to myself and the one-hundred-percent reliable bells going off in my head. But in the place where my head was, the bells sounded beautiful and heart warming, not anxious and foreboding. They were the sound of church bells announcing the end of the war, not warning of air raids. The other thing that should have alerted me was the information I had now garnered about him. I knew a lot about his childhood, his village and his parents. I knew a lot about his days as a student. However, after graduation, the picture suddenly became less clear. At the time, I put it down to a macho man not wanting to talk about how awful that time was – the lack of jobs, the hunger and the homelessness. Tunde and I had escaped it by working overseas, which was where Felicity met her man. It had been a bad time in Nigeria, what with the imposition of a so-called 'Structural Adjustment Programme', allegedly designed to help our economy recover from mismanagement and indebtedness. So which idiots loaned $30 billion to the illegal military regimes controlling Nigeria at the time? Why should ordinary Nigerians, most of whom were – and still are – poor, semi-literate, under-employed, dispossessed and ignorant of international financial deals, be held to account for the ensuing debt? Anyway, I didn't press Ojo at the time, because I thought he was hiding some terrible privation, as many others like him were.

Then one morning, it all fell apart. We were still in bed, although I was awake as I was listening to the 'Ojo bird'. The doorbell rang on the locked gate at the bottom of the steps leading to Ojo's first-floor flat. I was a bit put out; who could it be at this time on a weekday morning? I was about to say something rude out loud, when Ojo hastily clamped his hand over my mouth, and I realised something serious was about to go down. In my mind, I began to panic about where to hide. The doorbell rang again, and Ojo swore. I asked, 'What shall we do?' and he said, 'You must hide!' His car was visibly parked out front so he could not pretend to be out. He'd have to answer the door. I realised then that he wasn't behaving as if there were armed robbers out there, which is what I had thought of initially.

Only a few weeks ago, we had giggled at the story of a lecturer who lived about a mile away. His doorbell had rung similarly, the morning after payday. He managed to hide his wife and children in the loft before armed robbers broke in, and he had to pacify them not only with his pay packet (Nigeria's is a cash economy, especially on pay day), but also with all the alcohol and white goods in his house. Ojo was sweating now, and not wanting to add to his anxiety (it *could* have been his mother), I obediently got up and was shoved into a cupboard in the spare room.

I couldn't see anything, of course, and at first, I couldn't hear anything. Once the bell ringer had been let in the locked gate and brought upstairs and into the flat, however, I could hear every word. I heard a woman chatting animatedly and rather familiarly with Ojo. A horrible thought crossed my mind. It couldn't be his wife, could it? Please God, no! Then, another thought crossed my mind. If that *was* his wife, where had she been all this time? And how come she didn't have a key? No, she couldn't be, thank goodness. I'd already been taken for that ride before, and the momentary thought that it was happening again chilled my heart. Then the voices retreated; I heard the sound of a door being locked, then of footsteps on the stairs going down. Finally, Ojo's car, which was decrepit and had to be hot-wired to get it going, spluttered into life and rolled away.

How odd! I pushed open the cupboard door and stepped out

gingerly, as if the woman might still be around. But it was deadly quiet – just me and the 'Ojo bird'. I pottered around the flat all morning, as the locked front door prevented me from leaving. In the early afternoon, I heard a car draw up outside and peeped carefully out of the sitting room windows. It was Ojo, alone this time. He locked the car, mounted the stairs and opened the front door.

'Why did you lock me in?' I asked indignantly. For a minute, he looked startled and then he grinned, 'I must have done it out of habit!' I was too anxious to hear his answer to the next question, so I let that one go until later.

'And who was that woman?' He didn't answer at first, instead walking into the kitchen and taking a beer out of the fridge. I let him find the opener, open the beer, find a glass, walk back into the sitting room, sit down on the sofa and pour himself a drink. My heart was pounding louder and faster as the seconds and then minutes unfolded.

'Who was that woman?' I repeated. Over the rim of his glass, he stared at me expressionlessly, and then I knew.

My reaction makes me, with hindsight, proud to be Yoruba woman. There was no point in attacking him on a person-to-person basis. He was six foot two of muscled fitness, and I was five foot two of podgy city life. I do, however, believe in revenge – especially after the last time this happened to me – and my mind rapidly settled on an acceptable alternative. I wrecked the joint. Nothing escaped my fury. Anything that I could lift with my now super-human strength, I flung at things that I couldn't move. I attacked everything in that flat, and I screamed loud and long while doing it. The only object containing glass that survived was his television, and that's because he stood in front of it, defending it with his body. Every plate, cup and tumbler was destroyed, mostly by throwing them with all my might at the louvered windows, which were similarly, completely destroyed. I also successfully demolished much of his furniture. Even the bed was damaged – hopefully irreparably. Books were shredded. It seemed like hours, but it probably only lasted about twenty minutes. When there was nothing else to smash, I realised that I was wracked with sobbing.

I didn't want him near me then, so I put my shoes on and left. I walked just down the road to Tunde and Felicity's, where I found them trying to use the phone. It hadn't worked for many months and, in spite of my own problems, I was surprised and concerned. What other terrible thing could have happened to induce them to try something so futile? Felicity rushed to me and hugged me off my feet, while Tunde slumped with relief in his chair.

'What's going on?' I asked, over Felicity's shoulder. 'We could hear this terrible screaming coming from down the road! I was trying to call the police!' explained British-born Felicity, letting go of me. Then they both noticed that I was crying. Tunde sat up suddenly and said quietly, 'It was you, wasn't it?' I nodded miserably and collapsed on the sofa, crying fit to burst by this time.

'Has Ojo done something to hurt you?' Felicity asked. I nodded, as I was heaving too dramatically with sobs to talk. 'What?' they both demanded. Eventually, I calmed down enough to tell them, 'His wife came home today'. They were both shocked, especially Tunde, who thought he knew all there was to know about Ojo. He had not known about a wife – or he would have warned me from the start. The marriage must have happened while he was out of the country, though goodness knows why he hadn't seen the wife since he'd been back.

Tunde was so upset that he went off in search of the miscreant. He meant to challenge him about his behaviour, not only towards me, but towards Felicity and himself, who had openly given their approval to our relationship because they thought he was single.

Felicity spent the afternoon doing her best to help me get over this first bout of despair. Of course, there would be other, more keenly felt bouts, later. I told her what had happened and how I reacted, and she responded from time to time in that typically English way, 'No! You never! He didn't!' She let me talk myself out. We cooked a fabulous dinner, and had just put two-year-old Dotun to bed when Tunde came home. He strolled into the sitting room, grinning from ear to ear, showing all his teeth in a most indecorous way. He made straight for me. Felicity thought he was drunk, and tried to divert him, but he shrugged her off. He gave me a giant hug, held up my right arm like I had won a gold medal and declared, 'Behold! The lioness has spoken!' Now I also began to think he was drunk, though he didn't smell of alcohol.

We sat him down and demanded an explanation. I felt it was beneath me to ask directly about Ojo, so I just insisted on 'an explanation' of this statement. Tunde looked at me and said, 'Remind me *never* to be anywhere within arms' reach of you when you get angry!' Felicity and I grinned at each other, and I told Tunde what happened. By the time I finished, we were all crying, though Felicity and I could see that Tunde was crying with laughter. 'It's NOT FUNNY!' declared Felicity, bashing her husband over the head with a soft cushion. 'But you don't know why I am laughing,' choked Tunde.

Eventually, he told us what he had heard in the university staff club, a guaranteed source of the truth behind any gossip. Apparently, while I was smashing up Ojo's flat, one of his neighbours – a fellow lecturer at the university – just happened to be weeding his cassava plot a few yards away. This chap had heard the screams and roars and bangs and crashes. He'd even seen smashed louvers falling from the windows. Giving thanks that his wife and children were absent, the neighbour had crept stealthily to his car, let out the brakes and rolled it away from the scene of the assault. On reaching the laterite road, he switched the engine on and took off at speed. Did he rush to the police station? No. Did he go in search of help of any kind? No. He sped off to the staff club and announced to those present that Mr Ojo Olatunji, of the Physical Education and Health Sciences Department, had just had an encounter with a 'gang of armed robbers!'

The news spread like wild fire. When Ojo appeared at the club that evening with several plasters on his person, presumably to console himself over the day's disasters, he was startled to receive the commiseration of his colleagues. They bought him a large beer and plied him with questions: Why did he resist? How did he resist? How many were they? What were his wounds?

Ojo began to realise that no one knew what had really happened! After a few dry-throated half-sentences in reply, he began to wax lyrical about how he surprised them in the act. How there were two or three – he couldn't be sure – in the mêlée. How he fought them because he would not be taken for a fool! How he fended off their gun buts with karate chops.

In the midst of this flow, Ojo happened to glance up and what he saw drained the blood from his face. There was Tunde, sitting all alone in the corner, laughing his head off.

Anthonia C Kalu

Ebube Dike!

Adaaku shifted gears as the late afternoon traffic inched down Asa Road in both directions. They'd had the conversation many times about Adaaku having a car and knowing how to drive. She had learned to drive because the frequent trips to the village to look in on the grandmothers were not always voluntary. Although her parents lived only a few streets away from her, the message givers always managed to find Adaaku first.

Chike convinced her to buy the car. Although her business was doing very well, she had not thought of buying a car for herself. Rumour and the match-making mills had it that a woman alone with a car was not a good thing; for the men. Well-educated young women with tendencies for any type of personal independence were not for marrying. But Chike finally convinced her that a woman alone on foot or in a taxi at night could be worse than anything the rumour mills could dream up.

'Adaaku,' he said, at the end of his wits about how to convince her. 'To your family, Adaaku is the water, Adaaku is the firewood. You are at the core of everything in their lives. You cannot do anything about that. Your best option is to make yourself available to your many responsibilities while keeping control of your life. Knowing how to drive your own car will help you do that.'

Surprised by his passionate plea, Adaaku had no answer. Although she was familiar with the references to water and firewood, she had never understood them as applying to her or her life. In a few weeks, she learned to drive the car. It was a nice off-white Toyota Santana with plush brown seats. She loved driving herself around Enyimba City in her new car.

'I go drive myself!' She was jolted out of her thoughts by a jeering taxi driver who was stuck on the other side of the traffic.

'Yes, you fit drive well, well-o-o!' she jeered back, smiling cheekily at him. Nearby drivers laughed, glad to have something to divert their attention from the slow-moving traffic. Luckily, the lorry in front of her moved. She shifted gears again, pushing lightly on the pedal, mindful of the precariousness of a driver's life in the pothole-filled road. Although the air was hot and humid, she did not turn on the air conditioning because she wanted to hear all the noise outside. Despite the traffic jams, she loved the city at this time of the day. Mostly, she liked the different noises. There was the music blaring from the shops that lined both sides of the street; before she had the car, she loved to stop to listen to and buy some records. There were the horns of cars, lorries and trucks as drivers jostled each other, each one wanting to be in front of the person ahead of them. Driving in Aba was worth nothing if you did not join in the horn blaring. Drivers used them to tell pedestrians to move out of the way, give messages to one another or just add to the noise of traffic. There was also the laughter, the heat, the humidity. In short, it was life in Aba. The logic of it eluded her, especially since the result was almost always a traffic jam. But she'd decided that she would take her time and enjoy all of it.

Adaaku's high sense of connection to life made it easy for her to fully engage everyday problems like the evening jams in Aba traffic. Although she did not exactly like being in traffic jams, she always tried to solve the puzzle of which of the many cars would make it out of the predictable grid before the others, creating a small trickle of movement for those behind them. She scanned the traffic ahead, trying to gauge how much longer she would be stuck in the evening traffic on

Asa Road. Every day the drivers continued to make the same irrational driving decisions, turning the two-lane roads into a quandary of motionless cars and stagnant noise. For Adaaku, this was one of those days she was acutely sensitive to things around her and she wanted to reach the peace and quiet of her house soon.

Intimately connected with everything, Adaaku could imagine the airflow beyond the traffic jam and feel tickled by a bird flying overhead. When she was a teenager, she tried to explain her sense of connection to things to her father. He said she was either a mystic or a first-time visitor to earth. People like her, he said, danced to ancestral tunes no matter what. Sometimes, the flapping of bird wings could caress her funny bones as lightly as if her sides were touched by a friend's hands. At other times she could cry simply because a leaf fell off its tree and its falling reminded her of death, or a deeply felt love. But those feelings did not prevent her from cutting flowers to make bouquets which she gave as gifts to friends and relations who called her *ogbanje* because they could not explain her open demonstrations of fondness for nature. But, for Adaaku, this fondness did not stop her from eating chicken pieces in tomato stew made for rice or yams. In fact, it made her more determined to live life fully with delight and determination. She shifted gears; the traffic moved a few yards and stopped.

Feeling so close to things not only reminded her that life is borne on the wings of a passing bird but also that, throughout history, men had become used to the idea of giving the heads of other men to kings as tokens of respect, obedience or fealty. She knew that resurrection is the end of death and hoped that death is the beginning of reincarnation. She had learned from Nne that one did not have to give up deeply-held knowledge of the self to participate in the building of a nation or the sharing of life's gifts. But since she always immersed herself completely in everything she did, she often miscalculated people's ability to commit to ordinary things. That was the main problem she had with Chike, a lifelong friend and the love of her life. She could not guess what he was capable of.

When Adaaku was a child, her grandmother explained the mystery of sharing to her. She and Ukata were the youngest of four children and very close. Their two older brothers were already in a secondary boarding school. That year, Adaaku and Ukata were sent home to stay with Nne. Their mother was having a hard time with her cloth trading. Thieves had stolen all the bales of cloth in the big store, leaving her only with the smaller store near the edge of the market. She had to reinstate her business. Their father worked in a large company and always came home late. They sent the two youngest children back to the village so she could engage in the extended trips required to re-stock her business. One day, Nne returned from the market with the usual gifts of *akara* and groundnuts. She gave Adaaku one *akara*. As always, her brother Ukata wanted some of Adaaku's share. But Adaaku refused to share any of her *akara*. She ate it slowly, taunting her little brother until the last bit disappeared down her throat.

Nne watched. She did not scold Adaaku or punish her. Instead, a few minutes after Adaaku finished the last of that *akara,* Nne gave Ukata not one but two whole *akara*. Adaaku watched in dismay as Ukata ate the two big *akara* while sitting in the safety of Nne's lap. Long after he had finished eating, Nne called Adaaku aside.

'You must always share the things that make you feel sweet with the people you love,' Nne said. Adaaku understood immediately that she was talking about the *akara* incident with Ukata.

'But it didn't make me feel sweet; I was hungry and happy to have something to eat,' she said fretfully. She stiffened her shoulders, readying herself for the spanking she thought Nne was going to give her.

'No, you were happy because having the *akara* made your body feel sweet, powerful.' It was part statement, part question.

Adaaku thought about it. 'Yes,' she said. She understood. 'When I feel like that, it's as if there's a light shining through me and . . . and . . . , also . . . , I can feel there's a river, with very clear water that runs through it; inside me, I can feel it . . . ' she stopped, stunned by the effort of self-revelation.

'Yes. That's *ebube,* the wonder feeling of life. Not many people can feel it. Those who do must learn to control it as well as share it. Knowing how to do both is important in knowing how to live productively, properly. Only a person who can look in the face of life without flinching, the courageous, can feel it. Our people call such a person *dike*, husband-to-strength.'

Adaaku said nothing more about it. But over the years, she thought about it because the feeling came upon her again and again. Although she did not receive a beating that day, she remained angry with Nne and Ukata about the *akara* incident. She felt bad for days not because she had refused to share the *akara* but because she could not do anything to Ukata while he ate the two biggest *akara* she had ever seen in her life. A month later, Ukata complained of a stomach ache. They took him to the dispensary where he was given some medicine for worms. He died before daybreak. Adaaku was heartbroken. She missed Ukata with the unquenchable pain of childhood. Nothing anybody said helped. Nne refused to let her parents take her back to Aba.

'She'll not know how to mourn her brother there. Let her stay here where everybody knows him.'

For a long time, the *akara* incident was mixed up with Ukata's death. It became difficult for her to accept gifts from people because she did not know if the one they gave her was the best they could offer. Mostly, it made accepting Chike's friendship difficult. Did he really like her or was he only trying to find out if she was who she said she was? But it was not only the incident with Nne; it was also all the other encounters with people who tried to convince her that a girl should be seen and not heard. Now, as a fully grown woman and a graduate from Nigeria's premier university, she was not sure how to express her thoughts or plan her actions even though she had a great deal to share. Unlike Nne, who always said what she thought and did what she wanted, Adaaku's words and thoughts stuck in her throat. She glanced out of the window and felt the humidity descend on her – the evening traffic was beginning to move a few more yards at a time.

As she manoeuvred her car through the stop-and-go evening traffic, she began to plan what she would eat for dinner. But thoughts of her current quarrel with Chike kept intruding. She could not remember a time when she did not know Chike. As a child, she saw him as a tall, handsome, nice boy. Later, at the university, he looked out for her as one would a sister. She did not suspect that he was seriously interested in her until he surprised her by taking leave from his job in Lagos to attend her graduation at the University of Nigeria. Throughout that day, he had that special light in his eyes, or maybe it was the way she felt when he looked at her. His deep belly laugh seemed to her more than just laughter; it became a message to her, a message of his feelings for her.

Throughout that day there was an aura around him that made her tingle; it made her want to laugh and cry at the same time. She wanted to stand longer by his side after he gave her the graduation gift he brought for her and someone took a picture of them together. Even as she mingled with her guests, her ears were focused on his voice, his deep belly laugh. Her feelings were alert to every one of his movements. But Chike did not say anything about the force between them that day. Long after the graduation party, she remembered how they had looked into each other's eyes across the room full of people – twice. But Chike said nothing before he left and she wondered if she had imagined it.

After she passed her bar exams, she started working at a law office in Aba. She saw Chike during the Christmas season when everyone went home to the village. He had studied business and worked for a large company in Lagos. She wondered why he didn't marry but kept hoping he wouldn't. Every now and then there were rumours about him and some girl he wanted to marry. Two years after she started working in Aba, she opened a small boutique for women. Her shop also stocked expensive *lappas* and exquisite jewellery. The shop, which she called *Ebube*, became a popular spot for young women. Both young and old men wanting to impress their girlfriends and wives became her clientele. Her job and the store thrived. One of her cousins, Egodi, managed the store. She had completed the West African School Certificate exams with a grade one and was waiting to pass the entrance examination to the university. But after Adaaku made her the manager at Ebube, Egodi decided to work at the store for a few more years. Adaaku went to the shop two or three times a week to keep an eye on the inventory. But there was no need for her to worry. Egodi was an excellent saleswoman and the customers came steadily; Adaaku was even thinking of opening a second store. She swerved her car into a new space that opened up only to get stuck between a stationary lorry and a bus full of people. She exchanged a few 'I go drive myself' taunts and ritualised curses with nearby drivers as she steered her car back into the slow-moving traffic.

A few months after Adaaku's graduation, Chike came to visit her at Aba. He said he had felt that glow also but did not know what to say or do about it.

'So, why didn't you say anything?' she asked. They were sitting in her living room, as far away from each other as she could manage without seeming rude because she felt vulnerable.

'I don't know. I thought you'd treat it as a joke.' He sounded shy, uncertain.

'What are you talking about?' she said, gruffly.

'I didn't want to risk my reputation with you.' He was smiling, goading her; his confidence restored at the sign of her diffidence. 'Unlike you, I have a reputation to protect and your tendency for squashing replies in such situations is notorious. I have heard about all the suitors you've sent packing.'

She aimed an imaginary object at him; he ducked, laughing his deep belly laugh.

'Well, they deserved to be sent packing! Quite a few of the educated ones wanted a full-time housewife. Can you imagine me as a full-time housewife?' She joined in his laughter. They continued chatting for a while. He was easy to talk to and she liked spending the afternoon alone with him.

'So, why are you here?'

'Because I want to be the only witness to the quit notice you might serve me.'

'Wha-a-at, whaa . . . ?' she stuttered. 'What are you . . . ?'

He did not let her finish. In what felt like the longest minute of Adaaku's life, Chike crossed the room and sat down by her side on the sofa. He sat close enough to touch.

'I came here to ask you to marry me.' He said it fast; as if he was afraid he would not be able to speak otherwise.

'Is that all?' She felt herself glowing. Her whole body felt sweet. 'If I thought you were going to say "yes",' she said, 'I would have asked you many years ago.'

He pulled her close to him, squeezing the breath out of her. The rest of the day went by in that feel-great timelessness that all new couples feel is their sole preserve. They were hungry but wouldn't make time to eat. The conversation was endless, deep. Each wondered about what was growing steadily between them that day. Each one tried to explain why it had been so difficult to tell the other how they felt over the years. With the advantage of new knowledge, they told each other that they'd always known they were meant to be together. Together, they re-dreamed their past and planned a long peaceful future together.

'I didn't want you to blame me for stopping you from getting a university degree,' Chike said.

'I didn't want you to think I lacked good upbringing, but I kept hoping that you were not interested in someone else.'

They were sitting in the living room again after the light dinner they finally decided to eat.

'Well, I tried to make sure no one else would sideline me where you're concerned,' Chike said.

'Oh! Is that why you were always there at the university?'

'No, that's because I sort of like you,' he said, laughing. They lived years together that day as they came into the full awareness that no other couple had ever had or would ever have what they shared with each other.

However, it seemed the idea of getting married was the only thing they couldn't agree on. After that wonderful day, they began to think of the practical aspects of keeping what they found in each other. But they could not decide when he should carry the wine to her people or whether they should live in Lagos or Aba. There was her store, their parents, his big job in Lagos. He wanted to wait until his next visit to the east to carry the *mmanya ajuju* (the wine) to ask her people about her availability. They had waited all these years, he said. She wanted him to carry the wine now, before he left for Lagos again, but he was not ready. He had come to the east unprepared for that next step and did not have the money to buy all the items necessary for that first visit.

But Adaaku thought that Chike was watching her and quarrelled with him over something insignificant. She wanted to quarrel with him. But as usual, her anger stuck in her throat. She did not feel that she had known him long enough in the newly-declared phase of their relationship to risk a quarrel. On his part, Chike went back to Lagos more confused than Adaaku. Not knowing how to make things right between them, Adaaku wrote him a stinker and he fired one right back at her. They did not write to each other for a while. Adaaku missed Chike's belly laughs. Unable to convince himself of any reason beside Adaaku to go home, Chike reduced the frequency of his trips to the east. When he started visiting her again and brought up the subject of carrying the wine, Adaaku said he should wait. Their relationship developed into a close friendship. Everyone waited for the wedding invitation. The deadlock was now over two years old. Realising that the tension in her forehead was ebbing away, Adaaku relaxed her grip on the steering wheel, recognising that the traffic was moving more smoothly now. It was still moving slowly but there was less noise, fewer horns.

Throughout her educational career, Adaaku had focused on the necessary skills. All the women in her family encouraged her efforts because, according to them, a woman with a strong right arm could raise the world to her *chi* so both of them could observe it together in companionship. Eventually she chose law because it sounded like a reasonable career and a money-making avenue. Everyone told her that law is a profession for men. But she persisted, seeing it mostly as a route to a job that would make her independent. She would be able to take care of both her grandmothers, and her younger siblings. But most importantly, she would take care of her parents. Even while she was still in the university, everyone asked her about getting married. She always said that she would know when she met her husband. Among the family members, Nne was always there with her wisdom and a firm guiding hand.

'Listen to what people have to say. But with regard to marriage, make sure that the man you choose is your own husband. Life can be rough if you don't follow what your heart tells you. Often, a girl who's not paying attention chooses a man without thinking. One day, they wake up and realise that they married someone else's husband. Many women's lives are difficult because of that.' Adaaku listened. But over the years, it seemed that listening to Nne's wise words made her life more difficult. All her friends were married, and she couldn't decide if Chike was watching her or waiting for her.

Finally, Adaaku stopped the car outside her house. She was so tired she peeled off her sandals as soon as she stopped the engine. Swinging them from her index finger, she walked on the balls of her feet up the warm gravel path. She took the keys out of her handbag as she reached the door. As she reached for the door knob, the door was opened from the inside by a tall, slim, dark-skinned girl with soft brown eyes.

'Sister, Ndeewo!' Ola greeted her, taking Adaaku's bag and shoes. She was Chike's youngest sister. There was no mistaking the relationship. She could have been his twin if she were older. She was wearing a faded blue skirt suit but still managed to look like a fashion model.

'Mmm-hmh! *Odia*?'

'I'm fine,' Ola answered in English.

After a brief exchange, Adaaku discovered that Ola had arrived earlier in the day from the village.

'Have you eaten?'

'Yes. I ate some *garri* and that nice *egusi* soup.'

'So you haven't seen Chike?'

'No!' there was a smile in Ola's voice and a twinkle in her eye. Adaaku examined Ola's face for any traces of mischief. She could never predict what Chike would do in his efforts to make her give him an answer about the wine carrying. She'd continued to tell him she needed more time. Chike said he would wait.

'Because if Chike sent you, just tell him that my answer is final!'

'And what is your answer, Sister?' Ola was a student at the university and was one of the very few people who could talk back at Adaaku, who had a reputation for bluntness.

'The answer. . . ? I don't know!'

'Sister Adaaku, that's not an answer! It just means you don't know what to say.' Ola's eyes shone. She had attended the same secondary school with Egodi and stopped by often to visit her at the store. They were very good friends and there was not much Adaaku could do to keep Ola from her house. She always spent part of her visit at Adaaku's house. Although custom did not require Adaaku's hospitality toward Ola, it did not forbid it either. Adaaku could not refuse her visits without appearing ill-mannered. Besides, she liked the young woman.

'Let him come and carry the wine, you hear?' Ola pleaded.

But Adaaku was already looking for something to eat and did not reply. During dinner, Ola was full of news from home and talked nonstop with only a few interruptions from Adaaku. Later, they settled down and watched *Zebrudaya* and some other television programmes and went to bed.

The next morning, Adaaku was getting ready for work when Ola knocked at her bedroom door.

'Come in! What is it?'

'Sister, good morning!' Ola's worried face looked in the door.

'Good morning! What is it?'

'Are you ready to go to work yet?'

'I'm almost ready. What's wrong?'

'It's one of the taxi drivers from home.' She stepped into the room. 'It's Nne.'

'Is she all right? What's wrong with her?'

'I don't know. He says he wants to talk with you.'

Adaaku got dressed quickly and went to the living room. The driver was still standing near the door. 'Is my Nne dead?' Adaaku's lips began to quiver; she bit her lower lip.

'No. She's in the hospital. She wants you to come.'

'Which hospital did you take her to? Abiriba?'

'I didn't take her. They took her to Umuahia. I was sent to give you or your mother the message.'

'Please, sit down. Don't tell me any more. Ola, please help find something for him to eat. Send someone to tell Mama to get ready. She's coming to the hospital with me.'

Adaaku went into a frenzy of activity to get ready for the forty-mile drive to Umuahia. The fact that they took Nne to the hospital in Umuahia meant that the situation was serious. She packed a small bag and on Ola's insistence, ate some breakfast. Soon, Mama came and they left for Umuahia. Asa Road was not very busy. Adaaku kept up an incessant chatter, trying to distract Mama's attention from Nne's illness.

Nne was asleep when they arrived at the hospital. Two of Adaaku's uncles and one aunt were waiting on the veranda outside the ward. The nurse told them that Nne was doing well. The doctor had already given her some medicine. She had acute malaria and had been unable to eat for two days. She was delirious during the night. The nurse placed a chair for Adaaku near Nne's bed. Adaaku sat down, placing her hand in Nne's. Nne open her eyes, smiled weakly at Adaaku and went back to sleep. Nne looked so old and frail in the hospital bed. Adaaku's lips started trembling again as she contemplated the drip which was delivering a steady dose of liquid into Nne's body.

Adaaku stayed at the hospital for three days. But Nne's fever refused to go down and the doctor wouldn't discharge her. He ordered some more tests but could not figure out what was keeping her temperature high. On the fourth morning, Chike arrived at the hospital ward as Adaaku was giving Nne a bed bath.

'Good morning!'

Adaaku turned at the sound of the familiar voice. She dropped the wet towel and ran to Chike, who immediately enveloped her in a warm embrace. When he finally let her go, he kept her hand.

'Nne, *Odia*?'

'*Odi mma*. She's doing much better,' Adaaku said.

'That's what the doctors keep saying but they won't let me go home,' Nne added.

'I came as quickly as I could.'

'When did you arrive?' Adaaku asked as she continued to give Nne her bath.

'Last night. But it was too late to come here.'

'How did you know? Who told you?' Adaaku asked.

'Oh! Ola and Egodi sent me a message by local courier! One of the taxi drivers who ply between Aba and Lagos gave me the message,' he said. 'Does your mother know?' he asked.

'Yes. Mama left after the second day,' Adaaku answered,

accepting the change of subject. She would deal with it later. 'She says she'll be back tomorrow if we're still here. My uncles and aunt left yesterday afternoon.'

'I don't know why everyone had to come. I wasn't really that ill,' Nne said. 'It's all costing too much money.'

'Nne, don't worry about that. We just want you to get better,' Adaaku said, soothingly. They talked with her for a while until the doctor came.

'How is our Mother today?' The doctor asked Nne.

'I'm well.'

He laughed, 'You really are a very important woman. Look at all these people who have come to see you. You're going to get well soon.'

After the doctor left, Nne said she was hungry for some *akara* and *akamu*. That was the first time since Adaaku arrived at the hospital that Nne had asked for food without being prompted. She went outside to find an *akara* vendor. The nurses directed her toward a big mango tree where several women were selling some food items. One of the women was frying her *akara* right there. She had the *akara* mix in a large covered white basin. When it was her turn, the woman had only enough mix for three large *akara*. Adaaku bought some *akara*, fried plantains and *akamu* mix. She went to the make-shift kitchen used by relatives of the sick and boiled some water for the *akamu*. She went back to the ward with the food. Chike and Nne were conversing with the ease of old friends. Adaaku helped Nne to sit up. She and Chike encouraged Nne to eat as much as she could. But she could only eat two *akara*.

'You two should finish the rest.'

'Yes. I'm quite hungry this morning. I'll go and make some more *akamu*,' Adaaku volunteered.

Soon, she came back with two steaming bowls of *akamu*.

'Here is yours.' She handed a bowl to Chike. He picked up the large golden *akara*.

'That looks quite big,' Nne said. Adaaku felt rather than heard the inflection in Nne's voice. She looked from the *akara* in Chike's hand straight into Nne's eyes. And time flashed back. Adaaku could almost hear the years rolling back to her childhood. Nne held Adaaku's eyes with hers. Finally, Adaaku disengaged herself from what seemed like a long wordless conversation with Nne. But the exchange had only taken a few seconds.

Chike was holding the big golden *akara* toward her. She reached for it and broke off a piece. Chike, unaware of the exchange between Adaaku and Nne, took a bite of his *akara*.

'Mmmmm! This is sweet,' Chike said.

'Yes,' said Adaaku. She felt the light shinning inside her.

Nne's eyes twinkled as they caught Adaaku's again and held. She nodded ever so slightly at her granddaughter.

Antjie Krog

Three [Love] Stories in Brackets

1.
They say.
They say that my great grandmother, Helena Susanna Delport, owned all the land between Kroonstad and Renosterspruit. [ ] When her husband died, she was left with two daughters, one of them my grandmother.
They say she married bachelor Hennie Geldenhuys out of loneliness.
[ ]
They say that she became more and more diabetic until she fell into a coma. Her two daughters came immediately from their respective households elsewhere in the district.
[ ]
They say that within a day or two the first ampoule of insulin arrived at the infirmary of old doctor Dykman. He got into his car and sped to the large homestead to try this new cure. They say that on the dusty road he excitedly waved at oom Johnnie du Randt – the lawyer who was on his way back to the town.
They say as soon as the insulin was injected, ouma Lena showed signs of recovery. They say, as she was shakily drinking water, she asked where the ink on her right middle finger was coming from. 'Ask your husband,' they say was what her daughter, my grandmother, said.
The next morning she went to town to annul the will.
[ ]
They were married for six years after that before she died. Oupa Hennie had usufrucht and lived for another ten years.

2.

In the Voortrekker Museum in Pietermaritzburg are several self-made booklets – the diaries of Susanna Smit, wife of the Voortrekker dominee with Piet Retief. There is also a long, small tray filled with white cards – each with a Bible text. One gathers from the diary that Susanna Smit suffered insomnia; that she would meditate on a card and then pour religious and mystical thoughts into her diary.

[Deeply touched I got up from my bed and knelt, and sang this verse kneeling before the Lord with an out-floating emotional vision]

[ ]

[I was the most oppressed, even in my parents' house, the least loved of all the children of my mother] [ ] [ ] [I was given away into marriage, without even knowing what a marriage is or what it wants.]

From the marriage date, one gathers that she was thirteen when she married the stammering, unqualified missionary twenty-one years her senior. One gathers little information about the two children she had before she was seventeen. One gathers hardly anything about the fact that she trekked in a wagon, was present where battles were fought, oaths sworn and many people killed.

[But with what shall I show my thankfulness? I am a poor woman cramped, confined in the intestines of my meagre habitat. I do write on pieces of paper, but for who to read?]

[ ]

One gathers that Jesus **[His silver holy Face] [His fragrant Body]** was her Groom. **[lay down in ecstasy]**

One gathers that God was not an old man. **[my tender years when I was laying on the lap of God, suckling at His breasts]**

From the diary entries one gathers not a single word about the news in *The Graham's Town Journal*:

'At ten o'clock Commissioner Henry Cloete, robed and

bearing the insignia of his office, arrived and took his seat. While the Honourable Commissioner was reading the proclamation he was interrupted by the chief spokeswoman, Mrs Smit. Her husband at length endeavoured to check her volubility. But this only added fuel to the fire. To the kind expostulation of her husband – 'Stil vrouw, stil toch een wynig' (Quiet wife, be still a little) the virago vociferated, 'You wretch, shall I be still while you stand there silent – you boasted enough at first, but now I am obliged to wear the breeches'.

One gathers from a report by Commissioner Cloete that there was a second confrontation. Susanna Smit demanded voting rights for women – nearly a hundred years before it was granted in Europe.

'The spokeswoman, Mrs Smit, commenced by declaring that in consideration of the battles in which they had been engaged with their husbands, they had obtained a promise that they would be entitled to a voice in all matters concerning the state of this country; that they had claimed this privilege and although repelled by the Volksraad, they had been deputed to express their fixed determination never to yield to British authority; that they were fully aware that resistance would be of no avail, but they would walk out by the Draaksberg barefooted, to die in freedom, as death was dearer to them than the loss of liberty.'

'I endeavoured (but in vain) to impress upon them that such liberty as they seemed to dream of had never been recognized in any civil society; that I regretted that, as married ladies, they boasted of a freedom which even in a social state they could not claim; and that however much I sympathized in their feelings, I considered it a disgrace on their husbands to allow such a state of freedom.'

One also gathers that Susanna Smit was wearing a shawl.

'Cloete wanted to bring an end to the deputation and wanted to leave in order to get rid of the women. However his sabre got stuck in one of the shawls of the women. In his effort to break loose they surrounded him. But he escaped and locked himself in a house. The women put fire to the grass.'

Barely a day or so after this incident:

[in the afternoon I visited my friend, because I felt my soul was in motion, I left and walked back home as fast as I could to find the loneliness, was not even halfway when my soul-eye gauge up to the sky and found her most beloved Bridegroom, so utterly loveable and miraculously beautiful. How I managed to walk the rest of the way without tripping or falling over the tufts of grass, I do not know, because I was walking over unbuilt terrain where there was no street, with my heart and my eye cast to the heaven.]

One gathers that her husband was **[of infirm legs]** and often **[intoxicated]**. They were too poor to leave Natal. He outlived her.

3.

[They say she was as tough as a man. They say she was frigid. They say Nandi, the daughter of Mbengi, loved only her son. If she was praised, she was praised as a man.]

Usomqeni!
Father of trouble [ ]
[ ]
She whose thighs do not meet [ ]
They only meet on seeing her husband. [ ]
[ ]
[ ] **she, the loud voiced one**

[in footnote 3 the translator stipulates that Nandi was 'violent-tempered']

Sontanti [footnote 7 says Nandi's praise name indicates masculinity, and also 'he who drifts about']

She drinks the milk of a cow with horns [ ]
For fear of those who milk it [ ]

[footnote 8 says that this verse suggests Nandi's ambition: she did not want an insignificant commoner as a husband]

Sweetheart of the Mhlatuze valley [ ]
[ ]
Woman whose long staves [ ] are like those of a man
Who struck the army [ ] that it went up the Sabiza river.
She whose thighs do not meet
They only meet on seeing her husband.
She who was with the boys [ ] of Nguga,
Who came in a small group.

[footnote 13 says it refers to the day when she was quietly conducted to Senzangakhona's *kraal*, bearing the baby Shaka, to be installed as a wife subordinate to Mkabi, the chief wife. There was no ceremony for such a bride.]

Sweetheart of the Mhlatuze valley [ ]
[ ]

[This may refer to the indiscriminate massacre by her son after she died.]

Bibliography

IZIBONGO – Zulu Praise Poems edited by Trevor Cope (Oxford at the Clarendon Press, 1968)

Barrevoets oor Drakensberg by Anna de Villiers (Perskor Uitgewery, 1975)

Explanatory note

The brackets are to say: women's lives usually take place in secret, in brackets, in silence, in places that we don't know. They don't tell you about it, someone else tells you about it. So now you have the stories about women told by others, but the brackets remind you that the voice you hear is not that of the women, it is the voice of others.

Only in Susanna Smit's casc did she leave a very skewed diary, so hers is the only story where there are words within the brackets, but you also know that she is hardly telling you what is happening to her with her useless husband.

My great grandmother had a thief for a husband. What did she have to say about that?

Why the fixation with Nandi's thighs and male voice? In Shaka's mother's poem there are footnotes where the recorder of the praise poem makes calculated guesses of what is being meant, but what Nandi felt and said, we don't know. That is why all the stories have phrases such as: they said, apparently, one gathers.

Sindiwe Magona

Modi's Bride

Virginal inspection was the norm those days, a long time ago. No bride would leave her father's *kraal* without a few select senior women of her village, as well as those from the groom's village, having laid her flat on her back on a grass mat in a secluded rondavel – and looked. Following this would come the proclamation: 'She is still whole – *Usaphelele*!' And all knew she had done nothing to embarrass her family or her village; and all rejoiced, for life was communal then. The reputation of a village was the responsibility of all who lived in it and just as all took pride in the pursuits, successes and virtues of each and every villager, all felt themselves sullied, tarnished and reduced by the excesses of anyone in their midst.

Those were the days when, to their dying days, old women boasted, 'I have only ever had one man on my breast,' alluding to the fact of their faithfulness. A young woman left her father's home to be a man's wife. She was given a new name – a wifehood name. From then on, never again would she hear the name to which she had answered from birth. The girl's name is a thing of the past – shed – as are all things juvenile. There are changes too in the manner of dress; the head is covered now and dress length dropped to just above the ankle and so on. Later, often after the birth of the first child, the name may change to so-and-so's mama or Ma- followed by the clan name. An example is Madiba! Former President Mandela's clan name applies to all women of that clan. However, unlike him, a man, addressed would be addressed as Madiba, the women would be called Mamadiba.

But grandfather Modi's wife, my grandmother, was known to her dying day as Modi's Bride. She had a wifehood name – Nomzi (mother of the family) – but it did not catch on. Five children – two girls and three sons – suckled on her breast, but she was never called by any of her children's name. Naturally, she had a clan name and could have been called Mamkwayi; but that, too, never happened. Clearly, she was that rare thing – an exception. From the day she arrived in the village of Gungululu, Modi's bride and the manner of her coming into their midst so startled the people in Gungululu that for years they talked of nothing else but the love of the two – of Modi and his bride.

Today, in the cemetery of the little village a tomb stands testimony to that love.

Modi, the eldest of seven sons, had not only reached the age by which men of his times were expected to take a wife – he had exceeded that age by many, many years. Even if the family had had any daughters they would long have left this home to be wives to their husbands. Thus it was that Modi's mother, Nolenti, was often heard to say, '*Eyona nto, ndiyaguga mna, yaye zonk iintanga zam zinoomolokazana!*' 'I don't know if anyone is paying heed, but I'm getting on in years and all my age-mates already have daughters-in-law!'

As every village woman knows, the next best thing to a daughter is a daughter-in-law. Men do not help with the housework; that is woman's work. If Nolenti had had a sympathetic, considerate eldest son, why, he'd have thought of taking a wife as soon as he decently could, a year or so after he was circumcised and, therefore, a man. No Xhosa woman over the age of sixteen would have anything to do with an uncircumcised man; in her eyes, a boy.

It was ten long years since Modi had come back from the bush; a man. If his unhurried stroll to matrimony was an inconvenience to his mother, to his brothers it was torture. None of them could take a wife until he did, that was the custom. And many a maiden in the village viewed Modi with outright hatred. Was it not because of him they were stuck in their parents' home with no hope of becoming wives to the young men who were his younger brothers?

Modi's tardiness had a devastating domino effect on the lives of the young people of his village. It was not just the seven young women who wanted to marry who were affected. If any of these suffering women had younger sisters, none of those could leave their fathers' homes. It was generally held that the marriage of a younger daughter before an older one cast a shadow on the older girl's reputation. Surely, there must be something wrong with her... why was she skipped over?

Sokadala! (old young man) became the name by which Modi was hailed, for all his friends had long taken wives and some had several children to show for the passing of the years. Sokadala, he was hailed in jest. But many a jest hides bitterness and scorn. To his younger brothers' sweethearts, that scorn was heavily laced with anxiety and despair. When would this selfish, stupid, old goat get on with it?

But when anyone – family or friend – broached the subject with him, his reply was simple, unwavering: 'When I find the right girl, I will not hesitate!'

Daily, his mother complained and his brothers shook their heads in sheer exasperation. However, none dared voice criticism openly. It was not for naught that Modi was known throughout surrounding villages, as well as in Gungululu, as Nkomiyahlaba – the bull that gores – for he was a fierce fighter, a champion at stick fighting. His prowess was well known and respected, for miles around.

One day there was a wedding. Modi was into his twelfth year as a circumcised man. One of the girls of his village was going to her husband's home in a village a hard day's horse ride away. Modi was in the bridal party – uduli – accompanying her to her new home after a week's festivities at her village. The reputation of his village rested squarely on Modi's stout shoulders – was he not the champion stick fighter? The village in Tsomo was not to be allowed to rob Gungululu of a beautiful maiden and then beat their men at the stick fighting that would be part of the proceedings at the village of the groom.

As expected, Modi helped his side win the match. But then the unexpected happened: Modi lost his heart to Nonyibiba, a maiden of the Mkwayi clan in the village of Qutsa, in the town of Tsomo.

Nonyibiba – Lily – was tall and well put together as though sculptured by a master craftsman – a man of singular sensitivity and delicate touch who had woken up and brought his dream into reality in good-quality clay. She had deep eyes, set far apart; glowing pools of brilliance fringed with thick, double rows of black lashes that seemed in constant need of brushing out. An abundant black mane crowned the elegant figurine and recalled the tail of a well-kept horse. Straight, sleek and silky, it set off the girl's high yellow complexion to perfection. Her dimpled cheek and slow lingering smile split plump lips and revealed a gap through which half a crown could slide without a hitch. And he who had previously shown not the slightest inclination to get a wife suddenly unlocked his hitherto silent lips. Out poured words that proved Modi was neither a coward nor wanting in ways to woo and win the heart of a coy maiden.

By the time his horse Phikolomoya – wing of wind – pointed its nose towards Gungululu, a clear understanding between Nonyibiba and Modi had developed. As the returning bridal party left the village, leaving the bride in her new home, Nonyibiba stood at the top of a *kopje* and waved a white kerchief. She stayed there until the black stallion and his rider were but a speck in the distance . . . until the speck completely disappeared.

Before the end of that week, *oonozakuzaku* – marriage negotiators – had come to Nonyibiba's home in Qutsa village in the town of Tsomo. They had come all the way from Gungululu, a hard day's horse ride away. Within a month, all the *ikhazi*, the *lobola*, had been driven across eleven villages and through five towns: Umthatha, Idutywa, Gcuwa, Cofimvaba, Cala. Plans were not afoot; they were awing! Sokadala was getting married to a woman of the Mkwayi Clan, all the way from Qutsa Village in Tsomo!

This whirlwind courtship surprised all who knew Modi. The news of the coming wedding spread like wild fire. A song sprang and was sung throughout all the villages – from Gungululu in Tsolo to Qutsa, in Tsomo:

> Sokadala is smitten... He is smitten and that is true.
> He went to Qutsa to marry off a sister... But, instead,
> He returned raging, in fever, for a warm grass mat!
> He is smitten! He is smitten! Sokadala is smitten, indeed!

Now that he'd finally found the woman who filled his heart with the sweet music of growing flowers and low, slow-moving clouds, Modi couldn't bear to wait. He wanted his bride as quickly as in 'last year!'

But the bride's family demanded time to make fitting arrangements. They did not want to send off their beloved 'Lily' to her in-laws in unseemly haste as though they were driving away hail – unloved and unwelcome. They were not getting rid of her but giving her away in fellowship, a token of the love between two young people and the esteem between the two families now joined by their union. She was not a girl they were eager to get rid of, wash their hands of, but a beloved, respectful, obedient daughter they were reluctantly releasing... very, very reluctantly indeed, for rumour had reached them that their future son-in-law was a man of few words and hard, killing stick blows much feared by those who knew him and by some just from hearsay.

Now sporting a *doek* as befits a wife-to-be and dress length significantly lowered though not yet ankle length, Nonyibiba gave her age-mates the 'goodbye' parties expected of her. She had attended many in her time awaiting marriage, for this was the custom. Every weekend the young women of her village gathered at her father's *kraal* to help her in her preparations. Some went to gather *imizi*, others helped her in the weaving of these into mats of different kinds for the different functions for which they would be used: *izithebe* – trays *izicamba* – sleeping mats *imitshayelo* – brooms *iingobozi* – baskets. Those gifted in beadwork busied themselves making bangles, anklets, head circlets – *izacholo* – and necklaces.

And then, in the midst of this business and high expectations, calamity struck.

It was the time of day when the rays of the sun are long and strong and paint everything a soft warm yellow and make the ugliest person alluring – *xa libantu bahle* – when it is beautiful people time, say AmaXhosa. Nonyibiba and two of her friends took their pails and set off for the river nearby; a ritual of many a maiden before sunset. The herdsman was driving the cattle home as the girls made their way toward the river Tsomo, more a stream than a river in these parts.

The sun disappeared behind the far-away mountain tops and the evening frogs began their raucous evensong. But the girls had not returned from the river. Nonyibiba's mother began throwing her eyes down the path leading to the *kopje* below which the silent river ran. Where were these girls? What was taking them so long?

To still her unease, the mother poked the fire, lifted the lid from the pot and, brow wrinkled, peered at the bubbling evening meal, and although the meal was all but cooked, she took the ladle and stirred and stirred and stirred.

Suddenly, loud cries came hot on the thudding of hurried footsteps. Why would girls that age, pails on their heads, be running? Why were they screaming? The ladle clattered onto the lid of the pot on the mud floor, olive green from the cow dung with which it is smeared.

'Yintoni? What is the matter?' Screaming, in one swift move, the mother leapt to the door. The sight that met her eyes buckled her knees. And the words that hit her ears rent her heart.

'NguNonyibiba! It is Nonyibiba!'

'Utheni? What's happened to her?'

'Uthwelwe! She's been abducted!'

The wailing of the mother and the two girls, Nonyibiba's closest friends, brought the men on the double; wailing women usually announce a death or some other tragedy of equal import. Soon neighbours came, summoned by the same alarm. 'Nonyibiba has been abducted!'

As soon as the cause of the commotion was known, opinion sprouted, hotly differing. There were those who faulted the women for disturbing the peace unnecessarily. Irritated by the wailing, they asked, 'is being made a wife not cause for ululation? Since when is a daughter's abduction an abomination,' they asked, brows hitting the hairline in consternation. However, others – in the minority it must be admitted – saw the abduction as throwing a spanner in the works. There can be no feast or jollity when a wife is begot in such a manner. These reckoned they would be deprived of the feast they had foreseen in the man from Gungululu so eager to get his bride the *lobola* had come in one go. Did that not attest to the fact he was a man of means? Came from a family with many heads of cattle in their *kraal*? One man was seen to weep, wipe away tears from sheer frustration. The loss was irredeemable. Who knew what scoundrel of a man had abducted Nonyibiba? Usually men who resorted to this manner of taking a wife needed this short cut because they could not afford *lobola*. What was there to expect from such a man?

But the mother thought only of her child, the first born of her four daughters. Who was to know what kind of a man, from what kind of a family, had taken Nonyibiba? Then, as now, *ukuthwala* (abduction) was still a legal and honorable way of taking a wife. More and more men, with nothing in their *kraals*, not a cat or a dog to their names, pockets flat as a starving bug, resorted to *ukuthwala* to circumvent *lobola*. If it ever came, that *lobola* would come in dribs and drabs. It is not unheard of that a woman's life comes to an end before her family has seen all the *lobola* due.

On the other hand, the handsome young man who was Nonyibiba's husband to be – the one whose cattle were right there in her father's *kraal* – was from a family not ever likely to go hungry. Look how fast his *lobola* had come. Come, all at once, and within weeks of the initial negotiations... We have been robbed of what promised to be a wedding feast to outdo all feasts, said the young people of Nonyibiba's village. They had been looking forward to the festivities, the meat, the beer, the dancing, the stick fighting... all lost. Because Nonyibiba had been carried off to be made a wife. Everyone, old and young alike, believed that this nameless man who had snatched Nonyibiba was bound to be some mongrel from a home where the cat slept right on the hearth, cold from disuse; church-mouse poor people.

When these words came to the stricken mother's ears, her wailing would not cease. She wailed, some said, as though there had been a death. Eventually, calm returned, and brought new and searing problems. The family could do nothing but wait till whoever had abducted Nonyibiba came forward. That could take days. Meanwhile, the in-laws in Gungululu had to be alerted to the tragedy. Soon thereafter, their cattle would have to be returned; the wife for which the *lobola* had been given was no longer available. This had to be done in a hurry for before the cattle of the new suitor could be accepted those of the old suitor would have to have gone from this *kraal*. *Lobola* is not business and a man does not take it with the greed of a merchant, as though he were selling his daughter to the highest bidder.

It was a sad troop of three men that left Qutsa for Gungululu early the next day and returned, two days later, with news both unexpected and startling. Although Modi's parents were disappointed, they took the news sombrely and wanted to know when to fetch the *lobola*. And that is when Modi surprised them all – visitors and family alike.

'There shall be no return of the cattle,' he said, voice clear and strong, eyes ablaze with anger. 'I love her. I gave the cattle in her honour; and that has not changed.' He was a king giving a decree.

Even when the men in Nonyibiba's family sent a delegation to try to reason with him, show him they could not, in good faith, keep his *ikhazi* when another had the wife, Modi would not budge. He had given that *ikhazi* as a token of his love; a love he knew was returned; a love that would never die. 'That will never change,' he said, 'for as long as I live.'

Two weeks after the abduction, word came to Nonyibiba's family. 'Do not be alarmed. She is safe. We'll show ourselves in due course.' Nonyibiba's family had no choice. They waited. Weeks became months and still the family waited, for there were no further developments in the matter. And that was a bit unusual. Her mother began to fear the worst, her child had been stolen by ragged paupers and she was starving and would soon be dead. She knew that poverty kills. The poor do not become old. They are young and blooming and, a few years later, they are haggard from hunger and hard unrewarding work. Soon, they are dead. That would happen to her daughter. Daily, the mother grieved. Long were her lamentations. Long and ceaseless.

To the family of the abductor, fear of Modi's wrath was uppermost. And when Modi's twenty cows stayed stubbornly at Nonyibiba's father's *kraal*, this family's fear grew. What was that man from Gungululu up to? What did he mean, leaving his cattle at the woman's home when he could no longer want her? When he could no longer have her, why didn't he reclaim his *lobola*? Modi's reputation as a stick fighter was only surpassed by his reputation as hot tempered and fearless in battle.

The abductor's family bided its time. The moon died many times and still the family of the abductor did not return to Nonyibiba's home. Nonyibiba's family still had no idea who had taken her for a wife. They did not even know from which village that nameless man came. All they knew, all they had been told was, 'Do not be alarmed. She has come to no harm but has been taken for a wife. In due course, we shall come and show ourselves.'

The eighth time the moon was the horns of a cow caught in first morning light, crescent and sharp at the edges as though it could raze the sky till it bled, a man came driving before him three scrawny cattle, one blind of one eye. Now, the abductor had a name. Now, his village was known. He was Jonasi, a son of the Jwarha Clan. He was the son of a widow who had many children. The whole family depended on the kindness of others – landless, moneyless and without cattle. How they'd hustled the three cows was nothing short of a miracle.

A few days later, this knowledge became Modi's too.

Late that night, when everyone in the entire village was fast asleep, Modi saddled Phikolomoya and stole away. Without a word even to his parents, into the pitch black night he rode. Except for his horse, his knobkerrie, a spear and a shield was all the company Modi had as he galloped away, the beat of his heart louder than the sound of the horse's hoof on the hard dry ground of a winter's veldt.

All night through, Modi raced past sleeping village after sleeping village; across rivers; through mountain passes; and across wide lonesome fields bereft of crops, still as graves. The pale moon above kept watch, but the driven man paid it no heed. A burst of vermilion tinged the far sky as he reached the town of Tsomo. He neither paused nor slackened pace, but through the still-sleeping town he sped. He knew the village of Ngobozana lay toward those blinding rays that were even then beginning to turn a fierce scarlet slowly paling to gold.

Early shepherds were letting cattle out of *kraals* to go and graze on the scrubby veldt as he crested the hill and stopped. He cast a coldly smoldering eye to the foot of the hills. Several homes clustered on the thin edge before the drop that led to the River Tsomo. There was no mistaking the widow's shabby rondavels, only two in number.

The first cows were beginning to chomp on the scraggy grass when a storm whirled toward Ngobozana. Down the hill

Phikolomoya flew; down the hill, as though the very devil were behind him. Homestead after homestead, the apparition passed, a madman from hell, bent on Hades. On the wake of the fury, spectators sprung and gaped; relieved they were not the destination on which the one-man army was bent. For that he was on the warpath, was clear as the rising sun.

Loud rang the hooves on the hard, hard road. Loud they rang till they reached the small, sad, dilapidated rondavels at the foot of the hill. Loud they rang. Loud they rang.

Hearing the noise, the widow ran out of doors and screamed. From both rondavels, out poured the widow's family. Men, women and children, out they poured – each and every one of them, and each took one frightful look and took to heel. There was no need for words; the danger was clear, real and imminent. In all directions, they fled. Dogs yelping right behind them, they fled. Looking neither left nor right, heels hitting, back of tails between their legs. Even the two chickens the widow kept screeched and, feathers flying, took flight and perched atop the roof of one of the mud huts.

When Modi brought the stallion to a dust-spouting skid and stopped right at the centre of the courtyard, only one figure remained: Nonyibiba, large with child. Even had she wanted to, she could not have run. Silently she regarded him. Clear eyed, she stood and let him see what had been done to her; who she had become: a far cry from the wasp-waisted woman of months before. She looked at him, and never said a word. But the silent stream shimmering down her still cheeks was all the eloquence Modi needed; the language of soul and heart, loud, a clarion call to his singing soul.

His bride. His wife.

There was a tug in Modi's heart.

'I have come to take you home.'

'You come too late. This,' she said, eyes traveling the hill beneath her breast, 'this cannot be undone.'

'My will cannot be undone,' he said.

'And what do you will?'

'My love,' he said, 'you are my wife.'

'Then let it be according to your will.'

With one swoop, he lifted her, belly and all, onto Phiko. He turned the stallion around. The horse's hooves scattered the fire she had been tending, upset the pots she had been cooking and the lids flew off and the food spilled and doused the fire till it sputtered.

Looking neither left nor right, saying not one word more – not that there was any to hear that word, even had he uttered it – Modi spat on the ground, sent a long strong jet of saliva down, and rode away.

The widow's two rondavels stood empty. Not one person remained; not one was there to see Modi ride away. Ride away. Nonyibiba perched sideways on Phikolomoya in front of the furious rider as he rode back the way he had come. Only now, the stallion set off at a pace gentle and smooth.

Not one man pursued Modi that day he carried his bride to his home in far-away Gungululu; carried her away from the home of the man who had abducted her many moons before; carried her away two short months before she was to be married to her beau.

The first stars lit the sky as Modi rode into his father's yard. At once, doors burst open, heads craned and eyes popped.

'Here is my bride!' Those were the only words Modi spoke. The only announcement he made. Then he got off Phikolomoya and helped Nonyibiba down. All could see she was with child. All knew the child was not Modi's child. All knew this was no virgin Modi had brought. She was with child, about to be mother. And what was inside her was another man's calf.

'Are you sure you know what you're doing?' his father asked.

'Yes.'

'And the child?' asked his mother.

'She will be the child of my wife.'

Concessions had to be made. The women could see that

Modi's bride was near her time. It would not do for the young people to be together; the heat of young blood might overcome decorum and common sense. Nonyibiba was sent to Modi's grandmother's home, behind his father's homestead. She could not *hota* – do the ardous work expected of all new wives. It was time for her to rest before the big day arrived, when the baby would come. Needless to say, there was no grass mat to lay her on; her virginity no longer an issue. It seemed like a week – just a few days, a few days since Modi's bride had come to Gungululu to the home of her in-laws – and she became a mother.

The girl, Legina, grew up with Modi's own children, except that she bears her mother's clan name and her mother's surname. For Modi's bride had brought along, in her stomach, another man's calf. But except for that – for the surname and clan name – one could not tell her apart from the others. Gilbert was born three full years after Legina. In due course, two more girls and another boy followed. But to all of Gungululu and surrounding villages Nonyibiba remained Modi's Bride. Neither her wifehood name nor her clan name took on. She never once was called by any of her children's names. But Modi's Bride, UmkaModi, she remained.

Meanwhile, no one ever came to claim Nonyibiba. No one ever came to claim either wife or baby, to claim the child she was carrying when Modi came in a cloud of dust and carried her off on a jet black stallion called Phikolomoya. And through the long years of their marriage, when anyone would ask him why he'd done what he'd done, Modi's answer, ready, simple and constant was, 'She was the one in my heart.'

Sokadala was slow and late in finding love; but once he did, nothing and no one could diminish or change that love – least of all, stolen privileges. Five children, ten grandchildren, and two great-grandchildren later, Nonyibiba died cradled in Modi's arms. She was still known by all as Modi's Bride as though the fact might be in dispute – as though to still wagging tongues or answer a question not yet asked, to make a declaration.

The simple gravestone tells the story of this great love. Beneath two linked hearts, the legend reads 'Modi and his Bride'.

Sarah Ladipo Manyika

Modupe

I'm sitting in Charles de Gaulle airport wondering what to call her. Is she a woman or a girl? And does she realise just how sexily she's dancing? Surely she feels everyone in the departure lounge watching. We women are envying her while the men are busy making love to her in their heads. She dances alone in front of classmates with her back turned to us. She's oblivious to everyone except for her school friends, and that's what tells me she's young. Such freedom! Sixteen maybe. Seventeen? I used to have a body like hers. Look at her. Lucky girl! Enjoy, my dear, while it lasts because before you know it, your breasts will droop and your waist will disappear, but for now your hips are nicely curved and snug within the tight embrace of faded blue jeans. I imagine you dressing, like my daughters, heaving the denim over thighs, and then up and over hips before snapping tightly below the waist.

'*Ah, oui, c'est la mode. Il s'appelle, low-rider*,' was how the saleswoman described the style to me last week. Perhaps when she took my travellers cheques and saw my Nigerian passport, she supposed I'd never seen fashion like this before. Did she think I lived in the bush? Silly woman. Let her come to Lagos to see our modern ways any day, but I'll admit that I've never personally owned a pair of blue jeans. Frankly, they strike me as uniformly unattractive, and yet so many people wear them these days that I thought I should give it a try. But honestly, can you picture me strutting around in trousers like this young woman? My daughters would disown me and my husband would have a fit! Not that I care much about him any more, at least not for his views. I wouldn't be surprised if Segun's mistresses don these sorts of trousers every day. For all I know, he's the one who buys the goddamn things as they swan around Abuja on their weekend rendezvous. 'Business meetings,' he says. Stupid man! Does he think I'm blind?

It's not that I consider myself old, you must understand, but there is a certain biological reality that is simply not conducive to this tight, low-ride style at the age of sixty-three. Far better, is it not, to wear a long navy blue skirt with colourful *Hermes* scarf tied around the neck for a little panache? I might not be modern, but I'm always elegant. I look again and watch how the girl's bright yellow belt dangles between her legs rather than being threaded back around her waist. Girls these days are so carefree. She wears a white tank top – a striking contrast to her dark skin – tucked in, but open in a small 'V' at the neck. Her long, slim arms display no bracelets or watch, but the fingers that clutch the Discman are covered in silver rings. I wonder where these students are going. Is it a school tour to New York? The girl reminds me of my eldest – the one I'm about to visit, confident and theatrical. She stands there, dancing only a few feet from where I sit, as though she's completely alone in this airport lounge. What is she thinking? And her classmates, all these young, white Frenchmen strewn across the plastic chairs? They watch, through half-opened eyes, as she sways seductively. From time to time they joke amongst themselves when she sings a line or two out loud. I think of Achebe and those waists he once described swivelling like oiled ball bearings; only this is not just the waist, but also the hips – the whole body in fact. Headphone paraphernalia circles her neck, caressing the silver hoops that bulge as big as bracelets from her ears. She whisks her hips from side to side, then down, down, and up.

'Wow!' I marvel. Her classmates continue to laugh as though it's all a joke, as if the way she thrusts herself before them does nothing to their groins, but how can it not, especially when black women are all the rage in Europe these days. Isn't that so? You see it on TV – all these ebony singers, film stars, and tennis players. It's not like when I was young and nicknamed 'gollywog Mops' as the only black girl in a British boarding school. Even fat Fiona got boys to dance with her at school bashes, but not me. The funny thing is I don't remember it bothering me much as a girl. Perhaps it was because by the time I went to university, when boys really began to matter, many African men found me attractive. That was when we used to party down in London at the weekends – booze, cigarettes and men. Segun was the sexy one then, with his fast sports cars. Now he's just a sugar daddy to his useless Abuja girls and as long as he has foreign exchange they will continue to turn his foolish head. I'm sure he's with one of the mistresses now while I'm abroad, visiting our children. And me? Who notices me these days?

'Good book, isn't it,' someone says.

'Sorry?' I answer, roused from my reveries. 'Oh! This book, yes. *Atonement*.' I nod, revealing the cover before returning to where I'd left off. I try a few more sentences before I close it in exasperation. So much for a novel short-listed for the Booker! I've started chapter one at least three times, and still cannot fathom what is going on. I look back at the girl. One of her classmates is standing up. He reaches for her, wanting to dance, but she keeps him back, prodding his chest with her fingertips. Suddenly, she lets go and sashays towards him until their hips touch. The man can't keep up, and he's blushing, just like Andrew used to blush. Andrew. Oh Andrew!

What would have happened had I believed him? Would we have married? He told me once that he loved me, but I was so used to being ignored by white men that it was hard for me to take him seriously. The girl has started singing again in her Frenchified American accent, or is it rapping they call it these days? *Hey-ay*! What is she doing now! *Nawa-o*! Look at her winding her body back and forth, back and forth. *Na real wa!* Me too, I used to move like that before the knees started paining me. Oh yes! I remember the time Hugh Masekela came to London and I danced all night. Dancing and singing, *I won't forget the day the sun came shining in. Ew Mama!* Now what's wrong with the foolish old woman sitting opposite me and looking at me *one kind*? Is she trying to tell me I can't sing? We might even be the same age, but she looks terribly decrepit. Thank God I'm not haggard and wrinkled like her! And her sense of dress... good grief! Polyester tracksuit for travel? Must be an American.

I was with Andrew the night Masekala came to play. I remember Andrew's hands circling my hips in playful caress and his eyes undressing me well before his fingers touched my skin and played all sorts of havoc here, there and... *Oh Mama! A night time of ecstasy.* A baby starts to cry and the old woman stands up. She has arthritis, I can tell. She stoops. At least I carry myself with dignity. As soon as Madame has gone, her husband puts down his newspaper and looks at me. I smile back, and quickly look away. The three little children who have been scolded for making too much noise and waking the baby have grudgingly plonked themselves down on seats, and are also watching the dancer, for nothing better to do. I look again at the boy and wonder if Andrew is married. Divorced? Children?

The baby wails louder. Colic, no doubt. That's what my granddaughter has, or had, until I came and spent this month with them and calmed the child. How will Yemisi cope with the baby when I'm gone? It's not easy for them, you know, trying to juggle work, little ones and husband. In that respect we have it easy back home with our maids and house help. Now I must visit the second daughter halfway across the globe before returning home. Ahh, these children of ours! Why have they chosen such far-flung places? If Nigeria were not such a mess, perhaps they would come back.

Layo wants to be a photographer in New York. And what if she doesn't succeed? Then what? Layo can be so moody – takes that from me, unfortunately. When I arrive in New York, I know she'll talk nonstop of career, and I'm already tired *sha*.

And yet it's for these daughters, with all their *wahala*, that I've remained with Segun because that's what a mother does. We keep the nest intact even if our males go wandering, but it's high time I did something – something for me. And now a crazy little thought is brewing in my mind. It's just an idea, but a delicious one, a wild one. No I can't. Yes I can. No I can't. People will be shocked. They'll say, 'Modupe? No, Modupe couldn't do that!', 'How could she do that?' But I say, why not! If Segun can have his fun, then *pour quoi pas*? What will happen if I miss my flight to New York and go somewhere else instead? I've only brought hand luggage. I could simply tell Layo that I've been delayed.

I dial Layo's number and hear the answer machine. Background music lingers on after the message has ended. *Living my life like it's golden, golden*, I hear someone singing. I try again, but still get the machine and the woman singing *Living my life like it's golden, golden*. I look across at the dancer and it takes me back again to that night – thirty, forty years ago maybe – yet still vivid in my mind. I wore my tight white trousers and danced furiously to Masekela's 'Marketplace', pulling Andrew along. What would have happened if I'd believed Andrew when he told me he loved me? But he never stood a chance. I just couldn't trust his intentions, yet I trusted Segun. I hope this boy loves the girl and doesn't just lust over her or see her as some exotic queen. Did Andrew really love me? I still have the card he sent me last year congratulating me on the UNESCO appointment. He has stayed in touch, so that's saying something, isn't it? He's here in Paris. I could go and find him. The flight is boarding. I hear them calling my name.

'*C'est le dernier appel pour Modupe Oyafamee*.' Good gracious! How these Europeans butcher our Yoruba names! I stand up and walk past the stewardess holding the microphone. I'm walking back towards security. God knows what's got into me, but I'm swaying my hips and humming that tune. I'm Hugh Masekela's woman, *and I'm floating lazily through the market like a butterfly... Oh yeah!*

Blessing Musariri

Counting down the Hours

Vuso's soft belly is pressing against my back. His face in sleep is ugly to me. His quiet snoring is a soft tune that keeps me company in the long hours that challenge my sanity at night.

What would Marita say if she knew? Probably, 'Don't let me down. I know you'll do the right thing.' Marita knows nothing. She's in the UK working as a nurse; she left home when it was still free and easy to go that route. Now you have to pay to do the course and getting a visa is no walk in the park. Then there's Tawona. As big brothers go, I sometimes think he's a figment of my imagination. He left when the money started coming in and Mama and Baba could proudly send their son off to college in the States, full tuition paid. It's been three years and they don't even know that he dropped out of college to pursue his hip-hop dream. He calls himself Z3, 'Coz that's what I'm fina buy when I strike gold baby girl, coz Z stands for my country in the motherland, gotta keep it real ya kno'.'

He says it's a shame that no one speaks his mother-tongue over there because, 'I done forgot my words,' he says. 'Can't speak that shit no mo'.'

It's only been four years since he left but he's managed to completely disappear into the echoes of rap lyrics. I never even asked him what the significance was of '3'.

A dog barks outside and I think of Buster, at home. Did *mukoma* Givie remember to feed him? One day that dog will die of neglect. *Sisi* Marian doesn't seem to care. These are people who were left to look after me but their indifference to life in general has made them dependent on me. If I'm not there, nothing gets done. I'm too young for all that responsibility and I'm tired of it. Perhaps I won't go back. Ever. That house that swallows me up with its silences.

I was eating ice-cream as I walked back home from the shops when Vuso stopped the car. He thought I needed a ride. I let him think it. I'd met him several times before. He's married to mama's friend, Virginia, so it was okay to catch a ride with him. Even if I hadn't known him, I might have got in anyway. I invited him in for a drink – it was hot outside and he stayed a bit and talked. As he walked back to his car I stared at the roll of flesh at the back of his head and I wanted to take it between my fingers and pinch it. The thought made me giggle and he turned back and looked at me with a question. I just smiled at him with my secret thought glinting from my eyes.

'So, what are doing over half-term? Are you going to the farm to see your old man?'

I shook my head.

'Is your mother coming home from Namibia?'

Again I shook my head. She couldn't get away from work. There was a big conference going on so there wouldn't be any point in my going over. He seemed to hesitate, then making up his mind, he took a step closer.

'Well, I'm driving down to South Africa if you want to catch a ride and do some shopping.'

The 's' in seventeen doesn't stand for stupid. I looked at his dark, sweating face, his big belly and baggy trousers. Nothing to see there, but as I thought about it for a minute and before I could speak, my separate self jumped into my mouth and said, 'Okay.'

Vuso stirs and turns over in his sleep. This means I can change sides too. In the semi-darkness I can see that roll of flesh at the back of his head and I want to grab it and pull hard. Again, I feel the urge to laugh. He is so ridiculous.

If I was at home I would get out of bed and walk naked through the house. Moving slowly through rooms full of

Mama's precious furniture, but empty all the same. My body's just a thing, like the cherry-wood coffee tables from Dubai or another ornament found on special offer in a foreign mall. It was on one of these nocturnal wanderings when I felt it; like separating the yolk of an egg from the white, I felt my inner self separate from my outward self with a fluid tearing in my body, together but separate. My egg-yolk self curled up and went to sleep, tired of the endless journeys, and my egg-white self continued unfazed. I can't walk naked through this house; it's not empty like ours. I can feel Virginia's presence here and it castigates me even when I only think the thought.

It's only midnight. I've been gone from home for four whole days. *Sisi* Marian – a distant cousin who doubles as our maid – must be frantic but she will never tell on me because she would be found wanting as a guardian. She doesn't know that I've made it a point to call Baba every day and assure him that everything is fine. I even called him from Vuso's cellphone while I was in Jo'burg. It's tobacco planting season – there'll be no surprise visits from him for a while. Marian will tell Mama some lie or the other if she calls so I don't worry about that. To give them some credit, they did try and get me into boarding school when Baba decided he needed to be on the farm full time and mama was promoted to regional head of communications – my egg-yolk self knows the details. This was about six years ago. For a time they made an effort for one of them to always be at home, but I guess it was a strain on their jobs. It was only after Tawona left for college that I realised I'd been effectively left alone. *Mukoma* Givie had long been tasked to drive me to and from school so I didn't really feel the absences until the night I woke up in a silent house and couldn't get back to sleep again. I wasn't afraid but the darkness was a heavy thing that covered me as I lay, and suddenly I was stifling in my bed, gasping for air and sweating as if I'd been running away from something. I tore the covers off, I was crying, tears mingling with perspiration and my breath catching in loud sobs, but once free, it wasn't enough. I tore off my pyjamas too and ran to the door. Wrenching it open I stood there and called for my mother. I heard only the echo of my own voice fading into the night. I could feel the darkness around me breathing and shifting as it embraced me, filling in the spaces I had torn through as I struggled with myself.

Sisi Marian dies every night when she lays her head on her pillow and closes her eyes. Nothing wakes her until it is time for her to un-die. I couldn't go back to my bed, I couldn't sit down and so I began to wander around the house, stopping sometimes to stare out at lights in the distance. The darkness stroked my skin, soothed and caressed me and convinced me she meant me no harm. I haven't slept at night since.

Vuso really likes the weave I have in my hair. I bought the extensions in South Africa and had it sewn in yesterday. It's deep black (almost blue) with a straight fringe almost down to my eyebrows and so long at the back it almost reaches my waist. It makes me look like a black Barbie doll. My egg-white self grins every time she looks in the mirror and I toss my head to please her. It's almost fun. I bought some killer boots too, from Nine West, and lots of things I didn't need and don't really care about. Vuso's made a lot of money selling fuel since the shortages began, selling a lot of things that are scarce, including foreign currency. He spends his money almost as fast as he makes it – on stupid things.

My best friend Violet thinks I've gone too far.

'You've done some mad things but really! This takes the cup. What can you be thinking?' I couldn't even begin to tell her and so I just laughed.

'No really!! Do you realise you're putting yourself at risk of AIDS and other horrible diseases? And what will you do when his wife comes back?'

'I'm not planning to live here forever, Violet, just chill! I've got a whole big house of my own to go back to.'

Violet just wouldn't quit. Kept talking about morals and things like that and reminding me about all the crap they tell us at school about your body being God's temple and self worth and stuff. I stopped listening, then I said I had to go because Vuso had come in – but he was nowhere in sight. I had felt something deep inside me and, for a moment while I was listening to Violet, I wanted to cry.

Unlike *sisi* Marian, my egg-yolk self hears sounds in her sleep and stirs, but egg-white self steps up quickly and reminds me that it's just a body. I don't even really want to be in it.

Whenever Vuso tries to say 'no' to anything, I make everything inside me very still and quiet and I pretend that he's simply disappeared. He doesn't like that. He wanted to start the drive to the border but I wanted to go out to a club, so we went. I met a girl there, in the ladies, young like me, but only on the outside. Even with her bright red lipstick I could tell that the real colour of her smile had faded long ago. I smiled back at her and she offered me a cigarette.

'Who's the constipated hippo you were dancing with?'

When I realised she meant Vuso, I laughed until I cried. I decided to make her my friend. A lot of people just aren't funny, even when they are trying.

'Darling,' I said, 'he's a magic hippo, he shits money.' She knew the game – played it every night. I didn't even need to say the words.

I danced with my new friend but after a while she told me that fun was a luxury she couldn't afford. She left and I danced alone in the middle of everyone else. Vuso watched, sipping his drink, smoking his cigar and sometimes chatting to people who stopped by. I danced and danced in my new boots until Vuso came and took me from the dance floor. I could have danced all night.

The soft leather cushioned my weary body and I watched through the window as the darkness swallowed us. I didn't remember the name of the girl I'd been with. Had she even told me? I had so much more but it somehow seemed that both of us had nothing. I floated into the blackness and sighed. If only we could keep driving into the night, continuing into that distance with only the sound of quiet music and tyres on tarmac. Would we grow old travelling or would we stay forever as we were – frozen but in continuous motion? I would forget about sleep, untrue friend that she is; I would laugh in her face. But journeys always come to an end.

It's 3 a.m. Vuso has turned around and I realise that I've been lost in thought, staring at his face. It's a full moon outside and there's chink in the curtain that's letting in some light. I can see his features quite clearly. His eyelids are rounded over slightly protruding eyeballs, his nose broad and grooved. His pores are large in his skin – I can't see that in this light but I know from the harsh showcase of day. His lips are the best thing about his face – not thick or too thin. His mouth is wide and his lips are perfectly stretched across it with an attractive firmness. He's got a nice smile. That's all I like about him, otherwise he's just another person who has no clue about anything. He thinks I'm impressed by his spending power. I won't disabuse him. With his face relaxed in sleep, he looks like nobody I know, not even himself. Maybe I'm mistaken and it's not him. I'm lying here looking at a stranger and suddenly I'm afraid. I close my eyes and turn over, my heart beating like a village drum in the night. My mouth is dry and hundreds of tiny pins prick my tongue. What am I doing here?

I close my eyes and for a minute I don't think of anything. I just focus on breathing – I might start screaming otherwise. I want to get out of this bed and walk away from myself but this is not my house and my body refuses to move. I'm afraid Vuso will wake up and start touching me again. He says older men are more experienced and can give a woman more pleasure. That just goes to show how much he knows – I'm just a girl pretending to be a woman. How come he doesn't see that? Some experience is good for nothing.

It's quarter to four. A line from a song comes into my head, '. . . you're just a crazy fucked up man'. I think of Zuva. I went all the way with him – let him take my virginity. Two months ago he told me he needed a time out because things were getting too intense and he needed to concentrate on school. Violet says she sees him all the time with a girl called Fungisai from Girls High. He can just fuck off with his 'concentrating on school'. I hate it when people lie to me. He should have just told me that he didn't want to be with me anymore because he wanted to be with someone else. There's no truth in people, that's why nobody loves anybody. We're all in it together, mixing our lies, to ourselves and to each other; making egg-white omelettes – to be had with a pinch of salt.

I think Mama and Baba really believe that they're still married. They share children and property – where neither of them resides – and little else, but in their heads they are fully convinced of their union. I was a late baby. I don't think they meant to have me, however, I came along anyway – serves me right. I think they do love me, just not in the present. If their love for me were a tree or a plant, it would be a branchless, leafless, flowerless stem that is still alive only because the root hasn't died. I used to pretend Marita was my mother, followed her from room to room after school telling her all my childish imaginings. At night, I would curl my small hand around her side and fall asleep to the rhythm of her heart – the words to this lullaby – 'sleep tight little sis, sleep tight'.

I was angry when she tried to hug me goodbye. I stood stiff and unyielding, staring down at the speckled tiles of the airport floor. She didn't just leave. She left me.

Tawona packed his bags and left for a world of his own even before he got on the plane to America. In this world there was only him and his god – music. I don't know how he passed his O-Levels; it seemed the only words he knew were beats, rhythm, lyrics, bass line, vocals, sample, then beats, rhythm, lyrics, bass line, vocals and so it went on. Sometimes he would look and see me, as if for the first time in a long while, and I could see that he went through a process to recognise me.

'Hey!' he'd say, 'what's up little lady? Listen to this

jamming beat.' Then he would put his headphones over my ears for a time and I would listen to jamming beats while he smiled benevolently and nodded his head in time to a tune that remained with him even after it left his ears. I don't know where he picked up that phrase, 'little lady'. I hated it.

He left early one morning and no one woke me up to say goodbye. Of course I had known he was leaving but I never really felt his presence until he was gone.

It's ten to five and the light outside is changing. I'm dozing now, slipping into vivid conversations with people who aren't here, little broken adventures, and out again. Sleep is somewhere nearby. I can hear the early birds and my very last coherent thought is that eggs are altogether too easy to break.

I'm falling down a steep cliff and my weave catches on something and pulls and pulls. It won't save me, the tracks are ripping from the neat corn-rows, pulling hair out at the roots and my scalp is burning. I land in an ungainly heap on the ground. How is it I'm not dead? My breath is coming so fast it's all I can do to catch it. Someone is yelling in very high tones and at the same time a palm connects smartly with my cheek. I realise that I'm not dead because I'm awake. Someone has pulled me out of the bed by my hair and is raining abuse on me. I sit up awkwardly, one hand raised to cool my burning cheek and look through the strands of hair across my face.

Virginia.

She's marching to the dressing room. Dazed, I can't move. Sleep, so prolonged, is making me heavy.

At the first stinging lash across my shoulders I am released from my lethargy and I wince. There is no time though to feel the harsh lick of the last blow before the next one follows, and the next and the next. My breath is catching in my throat in dry gasps and I am whining like a stray dog tormented by cruel children. I curl up into a naked ball of burning flesh on the rough mat alongside the bed. I am powerless. Perhaps I did walk away from myself during the night and left my body empty and defenceless against such an attack. Perhaps I'm dreaming and will soon wake up. Why doesn't Vuso wake me? Can't he feel me twitching and gasping in my sleep?

'Sit up, let me see you, you little tramp!'

I am in a land of giants. Her voice comes from so high up that it takes an age to reach me. Perhaps I've shrunk.

'I said sit up!' So close now as she reaches down and pulls my limp hair. I'm sitting up and I can feel myself coming back, coming to. I hear Virginia's laboured breathing above me and I struggle to my feet but my body feels weak. I'm trembling but egg white steps up. I toss my head back and look Virginia directly in the eye. What land of giants?

My shoulders start to shake. I'm not sure what's coming next but I'm not surprised when the laughter comes. I hold my belly, head bent, and laugh until tears come streaming down my face. I earn myself another slap for my hilarity and something inside me snaps. I take off past Virginia at a sudden sprint. It's not a scream, but some high and winding note has caught in my throat and I'm letting it out in a loud sustained cry as I run. In the narrow hallway I let my hand run along the wall knocking down picture frames, ornaments, anything that's in my way. This house that wouldn't let me walk through it because of the absence of its owner. Now that she is here, I can run through and tear it down.

In the living room, I overturn glass-topped coffee tables and swipe at anything that stands on a surface so that it crashes to the floor and breaks or splinters. Then I take hold of one end of the long scalloped drape and wrap it around myself, falling into it so that it tears free from its rings and embraces me until I am half-sitting, half-leaning against the exposed French door. The sunlight hurts my eyes and I look away from the garden, back into the room I have destroyed. Virginia stands just inside the doorway, face disbelieving. I think for a minute she believes it's just a nightmare. We can't both be dreaming; we are trapped together in this hideous reality.

I am out of steam. I look at Virginia and Virginia looks at

me, uncomprehending. I see the very second that recognition opens the door to her thoughts. Her face crumbles into a mask of horror and tears gather in her eyes. Her hand across her mouth holds back her gasp of shock. My body feels like it has been dragged over rocky ground and left raw. It's a battered and bruised thing, and even though the pain is on the outside, I feel it from the inside; from the very centre of my being, spreading its sticky wetness through every part of me until I am nothing but pain.

'Rumbidzai?' she says. 'Is that you?'

I begin to cry. Finally, it is.

Monica Arac de Nyeko

Jambula Tree

I heard of your return home from Mama Atim, our next door neighbour. You remember her, don't you? We used to talk about her on our way to school, hand in hand, jumping, skipping, or playing runandcatchme. That woman's mouth worked at words like ants on a cob of maize. Ai! Everyone knows her quack-quack-quack mouth. But people are still left wordless by just how much she can shoot at and wreck things with her machinegun mouth. We nicknamed her lecturer. The woman speaks with the certainty of a lecturer at her podium claiming an uncontested mastery of her subject. I bet you are wondering how she got to know of your return. I could attempt a few guesses. Either way, it would not matter. I would be breaking a promise. I hate that. We made that promise never to mind her or be moved by her. We said that after that night. The one night no one could make us forget. You left without saying goodbye after that. You had to, I reasoned. Perhaps it was good for both of us. Maybe things could die down that way. Things never did die down. Our names became forever associated with the forbidden. Shame.

Anyango – Sanyu.

My mother has gotten over that night. It took a while, but she did. Maybe it is time for your mother to do the same. She should start to hold her head high and scatter dust at the women who laugh after her when she passes by their houses. Nakawa Housing Estates has never changed. Mr Wangolo our SST teacher once said those houses were just planned slums, with people with broken dreams and unplanned families for neighbours. Nakawa is still over one thousand families on an acre of land they call an estate. Most of the women don't work. Like Mama Atim they sit and talk, talk, talk and wait for their husbands to bring home a kilo of offal. Those are the kind of women we did not want to become. They bleached their skins with Mekako skin-lightening soap till they became tender and pale like a sun-scorched baby. They took over their children's *dool* and *kwepena* catfights till the local councillor had to be called in for arbitration. Then they did not talk to each for a year. Nakawa's women laugh at each other for wearing the cheapest sandals on sale by the hawkers. Sanyu, those women know every love charm by heart and every *juju* man's shrines because they need them to conjure up their husbands' love and penises from drinking places with smoking pipes filled with dried hen's throat artery. These women know that an even number is a bad sign as they watch the cowry shells and coffee beans fall onto cowhide when consulting the spirits about their husbands' fidelity. That's what we fought against when we walked to school each day. Me and you, hand in hand, towards school, running away from Nakawa Housing Estate's drifting tide which threatened to engulf us and turn us into noisy, gossiping and frightening housewives.

You said it yourself, we could be anything. Anything coming from your mouth was seasoned and alive. You said it to me, as we sat on a mango tree branch. We were not allowed to climb trees, but we did, and there, inside the green branches, you said – 'we can be anything'. You asked us to pause for a moment to make a wish. I was a nurse in a white dress. I did not frighten children with big injections. You wished for nothing. You just made a wish that you would not become what your father wanted you to be – an engineer, making building plans: for his mansion, for his office, for his railway village. The one he dreamt about when he went to bed at night.

Sanyu, after all these years, I still imagine shame trailing after me tagged onto the hem of my skirt. Other times, I see it, floating into your dreams across the desert and water to remind you of what lines we crossed. The things we should not have done when the brightness of Mama Atim's torch shone upon us – naked. How did she know exactly when to flash the light? Perhaps asking that question is a futile quest for answers. I won't get any! Perhaps it is as simple as accepting that the woman knows everything. I swear if you slept with a crocodile under the ocean, she would know. She is the only one who knows first hand whose husband is sleeping with whose daughter at the Estates, inside those one bed-roomed houses. She knows whose son was caught inside the fences at Lugogo Show Grounds – the fancy trade fair centre just across Jinja Road, the main road which meanders its way underneath the Estates. Mama Atim knows who is soon dying from gonorrhoea, who got it from someone, who got it from so-and-so who in turn got it from the soldiers who used to guard Lugogo Show Grounds, two years ago. You remember those soldiers, don't you? The way they sat in the sun with their green uniforms and guns hanging carelessly from their shoulders. With them the AK47 looked almost harmless – an object that was meant to be held close to the body – a black ornament. They whistled after young girls in tight mini skirts that held onto their bums. At night, they drank Nile Lager, tonto, Mobuku and sung *harambe*, *Soukous* or *Chaka-Chaka* songs.

Eh moto nawaka mama
Eh moto nawaka
I newaka tororo
Nawaka moto
Nawaka moto
Nawaka moto

Eh fire, burns mama
Eh fire, burns
It is burning in Tororo
It is burning
It is burning
It is burning

Mama Atim never did pass anywhere near where they had camped in their green tents. She twisted her mouth when she talked about them. What were soldiers doing guarding Lugogo, she asked. Was it a frontline? Mama Atim was terrified of soldiers. We never did find out why they instilled such fear in her. Either way it did not matter. Her fear became a secret weapon we used as we imagined ourselves being like goddesses dictating her fate. In our goddess-hands, we turned her into an effigy and had soldiers pelt her with stones. We imagined that pelting stones from a soldier was just enough to scare her into susuing in her XXL mother's union panties; the ones she got a tailor to hem for her from left-over materials from her children's nappies. How we wished those materials were green, so that she would see soldiers and stones in between her thighs every time she wore her green solider colour, stone pelting colour and AK 47 colour. We got used to the sight of green soldiers perched in our football fields. This was the new order. Soldiers doing policemen's work! No questions, *Uganda yetu, hakuna matata*. How strange it was, freedom in forbidden colours. Deep green – the colour of the morning when the dew dries on leaves to announce the arrival of shame and dirt. And everything suddenly seems so uncovered, so exposed, so naked.

Anyanyo – Sanyu.

Mama Atim tells me you have chosen to come back home, to Nakawa Housing Estates. She says you refuse to live in those areas on the bigger hills and terraced roads in Kololo. You are coming to us and to Nakawa Housing Estates, and to our many houses lined one after another on a small hill overlooking the market and Jinja Road, the football field and Lugogo Show Grounds. Sanyu, you have chosen to come here to children running on the red earth, in the morning shouting and yelling as they play *kwepena* and *dool* – familiar and stocked with memory and history. You return to dirt roads filled with thick brown mud on a rainy day, pools of water in every pothole and the sweet fresh smell of rain on hard soil. Sanyu, you have come back to find Mama Atim.

Mama Atim still waits for her husband to bring the food she is to cook each night. We used to say, after having nine sons and one daughter, she should try to take care of them. Why doesn't she try to find a job in the industrial area like many other women around the housing estates? Throw her hips and two large buttocks around and play at entrepreneurship? Why doesn't she borrow a little *entandikwa* from the mico finance unions so she can at least buy a bale of second-hand clothes at Owino market and retail them at Nakawa market? Second-hand clothes are in vogue, for sure. The Tommy Hilfiger and Versace labels are the 'in thing' for the young boys and girls who like to hang around the Estates at night. Second-hand clothes never stay on the clothes hangers too long; like water during a drought, they sell quickly.

Mummy used to say those second-hand clothes were stripped off corpses in London. That is why they had slogans written on them, such as 'You went to London and all you brought me was this lousy T-shirt!' When Mummy talked of London, we listened with our mouths open. She had travelled there not once, not twice, but three times to visit her sister. Each time she came back with her suitcase filled up with stories. When her sister died, Mummy's trips stopped like that bright sparkle in her eye and the Queen Elizabeth stories, which she lost the urge to retell again and again. By that time we were grown. You were long gone to a different place, a different time and to a new memory. By then, we had grown into two big girls with four large breasts and buttocks like pumpkins and we knew that the stories were not true. Mummy had been to Tanzania – just a boat trip away on Lake Victoria, not London. No Queen Elizabeth.

Mama Atim says you are tired of London. You cannot bear it anymore. London is cold. London is a monster which gives no jobs. London is no cosy exile for the banished. London is no refuge for the immoral. Mama Atim says this word 'immoral' to me – slowly and emphatically in *Jhapadhola*, so it can sink into my head. She wants me to hear the word in every breath, sniff it in every scent so it can haunt me like that day I first touched you. Like the day you first touched me. Mine was a cold, unsure hand placed over your right breast. Yours was a cold, scared hand, which held my waist and pressed it closer to you, under the jambula tree in front of her house. Mama Atim says you are returning on the wings of a metallic bird – Kenya Airways. You will land in the hot Kampala heat which bites at the skin like it has a quarrel with everyone. Your mother does not talk to me or my mother. Mama Atim cooks her kilo of offal which she talks about for one week until the next time she cooks the next kilo again, bending over her charcoal stove, her large and long breasts watching over her saucepan like cow udders in space. When someone passes by, she stops cooking. You can hear her whisper. Perhaps that's the source of her gonorrhoea and Lugogo Show Ground stories. Mama Atim commands the world to her kitchen like her nine sons and one daughter. None of them have amounted to anything. The way their mother talks about me and you, Sanyu, after all these years, you would think her sons are priests. You would think at least one of them had got a diploma and a low-paying job at a government ministry. You would think one of them could at least bring home a respectable wife. But *wapi*! Their wives are like used bicycles, ridden and exhausted by the entire Estate manhood. They say the monkey which is behind should not laugh at the other monkey's tail. Mama Atim laughs with her teeth out and on display like cowries. She laughs loudest and forgets that she, of all people, has no right to urinate at or lecture the entire Estate on the gospel according to St Morality.

Sometimes I wonder how much you have changed. How have you grown? You were much taller than I. Your eyes looked stern; created an air about you – one that made kids stop for a while, unsure if they should trample all over you or take time to see for sure if your eyes would validate their preconceived fears. After they had finally studied, analysed, added, multiplied and subtracted you, they knew you were for real. When the bigger kids tried to bully me, you stood tall and dared them to lay a finger on me. Just a finger, you said, grinding your teeth like they were aluminium. They knew you did not mince words and that your anger was worse than a teacher's bamboo whipping. Your anger and rage coiled itself like a python around anyone who dared, anyone who challenged. And that's how you fought, with your teeth and hands but mostly with your feet. You coiled them around Juma when he knocked my tooth out for refusing to let him have his way when he tried to cheat me out of my turn at the water tap.

I wore my deep dark green uniform. At lunch times the lines could be long and boys always jumped the queue. Juma got me just as I put my water container to get some drinking water after lunch. He pushed me away. He was strong, Sanyu. One push like that and I fell down. When I got up, I left my tooth on the ground and rose up with only blood on the green; deep green, the colour of the morning when the dew dries off leaves.

You were standing at a distance. You were not watching. But it did not take you too long to know what was going on. You pushed your way through the crowd and before the teachers could hear the commotion going on, you had your legs coiled around Juma. I don't know how you do it, Sanyu. He could not move.

Juma, passed out? Hahahahaha!

I know a lot of pupils who would be pleased with that. Finally his big boy muscles had been crushed, to sand, to earth and to paste. The thought of that tasted sweet and salty like grasshoppers seasoned with onion and *kamulari* – red, red-hot pepper.

Mr Wangolo came with his hand-on-the-knee-limp and a big bamboo cane. It was yellow and must have been freshly broken off from the mother bamboos just outside the school that morning. He pulled and threatened you with indefinite expulsion before you let big sand-earth-paste Juma go. Both you and Juma got off with a two-week suspension. It was explicitly stated in the school rules that no one should fight. You had broken the rules, but that was the lesser of the rules that you broke. That I broke. That we broke.

Much later, at home, your mother was so angry. On our way home, you had said we should not say how the fight started. We should just say he hit you and you hit him back. Your house was two blocks from ours and the school was the nearest primary school to the Estate. Most of the kids in the neighbourhood studied at Nakawa Katale Primary School all right, but everyone knew we were great friends. When your mother came and knocked upon our door, my mother had just put the onions on the charcoal stove to fry the goat's meat. Mummy bought goat's meat when she had just got her salary. The end of month was always goat's meat and maybe some rice if she was in a good mood. Mummy's food smelt good. When she cooked, she joked about it. Mummy said if Papa had any sense in his head, he would not have left her with three kids to raise on her own to settle for that slut he called a wife. Mummy said Papa's new wife could not cook and that she was young enough to be his daughter. They had to do a caesarean on her when she gave birth to her first son. What did he expect? That those wasp hips could let a baby's head pass through them?

When she talked of Papa, she had that voice. Not a 'hate voice' and not a 'like voice', but the kind of voice she would use to open the door for him and tell him welcome back even after all these years when he never sent us a single cent to buy food, books, soap or Christmas clothes. My papa is not like your papa, Sanyu. Your papa works at the Ministry of Transport. He manages the Uganda railways, which is why he wants you to engineer a railway village for him. You say he has gotten so intoxicated with the railway that every time he talks of it, he rubs his palms together like he is thinking of the best-ever memory in his life. You father has a lot of money. Most of the teachers knew him at school. The kids had heard about him. Perhaps that is why your stern and blank expression was interpreted with slight overtones. They viewed you with a mixture of fear and awe; a rich man's child. Sometimes Mummy spoke about your family with slight ridicule. She said no one with money lived in Nakawa Housing Estates of all places. If your family had so much money, why did you not go to live in Muyenga, Kololo and Kansanga with your Mercedes-Benz lot? But you had new shoes every term. You had two new green uniforms every term. Sanyu, your name was never called out aloud by teachers, like the rest of us whose parents had not paid school tuition on time and we had to be sent back home with circulars.

Dear Parent,
This is to remind you that unless this term's school fees are paid in full, you daughter/son... will not be allowed to sit for end of term exams...
Blah, blah, blah...

Mummy always got those letters and bit her lip as if she had just heard that her house had burnt down. That's when she started staring at the ceiling with her eyes transfixed on one particular spot on the brown tiles. On such days, she went searching through her old maroon suitcase. It was from another time. It was the kind that was not sold in shops anymore. It had lost its glitter and I wished she never brought it out to dry in the sun. It would be less embarrassing if she brought out the other ones she used for her Tanzania trips. At least those ones looked like the ones your mother brought out to dry in the sun when she did her weekly house cleaning. That suitcase had all Mummy's letters – the ones Papa had written her when, as she said, her breasts were firm like green mangoes. Against a kerosene lamp, she read aloud the letters, re-living every moment, every word and every promise.

I will never leave you.

You are mine forever.

Stars are for the sky, you are for me.

Hello my sweet supernatural colours of the rainbow.

You are the only bee on my flower.

If loving you is a crime I am the biggest criminal in the world.

Mummy read them out aloud and laughed as she read the words on each piece of stained paper. She had stored them in their original Air Mail envelopes with the green and blue decorations. Sometimes Papa had written to her in aerogramme. Those were opened with the keenest skill to keep them neat and almost new. He was a prolific letter-writer, my papa, with a neat handwriting. I know this because often I opened her case of memories. I never did get as far as opening any letter to read; it would have been trespassing. It did not feel right, even if Mummy had never scolded me for reading her 'To Josephine Athieno Best' letters.

I hated to see her like that. She was now a copy typist at Ramja Securities. Her salary was not much, but she managed to survive on it, somehow, somehow. There were people who spoke of her beauty as if she did not deserve to be husbandless. They said with some pity, 'Oh, and she has a long ringed neck, her eyes are large and sad. The woman has a voice, soft, kind and patient. How could the man leave her?'

Mummy might have been sad sometimes, but she did not deserve any pity. She lived her life like her own fingernails and temperament: so calm, so sober and level headed, except of course when it came to reading those Papa letters by the lantern lamp.

I told you about all this, Sanyu. How I wished she could be always happy, like your mother who went to the market and came back with two large boys carrying her load because she had shopped too much for your papa, for you, for your happy family. I did not tell you, but sometimes I stalked her as she made her way to buy things from the noisy market. She never saw me. There were simply too many people. From a distance, she pointed at things, fruit ripe like they had been waiting to be bought by her all along. Your mother went from market stall to market stall, flashing her white Colgate smile and her dimpled cheeks. Sometimes I wished I were like you; with a mother who bought happiness from the market. She looked like someone who summoned joy at her feet and it fell in salutation, humbly, like the *kabaka* subjects who lay prostate before him. When I went to your house to do homework, I watched her cook. Her hand stirred groundnut soup. I must admit, Mummy told me never to eat at other people's homes. It would make us appear poor and me rather greedy. I often left your home when the food was just about ready. Your mother said, in her summon-joy-voice, 'Supper is ready. Please eat.' But I, feigning time consciousness, always said, 'I have to run home. Mummy will be worried.' At such times, your father sat in the bedroom. He hardly ever came out from that room. Every day, like a ritual, he came home straight from work.

'A perfect husband,' Mummy said more times than I can count.

'I hate him,' you said, more times than I could count. It was not what he didn't do, you said. It was what he did. Those touches, his touches, you said. And you could not tell your mother. She would not believe you. She never did. Like that time she came home after the day you taught Juma a good lesson for messing around with me. She spoke to my mother in her voice which sounded like breaking china.

'She is not telling me everything. How can the boy beat her over nothing? At the school tap! These two must know. That is why I am here. To get to the bottom of this! Right now!'

She said this again and again, and Mummy called me from the kitchen where I had just escaped when I saw her knock on our back door holding your hands in hers and pulling you behind her like a goat!

'Anyango, Anyangooooo,' Mummy called out.

I came out, avoiding your eyes. Standing with her hands held in front of me with the same kind of embarrassment and fear that overwhelmed me each time I heard my name called by a teacher for school fees default.

They talked for hours. I was terrified, which was why I almost told the truth. You interrupted me quickly and repeated the story we had agreed on our way home. Your mother asked, 'What was Anyango going to say?' I repeated what you had just said, and your mother said, 'I know they are both lying. I will get to the bottom of this at school in two weeks' time when I report back with her.' And she did. You got a flogging that left you unable to sit down for a week.

When you left our house that day, they talked in low voices. They had sent us outside to be bitten by mosquitoes for a bit. When they called us back in, they said nothing. Your mother held your hand again, goat style. If Juma had seen you being pulled like that, he would have had a laugh one hundred times the size of your trodden-upon confidence. You never looked back. You avoided looking at me for a while after that.

Mummy had list of 'don'ts' after that for me too. They were many.

Don't walk back home with Sanyu after school.

Don't pass by their home each morning to pick her up.

Don't sit next to her in class.

Don't borrow her text books. I will buy you your own.

Don't even talk to her.

Don't, don't, don't do anymore Sanyu.

It was like that, but not for long. After we started to talk again and look each other in the eyes, our parents seemed not to notice, which is why our secondary school applications went largely unnoticed. If they complained that we had applied to the same schools and in the same order, we did not hear about them.

1. St Mary's College, Namagunga
2. Nabisunsa Girls School
3. City High School
4. Modern High School

You got admitted to your first choice. I got my third choice. It was during the holidays that we got a chance to see each other again. I told you about my school. That I hated the orange skirts, white shirts, white socks and black boy's Bata shoes. They made us look like flowers on display. The boys wore white trousers, white shorts, white socks and black shoes. At break time, we trooped like a bunch of moving orange and white flowers – to the school canteens, to the drama room and to the football field.

You said you loved your school. Sister Cephas your Irish

headmistress wanted to turn you all into black English girls. The girls there were the prettiest ever and were allowed to keep their hair long and held back in puffs, not one inch only as at my school.

We were seated under the jambula tree. It had grown so tall. The tree had been there for ages with its unreachable fruit. They said it was there even before the Estate houses were constructed. In April the tree carried small purple jambula fruit which tasted both sweet and tangy and turned our tongues purple. Every April morning, when the fruit started to fall, the ground became a blanket of purple.

When you came back during that holiday, your cheeks were bulging like you had hidden oranges inside them. Your eyes had grown small and sat like two short slits on your face. And your breasts, the two things you had watched and persuaded to grow during all your years at Nakawa Katale Primary School, were like two large jambulas on your chest. And that feeling that I had, the one that you had, that we had – never said, never spoken – swelled up inside us like fresh mandazies. I listened to your voice rise and fall. I envied you. I hated you. I could not wait for the next holidays when I could see you again. When I could dare place my itchy hand onto your two jambulas.

That time would be a night, two holidays later. You were not shocked. Not repelled. It did not occur to either of us, to you or me, that these were boundaries we should not cross nor think of crossing. Your jambulas and mine. Two plus two jambulas equals four jambulas – even numbers should stand for luck. Was this luck pulling us together? You pulled me to yourself, and we rolled on the brown earth that stuck to our hair in all its redness and dustiness. There in front of Mama Atim's house. She shone a torch at us. She had been watching. Steadily like a dog waiting for a bone it knew it would get; it was just a matter of time.

Sanyu, I went for confession the next day, right after Mass. I made the sign of the cross and smelt the fresh burning incense in St Jude's church. I had this sense of floating on air, confused, weak and exhausted. I told the priest, 'Forgive me father for I have sinned. It has been two months since my last confession.' And there in my head, two plus two jambulas equals four jambulas…

I was not sorry. But I was sorry when your father, with all his money from the railways, got you a passport and sent you on the wing of a bird. Hello London, here comes Sanyu.

Mama Atim says your plane will land tomorrow. Sanyu, I don't know what you expect to find here, but you will find my Mummy; you'll find that every word she types on her typewriter draws and digs deeper the wrinkles on her face. You will find the Housing Estates. Nothing has changed. The women sit in front of their houses and wait for their husbands to bring them offal. Mama Atim's sons eat her food and bring girls to sleep in her bed. Your mother walks with a stooped back. She has lost the zeal she had for her happiness-buying shopping trips. Your papa returns home every day as soon as he is done with work. Mummy says, 'That is a good husband.'

I come home every weekend to see Mummy. She has stopped looking inside her maroon case. But I do; I added the letter you wrote me from London. The only one I ever did get from you, five years after you left. You wrote:

A.
I miss you.
S.

Sanyu, I am a nurse at Mengo hospital. I have a small room by the hospital, decorated with two chairs, a table from Katwe, a black and white television set and two paintings of two big jambula trees which I got a downtown artist to do for me. These trees have purple leaves. I tell you, they smile.

I do mostly night shifts. I like them; I often see clearer at night. In the night you lift yourself up in my eyes each time, again and again. Sanyu, you rise like the sun and stand tall like the jambula tree in front of Mama Atim's house.

Promise Ogochukwu

Needles of the Heart

Nana is old now, but no one could tell her age as she excitedly moved her angular frame from one embrace to the next, kissing and shaking hands with people. She still has a youthful face. Her eyelashes have remained forever bushy, giving her a peculiar loveliness. As a rule, she never bothers her face with makeup, not even a mild lipstick. She was wearing a green nail polish that evening and her nails were rather long even though she was not one to wear artificial nails. People always thought that there was something about Nana which reminded them of nature and its perplexities. It was something they could not put a finger to, especially as she aged rather gracefully. Watching her as she threw her braided hair back, laughing heartily, one would think she was one of the few lucky and happy people left in the world. Indeed, looking around her as she was, surrounded by friends who wore their trammels of success and seeing that she was quite comfortable, one was tempted to envy her.

It was her birthday. Everybody in the city seemed to know about it. It was generously published and talked about in both the electronic and print media as countless people wished her a happy eightieth birthday. Almost every page of the daily newspapers had her photo, smiling at the world as though she was its queen. Some friends went to the extent of putting the pictures she took in her youthful days side by side with those she took in her old age. The difference was much but the similarities were greater, for she still had those broad, lovely brown eyes and arresting dark pigmentation which in those early days had made Ozolua lose his head over her in more ways than one.

Hers was a marble house with glittering opaque tiles, overlooking the bar beach in the highbrow Victoria Island extension of Lagos metropolis. She had quite a big compound to accommodate the impressive turnout of dignitaries that graced the occasion. But beyond the Governors and the Commissioners who spoke of her in glowing terms, there were two people in the crowd who, as they gazed at her smiling contentedly, saw not only the old Nana they were celebrating, but the many aspects of Nana. As their eyes focused on her, while returning her smile and wishing they could take a picture of it and hold it for all time, they knew also that that smile would not be complete without the needles in her heart. Jide, her son, was the one who witnessed much and Ene, her confidante, witnessed even more.

It was in the early hours of the morning after Nana's wedding day that the monster in Nana's husband decided to disrupt the tranquility of the day. Ene had been her chief bridesmaid and was meant to return to her apartment in Ibadan that morning. She was having her bath when she heard a sharp cry from Nana's room. The cry was followed by the shattering of a glass and an angry voice, swearing at someone, seeming to thunder above them, shaking the entire house. She froze with fear as she applied caution and listened. The angry voice thundered on. It was Ozolua's voice. He seemed to be slapping someone around as he shouted all the more, cursing. Then she heard a muffled voice which was obviously Nana's. It was the very voice of agony: controlled, ashamed, almost soundless. The noise of another shattering glass jolted Ene from her frozen position and she ran to the direction of the sound. What she met would remain in her mind all her life.

There, in Nana's room, was Ozolua still roaring like a lion. She could not believe he was the same man she had always admired for his strong physique and calm disposition when he was courting Nana, when he would carry Nana up, proudly showing her off as the core of his existence and telling everyone who cared to know how deeply he loved her. He would call her all the time, even at odd times, waking her up to tell her how much she meant to him, filling her arms with gifts; some he brought, some sent by express delivery services, some through friends or other means. He was all over her so that eight months later, when they went down the aisle to declare their love before God and man, people were not taken unawares. But the very next morning, Ene nearly fainted over what she saw when she forced her way into Nana's room. There was Ozolua with his furious muscles flexed like those of a boxing champion. He had his mighty feet on Nana's thin neck as she crouched by the iron foot of the bed, shielding her face with her hands as she tried unsuccessfully to ward him off.

Charged with anger, Ene tore at him, hitting him with all her strength as she struggled to rescue the tiny woman about to be crushed. Nana held the foot of the bed firmly as she whimpered, surprised by the raging anger of the man she just married and the fear of the death reaching out for her so early in life. Ene saw her friend's fear and heard the whimper and became more enraged as she pummelled him, blinded by rage, not minding if she was making much impact or not.

Apparently, Nana's worry increased. Ene's rush into the room and the angry manner she was hitting at Ozolua must have scared Nana further for it was possible she feared that instead of killing one woman, Ozolua would now kill two and strangely she might have thought this was not good for him. She whispered, 'Ene, please go away. Don't let him harm you. I don't want him to be charged with manslaughter. Please don't let him kill two people. It's not good for him!'

It might have been her words or Ene's presence that made Ozolua stop and gaze at Ene, as though he was seeing her for the first time since she entered the room. But his eyes were no longer glaring with anger. They softened as they turned in the direction of the source of the words, by which time Ene had rushed to take Nana in her arms. Ozolua focused his gaze on Nana, still crouched by the foot of the bed. Her head which Ene held tenderly was bleeding. In tears, Ene's eyes sent daggers at Ozolua who hurried to Nana, kneeling beside her.

But Ene could not take it as she blurted out, 'Don't dare touch her! How could you! How could you! You!'

'Nana,' he said in a desperate voice. 'My God! What did I do?' he whispered.

Ene's face was contorted in contempt as she pulled away from him, holding Nana as though she was a child that badly needed protection.

'Let me take her, let me sort this out.' Ozolua reached out for Nana.

Ene shoved off his hands and turned to Nana. 'Come, let me help you up. Can you manage? I need to rush you to the hospital. We need to get out of here!'

'Look, I am sorry. Let me handle it.' He looked sober as he reached out to hold Nana, but Ene would not let him. He hurried outside to bring out his car, obviously shaken by the sight of the blood.

Nana had managed to get up as her blood dripped onto the floor. The sight of it seemed to anger her as she allowed Ene to lead her away. His car was already waiting by the stairway. He hurried out of the car to help them into it. Ene noticed that his hands were shaking on the wheel and wondered what kind of man he really was. He kept turning to look at Nana with concern as he drove. At the hospital he told his doctor the cause of the injury almost with tears in his eyes. Nana received treatment and was sleeping when the doctor reprimanded Ozolua and told him how disappointed he was in him. Ene, who overheard them, frowned at Ozolua's response:

'Dr J. I have to do something about my hot temper!'

'You'd better and fast too. You can't do this to anybody let alone your newly wedded wife. What's wrong with you?'

'I only know it won't happen again. I am sure her friend thinks I am mad.'

Again, Ene frowned, wondering if he was not suffering from something worse than madness. She knew she would have a heart to heart talk with Nana when she recovered. And she did.

'Nana, you did not tell me Ozolua was a violent man. Has he been putting your life in danger in this manner?' They were in Ene's room. Ozolua had gone to his laboratory which was a walking distance from their beautiful bungalow, one of the assets he inherited from his father.

Nana took her time to answer as she gazed into the wall. 'Ene, I can't really say if he has always been like this. But you know, this is the very first time he is beating me. I still can't believe he beat me. He has been so nice to me and all of a sudden, this . . . ' there were still tears in her eyes.

Ene breathed in. 'Wipe your tears. Tell me why a man who was so nice could begin suddenly to beat the woman he has just married?'

Nana looked up sharply as though stung. 'I must tell you, it worries me.'

'Why did he beat you?'

'Come to think of it,' she began slowly as though she was weighing the matter and thinking aloud, 'it's for something so ridiculous. I was looking at his collection and he said I was admiring a particular man in the collection. That he saw how I gazed at the man the first day I met him and that I was looking at his photo lustfully. As I protested, he hit me. His countenance had changed. He tore the man's picture and smashed the glass.' Her voice rose progressively, but it was never really loud.

'Look, Nana, this is a bad symptom,' Ene cautioned. 'You have to do something serious about this. I don't understand it. But I know I can't take a man hitting me for whatever reason.'

Three days after Ene left, Nana called to explain that it was just a mistake and that it would not happen again. Indeed it did not happen until two years after the birth of their baby, Jide. Then the call came through one evening in harmattan.

Everybody had been complaining about the weather, how it seemed to dry up and shrivel the skin, filling everywhere with dust, removing doors from their staples and breaking people's lips. It was a bad time for anybody to be wounded because wounds had a way of multiplying their pains during harmattan.

When the telephone operator told Ene to hold on for her caller, little did Ene know the next voice she would hear was Nana's. It was a tearful voice subdued in pains. In the background was the cry of a baby.

'Nana, what is it? Why are you crying? You are not using your phone, what is the matter?'

'Please come and get us. We are at Okene. We are hiding in someone's house. Ozolua threw us out.'

'Christ! Where? Where exactly are you?'

Nana told her and Ene went with her driver to fetch them. Nana who had always been petite had lost so much weight and was almost as dry as a stockfish. She had cut her long hair almost to the skin and tried to cover it with a head tie. But when Ene yanked it off, she saw that it was actually covering a mound of plaster over a terrible wound.

'Jesus Christ! Who did this to you, Nana?'

Nana managed a smile and fought her tears. 'I don't know. He was not like this. There was a problem in his office. I think he was under pressure. I must have uttered the wrong words. I don't know, but he hit me hard and broke my head. I told myself I had to escape, at least for a while. He didn't know when I left the house and went to his sister's at Okene, but on getting there, we realised she had travelled. So, I had to give you a call.'

'That son of the jungle! What beast will tear a woman's head apart in this manner! Someone needs to tell him a few home-truths!' Ene was already with the phone before Nana could stop her.

'Don't! Don't. I don't want him to know we are here.'

'So that what will happen? He won't dare come looking for you here. Let him try it!'

'Please, let him suffer a bit. Let him look for us.'

'And you think he will look for you?'

'I know him; he will be going crazy now in search of us. It's difficult to admit, but he is otherwise a good man. He really takes care of me in his good moments. He even bathes the baby, backs me at the beach, his heart actually embraces mine. I know it when he is near me and he is really near. I don't know where he got this madness. It worries him too.'

Ene shuddered, listening to her. 'He must be a good man, my dear, breaking your head so, yet his madness never allows him even to hit his own head against the wall! Nana, don't annoy me any further. If you are going to sit down there reeling out his sterling qualities with that open head of yours, then you are really pushing me hard. Just keep him out of our conversations. I don't want to talk about this anymore.'

That same evening, Ozolua called her. She did not give him a chance. 'If you don't know where your wife is, how do you think I will know? Have you made a formal report at the police station? Try that.'

He kept calling her. That night he arrived at Ibadan and stood at the gate after ringing her bell.

'Please, Ene, just let me see her!' he pleaded.

'Didn't I tell you she is not here?'

'You did, but I also know from your response that she is there.'

'I am sorry, you read me wrong!' She left him at the gate and walked back into the house. It was not until he started calling Nana desperately, disturbing the neighbourhood so shamelessly that Ene went back to the gate to speak to him again, by which time, a few people had gathered at her gate.

'I need to see my wife, after all, she is my wife.' He was getting angry.

'Look Ozolua, you are causing a scene. Can you please behave yourself!'

Ozolua stood there stubbornly.

By the time Ene got back inside the house, Nana was all

dressed up to see her husband. Touching Ene's cheek, she smiled. 'Please let him in,' she pleaded, teasing Ene. 'You know, he is just like a lost child. He can't go away. This is where his hope lies. I have forgiven him. Poor child! Poor soul!'

Ene marvelled at her and shook her head.

'Don't worry,' she said, 'you will understand when you get married.'

Ene knew that she would never understand it, especially as Nana flew into his arms the moment he got in. But at least, Nana spared her the details of their life together from then on. All Ene heard were snippets of their story, how on one occasion he beat her so badly that three of her brothers besieged his residence and almost killed him. Afterwards, they took their sister away with all her belongings.

But a week later after Ozolua had sobered up and begged, calling Nana every second, she escaped from her brothers and returned to her husband. At that point, the brothers gave up. For over three decades, Nana did not complain to anyone about Ozolua. Ene wondered if everything was all right or if she was merely bearing her pains privately. She refused to ask her friend but made sure she prayed for her every time.

Then Jide shocked her when she attended his wedding. 'My father left. It's an old story now. He left with Brenda.'

'Who is Brenda?' Ene held on to the chair beside her so she wouldn't faint.

'The woman he has been dating. Mama kept saying she took him away through diabolical means. Someone told her the woman was the daughter of a chief priest from some place where they could easily make a man do their bidding. This woman had boasted that she would make my father hers. Mama was told that she succeeded because my father previously dated her for nine years and instead of marrying her, as she expected, dropped her for Mama, so she swore to wreck his marriage and so on and so forth, but you know...'

'Wait a minute. This woman, did Nana say she knew her?'

'No, but she realised he actually had dated her that long and sadly, Aunt Ene, sadly continued to date her after wedding Mama.'

'No, please!'

'Yes, Aunt Ene. When Mama was told after he left, she saw a lot of the letters they exchanged. She saw much that nearly broke her heart, but she is a strong woman and I think her love for him is even stronger, so she kept defending him, believing that it was Brenda that was manipulating him. But I think it was the way I held him the last time he beat Mama that made him go away. I told him that it was going to be the very last time indeed and he read my lips right. I could no longer watch him do that to my mama.'

Ene ran to Nana and they cried on each other's shoulder even as Nana kept saying, 'I know my man will come back! He didn't leave intentionally, he didn't!'

Many years have passed since then and now there was Nana on her eightieth birthday, standing regally with friends, clicking wine glasses and savouring a throaty laughter. Things had turned out quite well for her. She had become very successful in the clothing business she started shortly after her husband left, designing clothes so excellently that she caught the attention of the President's wife, who introduced her to many people. As her designs won many local and international awards, she shot into the limelight and remained there to the joy of many who really loved her, especially as she also took time to design for the poor and the middle class even though she was surrounded by the rich and powerful. She never remarried despite all the numerous proposals that flooded her path.

That evening as she moved around greeting her friends and admirers, someone sneaked into the crowd. It was not until Nana's glass dropped and shattered as she stared at someone that Ene saw who it was.

The night stood still.

He walked towards her, his shoulders slacked, his face wan

even as he mustered a smile. Her feet moved slowly, then faster as her arms flew around him.

He was in tears and so was she.

'Where is she?' she asked.

'Dead...I shot her.'

Molara Ogundipe

Give Us That Spade!

Joko was now a Dean of Sciences at her school, no longer the anxious and unsure young woman she was when she met Kole, at the time already a full Professor of African Studies. A young scholar returning to Nigeria with a fresh PhD, Joko was trying hard, twenty-one years ago, to find her place at the University of African Heritages in Science and the Arts. Kole was a dean and the most senior of them, that is, one of the first to be dean at the same university. He was brilliant, admired and on the way to great things as everybody thought on the campus and in the country. Nobody knew the source of their attraction to each other, but the rumour mill against Joko was that she was after his position and fame and what it could do for her on campus. She believed herself to be in love with him and did not care about the stigma attached to being with Kole, who was married with children.

Now he was dead and Joko was as shocked as anyone else. What hurt her most was that his family never got in touch with her or informed her in any way although she had had a daughter with him. Not to be told of the death of one's daughter's father! She knew nothing of the funeral arrangements either. Her Yoruba culture made her Kole's relative for life because the sacred cord of life bound them through a child. She was socially considered in both the traditional and the little more confused contemporary cultures at a status higher than that of a concubine or a girlfriend. A longstanding traditional saying goes *Ka bimo fun ni kuro ni ale eni*: to have a child with one removes one from the status of the unmarried/lover. The concept was dually gendered, applying to both men and women.

After having therefore done her own research about the event of Kole's death, and having not been invited, Joko was now sitting in a middle pew of the church for the funeral with her best friend, Moradeke, or Deke, for short. Her daughter by Kole, Moriyike, now nineteen years old, was sitting between them. Joko was at the church part of the funeral which usually had many cultural sequences. There had been other Yoruba rites of the funeral which she had chosen to avoid. Joko certainly did not wish to participate in the preparation of the body, or turn up after the church service at the all-night fiesta usually held to celebrate the life of the dead and flaunt his biological and other material achievements. A life well-lived was cause for joy, not an occasion for glum faces and frightening black clothes. Being sad merely underscores the loss of the survivors, a selfish response to the life of the departed. Rejoicing after a death gracefully and generously gives the dead his or her freedom to go, accords him or her much dignity by remembering great doings of the deceased when alive, while minimising the human focus on loss as well as helping the bereaved to surmount their loss.

By the time the prolonged burial rites are completed, most of the bereaved would have moved to a state of much emotional relief. Funerals were and are the most important of the life rites of Joko's people. Perhaps the indigenous idea of reincarnation also had helped in the past to soften the grief of death and loss. The closest relatives are supposed to dance in triumph and glory. In Joko's status as mother-of -a-child-with-the-deceased, she could acceptably contribute her own marquees of invitees and provide food and entertainment with the rest of the family, even dance on that evening too, all at her own risk, of course. She was, by received thinking, bound to Kole's family for life, marriage or no marriage, divorce or no divorce, speaking of formerly married wives too. Joko was not, however, going to subject herself to any public scenes and challenges.

She sat quietly now in the church with her friend, Deke, and her daughter waiting for the funeral to begin, as the organist played sad hymnal tunes.

'Why are we sitting in the middle of the church, so far away from the front pew, so far away from Daddy's body?' Moriyike – Riyike for short – suddenly whispered loudly and urgently to her mother in the solemn silence. 'From where his body will be, I mean?'

Joko cringed at her calling Kole 'Daddy'. Moriyike always called him 'my father'. Now at his burial she was saying Daddy so intimately and even fondly, though she had not seen her father in eighteen years and did not grow up with him. He had come once to see her mother when Moriyike was still in her first year only to tell Joko that he could have nothing to do with the child. In the situation, Moriyike was a love child for Joko only, not for him. Foreseeing the rejection, she had named her daughter, Moriyike, meaning 'I have this one to pamper'. Some of the rumour mill members, the invisible talkers, reportedly mocked her for that name, saying 'pamper what? Who cares what she pampers? Don't mind her, *ojare*'. After that visit from Kole, Moriyike and her mother never saw him again – and now 'Daddy'?

Moriyike was antsy now, where she sat between her mother and her friend whom she called Auntie.

'Mummy,' she said again, 'why are we sitting so far away from the front? From where the body will be, Mama, and from the other children?'

Like most Nigerian middle-class children, Riyike spoke, most of the time, a certain kind of English: a Nigerianese that some mocked as International School English. Joko looked in consternation at her friend, Deke, who looked back into her friend's eyes with concern, and then looked down at her own hands lying quietly in her lap.

Moriyike rose and walked down the middle of the church to the front pew, usually reserved for the closest relatives of the deceased. Her mother was a little amazed that she would walk down the middle passage of the church, all by herself, in a huge church, a cathedral really, where such a large crowd from all walks of national life sat waiting, dressed to the tee to honour and witness the burial of the famous professor.

Joko nudged Deke and whispered, 'Look at Moriyike.'

'I see her,' Deke whispered back.

Riyike stopped between the first two pews where the public family of the distinguished deceased had been placed. The legal wife, sometimes called the 'madam' in the local English of the country, and her six grown children, all born one year apart in the modern style of national child reproduction, stiffened in their seats and did not move to accommodate her. Riyike then moved to the pew directly behind them, whispering 'Excuse me' to the people seated there. One man shifted so that Riyike got a foot in and sat down closer to the altar than she had been. The officiating clergyman coughed and fingered his Bible and notes.

The congregation and choir sang lustily during the service, perhaps trying to show in this way their pride in the man who had passed. Most probably they felt that the funeral should be one of joy and triumph since he had had a distinguished academic life and died not too young. To die in one's sixties was not to die young in that part of the world, so everyone was dressed in his or her most expensive and most 'see-what-I've-got' outfits. Wearing black was for tragedy, such as dying too young to have any achievements.

At sermon time, the officiating pastor who had fidgeted with his hands rose to speak. He reminded the church that to die in the Lord was to die well. More so, to die after having been chair of a university department, a dean, and a potential president, not to mention membership of the board of trustees of many universities in the land, was to die well indeed. The congregation agreed with him with sighs, firm nods and some regretful sucking of teeth. Some shifted in their seats or fanned themselves vigorously while others murmured under their breath:

'*Abi o.*' (Not so.)

'*A o wa ti se?*' (What can we do about it?)

'*Jesu seun.*' (Jesus has done something deserving thanks.)

'*Adupe o, Jesu.*' (Thank you, Jesus.)

Suddenly the pastor launched into a harangue about wives in the lord. He cried, 'We only know one Mrs Kole Olatunji in this church, don't we? Am I in the Lord? Am I saying something? I say we only know one Mrs Olatunji in this church community and fellowship of God. Am I right?' he concluded fiercely, looking to the right and the left, his eyes suddenly getting redder and redder. After a short pause, he cried, 'If anyone knows another Mrs Olatunji, will that person stand up now and declare it?'

The church was quiet as death. Not a sound could be heard in a church that had been full of different kinds of quiet, personal and pious sounds. Finally the pastor said slowly and clearly in a louder voice, 'and if there is any other Mrs Olatunji in this church today, will she stand up and meet us?'

When no response came from the audience, he proceeded to say quietly, 'Let us then bow our heads in prayer'.

As they prayed, Moriyike left by a side door and stood outside waiting for her mother and auntie. Both of them had risen with her, exited the church and were walking towards her.

'Did you hear that, Mummy?' Riyike said insistently, looking excitedly from one to the other. 'Did you hear that, Auntie?'

Joko and Deke raised their arms towards her almost at the same time. Joko moved towards Riyike to hug her as Deke held one of her hands.

'Don't be angry,' her mother said in English.

'*Ma dahun. Ma da won lohun,*' her auntie said in Yoruba. (Don't respond. Don't mind them all.)

'He was probably sent to say that, I am sure,' Joko mused aloud. 'To whom is he sending innuendos? *Ta lo npowe mo*?' she concluded, reverting to Yoruba.

'More than *owe* or innuendo, Mummy, he was directly provoking us,' Riyike fired back.

'Let us to go to the cemetery before they all come,' said Joko, as if to change the conversation and move them from where they were standing outside the church.

'Yes, let us avoid the rampage and the show off,' said Riyike.

They walked to the parking lot with Riyike stormily walking slightly ahead of her mother and her auntie. She went into the back seat of her mother's car and slammed its door. Her mother climbed into the driver's seat, looked back over her seat and said to her daughter slowly in Yoruba, deliberately enunciating each syllable to remind her of the meaning of her name:

'*Mo-ri-yi-ke, ni suuru.*' (Moriyike, have patience.)

Riyike gazed steadily out of the side window of the car and only replied in one word, meaningfully.

'Mummy.'

When they arrived at the cemetery, the immediate family of the professor had gathered round the casket, laid now across the grave. On one side of the length of the grave was a heap of earth. Beside it lay a small and ribboned spade. The pastor walked quickly to the graveside and intoned the appropriate liturgy, all in English as the main service had been, except for Yoruba praise songs, composed locally for African worship through dance. As the crowd began to sing a hymn at the graveside, Riyike's attention began to wander. She stared for a while at the heap of earth. She wondered how she could get close to the graveside. Slowly she inched away from her mother and auntie. She moved towards the nuclear family and stood by her siblings of the other mother. They instinctively closed ranks to form a tight straight line. Riyike pushed the one nearest to her unwittingly in order to find some space in which to stand. She stood in the same straight line with them and was now nearest to the heap of earth.

The casket was lowered slowly into the grave to the tune of 'Abide with Me'.

'Dust to dust and ashes to ashes,' intoned the clergyman as he threw some earth into the grave with his hands. 'The family of our dearly beloved departed will perform the last respects. They will take the spade over there and, in turn, throw some earth onto the grave after me. From the earth we came and to it we shall return,' he concluded.

The spade was passed to the pastor, who handed it to Mrs Olatunji. She adjusted her elaborate headtie, making sure it did not fall into the grave. She then gave her handbag to her eldest son, a young man of about thirty-four years. As she moved slowly towards the heap of earth, one of her daughters, now thirty-three years old, rushed to support her in her staggering widow's walk. She picked up some earth gingerly with the spade and in a frail and tear-laden voice whispered, 'Goodbye, my dear, till we meet to part no more.' She threw the earth into the grave and laid the spade down.

Riyike, standing next to the spade now, picked it up in a determined manner. She shovelled some earth and was about to throw it when pandemonium broke loose.

'Put that spade down!' came a shout from the unified voices of her father's wife and her children, in English.

'Put that spade down!'

'Give us that spade!

Then came shouts from individual voices. 'Put the thing down!'

'*Gbe kini sile*,' in Yoruba. (Put the thing down.)

'*E gba a lowo e,*' again in Yoruba. (Take it from her.)

The youngest of the three boys, now twenty-nine years old, detached himself from the sibling line to confront Riyike aggressively.

'Give me that spade!' he said at first. Then in his thick baritone he yelled again, 'Give us that spade!'

Riyike stood aghast. However, she held on to the spade in a more determined manner. As she held it tightly to her chest, not caring about soiling the beautiful lace she was wearing, she also shouted in a clear but shaking voice, 'He is my father too!'

'Give us that spade,' the public family all yelled back in unison.

The stunned pastor moved into the mêlée and grabbed the spade that Riyike still held, now to her middle. Suddenly hands were all over the place fighting over the decorated spade. The married woman and widow could not believe the scene. She burst into tears as she screamed loudly in Yoruba, '*Se e ri nkan bayi?*' (Do you see this now?)

'*Se e ri nkan bayi?*'

Somehow Moriyike had secured the spade from all the clutching hands. The many coloured ribbons tied fancifully to the handle of the spade had broken loose into streamers. Deftly manoeuvring the spade from the many hands, Riyike, in a flinging movement of her arms, threw a sizeable quantity of earth on to the casket.

'Goodbye, Daddy,' she shouted. 'You were and are my father too. I never knew you but, *orun ire o.* Sweet heaven to you.' She then turned to the now flabbergasted family and the flummoxed pastor, saying calmly, 'He was my father too and will always be.' She was still holding the spade in a kind of forgetfulness. She looked at herself and saw the spade in her hands, muddying her clothes. She held it aloft with its streamers for a minute before throwing the spade down. Turning around, she walked with sure steps over the grass lawn of the cemetery, away from the grave, not looking back once, her back straight as an arrow, her eyes looking in the distance. She walked towards her mother and auntie, who had stood discreetly some distance away from the open grave and the acknowledged family. As she approached them, her mother said quietly but admiringly in Yoruba, '*E gba mi lowo omo yi.*' (Save me from this child.)

Her flummoxed mother and broadly smiling auntie followed Moriyike as she led the way out of the church grounds.

Helen Oyeyemi

The Telltale Heart

Once, in Asyut, east of Cairo, a boy was born to a market trading family fallen on hard times; a family too poor to keep him unless he had somehow been born full-grown and ready to work. The boy's tiny mother had given birth to five big, healthy, noisy boys before him, but the first thing this particular boy did when he was born into the frame of cedar and rosewater that was his parents' bedroom, was cough quietly and turn a blind, bewildered glare on his brothers, who, suddenly as quiet as stone, elbowed each other and watched him closely. He was far too small. He had to be spanked six times before he proved his lungs to the midwife, and even then, his cry wasn't lusty enough. He was limp and wouldn't cling to an adult finger when it was placed in his palm. He refused his mother's breast, wrinkling his nose at the knotty brown bud of her nipple with slow bafflement.

Yet his eyes said that he needed something.

The boy's mother, who ran a meagre stall herself, saw into the future. Her mind hunkered down in the midst of her tiredness and spread the dead circle of her nerves until it overlapped into her next life, her next fatigue. The boy's mother saw that she did not have, and could not make, the time or energy to coax this son, to coddle him, to silently cherish him, to let him fall and find no help, to permit the breakage of parts of his spirit so that his heart could remain whole; to do all of the things that it would take for this boy to survive into his strength as a man. Her own spirit could not bear much when it came right down to it. (She looked into his puzzled, unhappy face and his eyes were like famine, like looking into hot, harsh hunger; seeing them sent hurt and light through her bloodstream, seeing those eyes made her certain that inside she was getting darker so that her happiness could hide from the brown mist that would take it, and like famine his eyes kept asking, asking, and she knew that to love him would be to die for him.) So if it hadn't been certain before, the decision not to keep the boy was now absolute and instantaneous.

'He will not be strong,' the boy's father winced, when news of the birth was brought to him at his sand-blown stall. He didn't tell the other men whose threadbare robes jostled his at market because it was not a good thing to have to send a child away.

'He will not be strong,' the midwife said, averting her gaze from the child's. She left as soon as she could, with promises that she would tell all the doctors she knew about the child, in the hope that they knew of some infertile couple.

Sunset on the outskirts of Asyut brought clarity. The boy's mother was comforted by sunset, and she closed the shutters and began preparing her new son's cot. The next day's noon came like a blazing hoop, and the sun spat yellow razorblades through it. People did what they had to, to keep from wilting. Slim women waddled, fat women crept close to the ground, barely taking steps. Among them came a tall, ramrod-straight woman in pure black; she parted the jostling knots of people in bounding spurts, like dark cognition. She was accompanied by the boy's midwife.

The woman took the market traders' son away with her because, she said, she needed a seeker, and he was one. The woman's voice was soft and you had to listen hard for it, otherwise you thought she was trying to speak to you only with her eyes, which lacked lustre and were not very expressive. You could tell that this woman was wealthy in some way that dulled her ability to inhabit the same moment as ordinary people – the atmosphere around her told of books and fine rugs. The boy's mother cried and held herself, held her leaking breasts as the woman took her son away. But she didn't change her mind.

A girl was born in Osogbo, in a small, off-white hospital a few feet away from a stone shrine to love. The girl was a heavy baby, with features that were pleasing because they were fluid and made her simple to look at, as if she was carved all of a piece. The girl's parents were disappointed that she was not a boy, but because the girl was so docile, she more than made up for it. The girl was very quick in learning to walk, to speak in both English and Yoruba, eat solids, use her potty, smile in a lasting, convincing way that brought maturity down like an axe on her face and put people much older than her at their ease with her. At six years old, she prostrated herself for her elders unasked. She clambered over her milestones with unassailable, business-like calm, as if this was her job, to be in order, and she had a mental checklist to get through. She passed through her milestones with minimal idiosyncrasy – no cute lisping, no unusual habits. It took a long time for the girl's parents to realise that their daughter's docility and sweetness was in fact vacancy, a kind of sleepiness and an instinctual longing for ease that translated itself to her entire body. From a very early age, the girl's hair grew soft and light so that combs flashed through it without tangling, so that it sat well in plaits, and blemishes fell away from her skin with simple soap and water. The same question put to this girl two times in a row would yield two different answers, depending on who asked the girl the question, and in what tone. Before it was finally made clear to her with a beating at the age of ten, the girl would often go with anyone who asked her to follow them home. The day that he saw that it was enough, the girl's father was chauffeuring a sweaty, bearded oil executive to the airport, and he looked away from the well-fed face, from the firm, confident mouth of his passenger in the rear-view mirror for a moment and saw his daughter following a street vendor home, talking respectfully, nodding and smiling in the shade of the bush-lined thoroughfare, a sack of rice piled across her shoulders with a sturdy, troubling grace. He bundled her into the car without ceremony or apology to his passenger, and at home he thrashed her with a mahogany walking cane. He held her head down on the kitchen table as he beat her, and his fingers dug into her scalp, but he did not feel her neck tensing against him as it does when funnelling pain, and she didn't make a sound. He kept on hitting her because he wasn't sure whether she was feeling this or not. The neighbours came *en masse*, some with their fingers entwined in the fur at the scruff of their goats' necks, and they remonstrated with him; women pulled off their head wraps and wrung their hands. 'It is too much,' everyone told him. He stopped when he was tired of hammering on her bones, and he still didn't know whether she had been hurt. He thought she might be dead. But no, he saw her breathing, her shoulder blades rose and fell with her head turned away from him and into the table. When she lifted her head, she was sorrowful, but calm. She said unsteadily, 'Sorry, Daddy.' Blood welled from the space between her lips and claimed the tabletop like a holy name.

The boy grew up with a hard smile, a complicated manner that was at once condescending and eager, and he developed a gait that made him seem arrogant, all strategies that he began from an early age in an attempt to counteract his eyes and their treacherous tendency to ask. He wasn't handsome, or talkative, but his adoptive mother made sure that he dressed well, in English tailoring and American denim, which differentiated him from the muted cotton and khaki trousers that Asyut people dressed in. And besides, this boy's sadness was luminous, and that called for addressing. Girls his age gave him kisses and held his hand even when they shied away from other boys. Women offered him honeyed pastries, warm chopped nuts, confidences, concern. He walked the markets and chugged pipe smoke in corner tea houses, breathed in the spice-pod musk of men and took their advice with throwaway thanks in Arabic. Had he simply drunk in all the love that was offered him, people would have stopped offering. His adoptive mother was a widow, and it was possible that her bereavement had made her mad. She lived in a large house that had used to terrify him when he was younger because the downstairs was bright and softly pastel-coloured and air-conditioned, but the upstairs was cordoned off with a festoon of silk ribbons and you could see it clearly from the foot of the staircase, and it made him understand that, if the downstairs was the bright match-flare, the upstairs was consequences. The upstairs festered like a dark flame blister that sucked up all of the day. If he looked hard enough, he could make out doors and bare floors, but that was all. At night he slept on a couch beside the woman who had adopted him. The woman herself slept on a boat-shaped ivory chaise longue; it took to her body in a way that he would never see again, let her sleep with grace although her arms and legs were bunched up and her feet were hanging off the end of the couch. The woman was very beautiful beneath her scarves; her face was sweetly composed dusk and her lips were rose petals that always seemed swollen with kisses, although these didn't trouble him until the years when he began to add kisses and a woman to sigh beneath his hand to his comprehensive list of wants. It didn't seem to matter very much that the woman didn't grow older as he grew older, either, though he suspected that something about the woman herself slowed him down, bathed his thoughts in perfume, set his dreams afloat so that his mind was abuzz with stranger things than her age, or her solitude, or the silent upstairs. Even when he was smaller, she would take his hand and smile mysteriously at him and say, 'And now, we are going to...'

And they did, and he did with all his heart, although he never remembered what it was that they did, or how she finished her sentence, or even whether it was the same thing she said every time, or different things. Afterwards he felt pain throughout his hands, so much they grew rictus stiff and the woman had to spend hours massaging them with oils that madc him golden for moments at a time.

One day, with free pomegranates from a market stall owner weighing down his pockets, the boy walked past his midwife and, even in a crush, they noticed each other. They did not recognise each other, but each looked in the other direction, troubled. The woman who had adopted him, who insisted on being called mother – which he did, but with a secret hiss that came from some place inside of that him he did not understand; inside his head her name became *motherhhhhhhh*, smothered myrhh – was an art collector. But she only collected art that was body pieces, one piece of each, one considered piece at a time, painstaking finds because she was looking for a collection that, when put together in a room, would create the suggestion of a woman's beauty, a woman who crammed the room from wall to wall. He never asked her how she could afford all of these things, how she could afford to spend her days pacing the kitchen, where, amongst lace tablecloths and shiny, unused utensils – the woman had supper and breakfast brought to them, mounds of herbed rice and spiced meats at dinner, and sweet tea and rainbows of fruit in the morning – all her artefacts were assembled like quaint restaurant bric-a-brac. The boy did not ask her anything. He took telephone calls and messages left for the woman by her contacts all over the world. He travelled Egypt with her and observed cemetery graffiti as she did, so closely that she almost inhaled it – in hundreds of perfumeries they watched glass blowers torture air between their hands until the air was forced to remain solid, brittle and distressed in several tints. In New York, they spent a long time in one particular museum, looking at a painting that a black man had done, that everyone was talking about. The painting was a reinterpretation of another painting, that a white man had done, that had made a plain woman look mysterious and glad in her infiniteness. What the black man had done in this new painting was to make the white woman look like any old woman, any thing –

unfinished and lacking in colour. The numbness of the painting was such that the boy knew that even if the black man had painted a black woman, the new woman would be the same or even worse. The boy's new mother liked it. The boy did not, as he wanted the woman from the first painting, the one who was more than the paint, or the painting, or the painter, back. Always, as they travelled, she pointed and asked him, 'Do you like that? What do you see there? Do you want what you see there? Do you want her?'

He told her the truth, and she always listened to him. She said that he chose well.

But when they got home, the boy did not ever feel anything in the presence of these well turned ankles and smooth calves, these arms and shoulders captured in shade and the moment of motion. They were a collection, not a woman. They had a face, a photograph of a girl who had died with her family one night when her neighbours smashed the door down and took an axe to all the living inside that house. The neighbours did this because a radio broadcast which, although run by people and read aloud by people, was not a person and thus had an icily accurate, objective view of human life, had advised them not to wait for the evil that lived next door to grow and get the better of them. The neighbours had not touched anything else in the girl's house, which is how the boy and his new mother, picking over this living room at the end of a series of shattered living rooms, found the girl's picture. At first the boy thought that it would be wrong to take the picture, but then he saw how this girl could not be dead as long as the picture survived, because this picture was unlike any other picture – it had been taken in the back yard of the house, at a moment between the sun's departure and the coming on of a braid-tweaking evening breeze. Her smile did not seem to correspond to the presence of the camera, or even to a joke told off-camera, and because the smile had no reason, it was unnerving. The boy could see how it would be frightening to live next door to someone like that. They took the picture home, even though the boy's new mother complained that it wasn't art.

But when they got home, the boy did not ever feel anything in the presence of these well turned ankles and smooth calves, these arms and shoulders captured in shade and the moment of motion. They were a collection, not a woman. When the boy's new mother asked him what he thought of their almost complete collection, waved her arms at all the fineness and said, 'Do you want her? Do you need her?', he said, 'No.'

'We need a heart,' the boy's new mother said, and when she looked at him, in that moment, she seemed to him so high just then, it seemed that her feet connected to the ground only tenuously and it was her shadow that bore her up and prepared the way for her. As ever, her eyes were dull. He thought in that moment that this woman must be beautiful because all of her features were correctly exaggerated, all of her features the right shade and shape, but at the same time he thought that his new mother must be a spider.

What nobody knew about the docile girl from Osogbo was that her heart was too heavy, and that from the first moment she understood that she could feel, she had felt that weight, a gravitational pull that invited her to her grave. She knew that she needed to be lighter. Her heart was heavy because it was open, and so things filled it, and so things rushed out of it, but still the heart kept beating, tough and frighteningly powerful and meaning to shrug off the rest of her and continue on its own. People soon learnt that they could play on her sympathy even if they couldn't touch her empathy, and, because she was terrified that one day this unasked-for conscience of hers might kill her, she gave away whatever money she earned baking and selling bread, gave away bread, gave huge discounts, was poor and paid her protesting parents rent for the propriety of the thing. She tried, several times, to give her love away, but it would not stay with the person she gave it to and snuck back to her heart without a sound. What people didn't know about this girl was that the ancestral dead kept her company – they came to find her at bath-time and sat four at a time in the bath with her, cooing wistfully and washing her hair with wasted, insubstantial claws. She urged them to take care of their own children, but they refused. Her head lolled at these times and she was overcome with gratitude that her helpers did not demand that she cared for them. At bedtime the dead took her with them, and in her dreams, she visited their graves.

At first, in rebellion against her heaviness, she thought that she needed to be thinner, and she took to reading imported women's magazines on credit from a bookstall owner. The magazines talked about calories and saving calories and keeping some back so that you could have a glass of wine, and the girl started thinking about calories. One day at the dinner table, she ask her mother for an estimate of how many calories there were in the fried stew that bubbled at the bottom of her bowl beneath a layer of *eba*. There is no Yoruba word for calories, and so her mother just looked at her and said musingly, smilingly, in English, 'calories', as if she was trying to understand a punch line hidden in between the syllables. Then the girl didn't ask anymore and sat looking at the food, which was bottomless and made to sink hunger, but what happened when in fact you were too full?

It made her decide that she had to hide her heart somewhere until she was big enough to keep hold of its weight, and one night the dead helped her, some stroking her hair and soothing her while others hooked their fingers into her and carefully lifted a strand of fine steam from the cracked cusp of her chest. She took her heart and hid it in the shrine to love, and that cool night she was frightened even though she walked amidst a crowd of other people's ancestors and the moon and stars held off the spears of darkness that would otherwise attack. The shrine was a rectangle of stone arches that bore the marks of violent, harsh minds that conceived of another kind of love – strange, ugly, smoke and choking sort of love, carvings of cruel hands that killed candle flames to break refusal in the dark, women thrusting out hard breasts and genitals and a still knowingness, and also in the carvings was the kind of love that wakes you up from nightmares and into a new world that consists of one person who is, in turn, all people and a sundial of wise children's faces. The shrine was the kind of place where a Valentine's heart would have trembled and wilted. She heard a shrieking like a bird, and it hurried her, she refused aid and, with her fingers, she scratched a place for herself in the grey north wall that night and when she exposed a chink, she slipped her heart through into the dry moss behind the stone, and she walked away, and she walked away, and that was that, and that was that.

Because he had been told to, the boy looked for hearts. He examined unusual playing cards and alabaster chess pieces and went to London with his new mother to examine posters plastered onto the walls of public transport. He turned twenty-one, and on his birthday, his new mother took him to the west coast of his continent to view a shrine, a shrine where, one of their contacts had told her, you could hear and feel a heart beating when it grew dark. They stood, amidst a small crowd of other curious people, and waited for sunset, which came with a slow earthquake that sent the ground slipping away until they realised that it was the legendary heartbeat. The boy, now a man, stood a little apart from his new mother, who listened intently, and the heartbeat said things to them both, things that made the boy smile with all of his soul in his face, things that made the new mother suck in her cheeks and look suddenly pinched and old. They stayed long after everyone had gone, and fell asleep at dawn with their heads laid on rocks converted to pillows with thick cashmere shawls.

When the next morning came around, the asking in the man's eyes was intensified as if refracted through a new lens, and no one could look at him without offering, offering, offering.

The girl was lighter without her heart. She danced barefoot on the hot roads and her feet were not cut by the stones or glass that studded her way. She spoke to the dead whenever they visited her, tried to be kind, but they realised that they no longer had anything in common with her, and she realised it too, and they went their separate ways. Other people were closed to her, and she enjoyed it this way – at the market place she handed over her bread and exacted the correct payment for it with a slight pressure of the hand and an uncaring smile, and when she moved amongst people, she felt as if she were walking in a public place at an hour of the night when it was too dark to come out, or at noon, when it was too hot to be out, and all the doors around were closed and barred. The girl felt this aloneness to be an adventure. She moved away from her parents and went to live by herself on the ground floor of a tenement, even though this was frowned upon. When she was not working or wandering, she listened to the white noise inside her head, or she sat on her bare floor and listened to people arguing, romancing, accusing, the people all around her; she let their words fall into her body like a coin into a bottomless well when once she had tried to carry them. Sometimes she thought about her heart, and wondered how it was doing without her, but she was never curious enough, or brave enough, to go and find out. Except once, when she almost went back to see. Except once, when she woke up one morning convinced that she was in love. All over her, her skin felt softer even than her breath, and her eyes felt wider, clearer, dreamy, lashed and lidded with an unknown stuff that had drawn a man in. For a week, she washed and dried and rubbed cream into her body with a special, happy care, and she realised that she was preparing herself to be caressed. She found a taste for cold things that released their sweetness slowly – ice cream that slid down her throat before she could taste it, tinned peaches in chill syrup.

But no man arrived, and there was no heart for her to love with. When the girl fully remembered this, she forced herself to eat a bite of mashed plantain, and the first swallow was hard, but after that, life stepped straight again.

The man's new mother told him, 'That heart, that heart in

the shrine, it's the heart that we must take for my collection.' With the addition of the heart, the art collection, the beautiful woman, the new mother's obsession, would be complete. 'If only we can locate the heart and take it with us,' the man's new mother said, watching him closely, as if she knew that he already knew exactly where the heart was.

And it was true; the heart had told him, it had called to him, 'come and claim me, take from me, I am inexhaustible'.

'I know that you know where that heart is,' the man's new mother said, and she bared teeth as sharp as daggers. 'You are a seeker, you find things. Bring it to me, or I will kill you.'

The man was afraid of his new mother, but he was more afraid of another thing too large for him to understand. The fear had to do with giving the heart away when it belonged to both him and someone else. He told his new mother to give him five days, and he ground valerian root into her tea to make her sleep. (He almost put enough in to kill her, but her death was not what he wanted.) The new mother slept with a beauty like rose and earth, and her bitterness was a weed whose roots were scourged by her sleep, and it fell away.

The man moved the collection, in carefully packaged batches, to the Osogbo shrine. It was a call to the owner of the heart, this offering; he would not take the heart from the walls of the shrine until she came. He looked at all the love carved into the stone, and it was a lot of love, and he believed that it must be enough; he had to believe that it was enough. He arranged the fragmented woman as best he could, and sometimes he felt as if unseen hands helped him, propped a canvas in such a way that the light enhanced its beauty. He was desperate, and he asked the heart to call to its owner, for she was the strength that he had somehow been born separately from. The heart called. The heart called. The man called. The girl didn't hear, but the gathered woman, scattered across sculptures and glass and photographs and scraps of paper, the gathered woman became complete and almost breathed, and she was rapture, but she was not enough. The man waited for five days, and he thought that he must die under the sun and the pain of this disaster, but he didn't die because the shrine stones protected him.

And when the five days were over, he saw that the heart's owner did not come, or would not come, and he left that place.

Nawal El Saadawi

The Veil

All of a sudden I awake to find myself sitting with a bottle of wine in front of me, of which only a little remains, and an ashtray full of cigarette ends of a strange kind I have not seen before, until I remember that they are the new brand I began smoking three or four years ago.

I look up from the ashtray to see a man I've never seen before. He is naked, apart from a silken robe which is open to reveal a hairy chest and thighs. Between the chest and thighs is a pair of close-fitting striped shorts. I raise my surprised eyes to his face. Only now do I realise that I've seen him before. My eyes rest on his for a moment and I smile – a strange, automatic smile, as fleeting as a flash of light or an electric current, leaving behind no trace other than a curious kind of perplexity like the eternal confusion of a person in search of God or happiness. Why is there such confusion in the world and in my body at this particular moment, even though each day my eyes meet hundreds of thousands of eyes and the world and my body remain as they are? But it is soon over. The world and my body return to normal and life continues as usual. It is three or four years since I saw him for the first time and I'd almost forgotten him in the tumult of work and home and people.

My eyes fall on his naked body and hairy thighs once more. The expression on my face, as I look at his body, is not the same as when I look into his eyes, for my problem is that what I feel inside shows instantly on my face. His eyes are the only part of his body with which I have real contact. They dispel strangeness and ugliness and make my relationship with him real in the midst of numerous unreal ones. Three years, maybe four, and every time I run into him in a street or office or corridor, I stop for a moment in surprise and confusion. Then I continue on my way, knowing that while this relationship is very strange, it is at the same time familiar and accepted, among numerous unfamiliar and unaccepted relationships.

When we began meeting regularly or semi-regularly, my relationship with him did not extend to parts of his body other than his eyes. For long hours we would sit and talk, my eyes never leaving his. It was a sort of meeting of minds, and gratifying, but the gratification was somehow lacking. What did it lack?

I asked myself whether it was the body's desire for contact with another body. And why not? In the final analysis, isn't he a man and I a woman? The idea strikes me as new, even strange, and a frightening curiosity takes hold of me. I wonder what the meeting of my body with his could be like. A violent desire to find out can sometimes be more compelling than the desire for love and can, at times, draw me into loveless contacts simply in order to satisfy that curiosity. And every time that happens, I experience a repulsion, certain in my mind that my body repulses the body of a man except in one situation – that of love.

I understand the cause of this repulsion. It's an explicable repulsion linked not to the body but to history. To the extent that man worships his masculinity, so woman repulses him. A woman's repulsion is the other face of the worship of the male deity. No power on earth can rid woman of her repulsion other than the victory of love over the male deity. Then history will go back six thousand years to when the deity was female. Will love be victorious? Is the relationship between us love? I do not know. I have no proof. Can love be proved? Is it the desire which rises to the surface of my crowded life, to look into his eyes? Like a person who, from time to time, goes to a holy water spring to kneel down and pray and then goes home? I do not kneel down and neither do I pray. I recognise no deity other than my mind inside my head. What is it that draws me to his eyes?

Is love simply a fairy tale, like the stories of Adam and Eve, or Cinderella, or Hassan the Wise? All the fairy tales came to an end and the veil fell from each of them. Many veils fell from my mind as I grew up. Each time a veil fell, I would cry at night in sadness for the beautiful illusion which was lost. But in the morning, I'd see my eyes shining, washed by tears as the dew washes the blossom, the jasmine and the rose. I would leave the mirror, trample the fallen veil underfoot and stamp on it with a new-found strength, with more strength than I'd had the previous day.

He has filled the tenth or twentieth glass. My hand trembles a little as I hold it, but the deity inside my head is as steady and immobile as the Sphinx. My eyes are still on his and do not leave them, even though I realise, somehow, that he is no longer wearing the silken robe nor even the tight striped shorts.

I notice that his body is white, blushed with red, revealing strength, youthfulness, cleanliness and good eating. My eyes must still have been staring into his, for in another moment, I realise that he has taken my head in his hands and moved it so that my eyes fall on to his body. I look at him steadily and once again see the strength, and youthfulness, and cleanliness, and good eating. I almost tell him what it is I see.

But I look up and my eyes meet his. I do not know whether it is he who looks surprised or whether the surprise is in my eyes. I tell myself that the situation calls for surprise, for it is nearly three in the morning. The glass is empty. There is no one in the house and the world outside is silent, dark, dead, fallen into oblivion. What is happening between my body and his?

When I next turn towards him, he is sitting, dressed in the robe with the belt carefully tied around his waist, hiding his chest and thighs. I no longer see anything of him other than his head and eyes and feet inside a pair of light house shoes. From the side, his face looks tired, as though he's suddenly grown old and weary. His features hang loose, like a child needing to sleep after staying up late. I put out a hand, like a mother does to stroke the face of a child, and place a tender motherly kiss on his forehead.

In the street I lift my burning face to the cold and humid dawn breeze. Mysterious feelings of joy mingle with strange feelings of sadness. I put my head on my pillow, my eyes open, filled with tears. My mind had got the better of the wine until I put my head on the pillow; but then the wine took over and sadness replaced joy.

When I open my eyes the following day, the effect of the wine has gone and the veil has lifted from my eyes. I look in the mirror at my shining eyes washed with tears. I am about to walk away from the mirror, like every other time, to trample on the fallen veil at my feet and stamp on it with new-found strength. But this time I do not leave my place. I bend down, pick up the veil from the ground and replace it once again on my face.

Véronique Tadjo

A Sunny Afternoon

He shouldn't have shown her his home, taking her through each room, pointing at the paintings on the walls, commenting on them. She loved every bit of it. And he should definitely not have taken her to his bedroom. A bedroom is an intimate space. It is the place where you hide your soul, your secrets, and your vulnerability. Only a few carefully chosen people are normally allowed in. And it was such a beautiful bedroom! On that sunny afternoon, a bright light shone through the windows and touched everything with a glow. The bed was in brown wood, taking the centre of the room and facing the balcony. It had been made and looked neat, but it was all too easy for her to imagine him sleeping between the sheets, half naked.

They stood for a moment looking at the garden from high up. The tall trees hid the road from which she had come and flowers flashed bright smiles at them. The grass had been freshly cut and its scent travelled upwards. He explained that during the past rainy season half the garden had been flooded. It was only drying up now. They could see the city centre in the distance. She thought, 'this is wonderful, so peaceful, so green, so promising. I feel miles away from everything'.

She turned round to admire the bedroom one more time. She thought he had taken her into his private world, revealed himself to her. Surely, it meant that he wanted to embark on a journey together. His bedroom would be their ship, or should she say their raft, their canoe on a tumultuous sea.

He really shouldn't have done that, catching her off guard in this foreign country where she was alone and vulnerable.

She had a flight to take in the evening so why this display of intimacy now? Why did he show her so much when he knew she would be leaving soon?

After having breathed in the powerful scent of the garden one more time, he told her they should go downstairs for a drink. She was startled by what he said, totally shaken as if she had been allowed to have a glimpse at a treasure and then told to abandon it. She thought, 'when we go, love will stay behind in this bedroom, hidden away in the cool shade, blooming in the light, fragrant with anticipation. This must be the most beautiful house to make love in'. And she had wanted, here and then, to ignore the rest of the world and take his hand.

But she did nothing of that. Instead, they went down the stairs. She looked again at the paintings on the walls. She was amazed to realise how each one of them spoke to her. They told her that she shared the same taste with their owner, a taste for bright colours and bold strokes. Some of the figures on the pictures were half animal, half human, possessing eyes that looked back at the viewer in total amazement. They were like the keepers of his house, radiating a powerful presence. For her, that was it. Anybody who was on such a par with her could only be a kindred spirit. Moreover, virtually every other object she saw around her, she could have chosen herself. She could not deny such an incredible level of connectedness. His vision, his mental landscape, seemed to be the same as hers.

She could not bring herself to say anything about her feelings for fear one wrong word would break the spell. Instead, she chose to memorise every last detail of the afternoon. She had a photographic memory. She knew she could be relying heavily on it in the days to come. How could she let these moments erase themselves? She descended downstairs slowly. But as she walked onto the terrace, she saw that the light had fallen. Evening was approaching rapidly.

Her other life was calling her. She needed to go back home to her routine and all her unaccomplished wishes. Her car was parked in the driveway, ready to go. The clock was ticking away, refusing to stop for one single moment, refusing to acknowledge the particular quality of their encounter. She said, 'Let me go now. It is time for me to pack my suitcase and get ready for my flight.'

While saying goodbye, she wanted nothing more than to go back into the house and rewrite the afternoon. But she knew it was impossible, far too late for changes. So she parted as calmly as she could, even managing to wave to him as if she would be returning soon, as if she would be parking her car in his yard on many occasions to come. She would have her own spot somewhere by the edge, next to that tall soapstone sculpture. She would come back on a similar afternoon; sunny and crisp, bright and overpowering.

She drove straight to the hotel. She was changing the gears of her hired car mechanically, lost in her thoughts. It wasn't so much the act of love-making she was longing for but the reassurance that harmony did exist in a simple and wonderful way and that she had been very close to it. She could have stretched her arm and touched it. She could have bathed in it, listened to its murmur. It was unexpected and rich, yet achingly sad.

She went to the airport, took her flight, found herself in the sky for several hours, was lulled by the humming of the place and transported into a fretful sleep. She was engulfed by the undercurrents of her dreams. Sensations took hold of her, flinging her in the air, tossing her body around and leaving her feeling she had never closed her eyes during the whole journey. 'My life has entered a turbulent zone,' she reflected. 'I am disconnected from the outside world. On either side of reality, I can fall. I cannot hide behind the clouds. The sun could burn my eyes, my skin. Yet I have to uncover myself.'

In her dream, she had embraced him may times and he had done the same. It was more real than anything she had experienced before. What was the difference anyway if she believed in it?

Finally, she landed back in her country, re-entering her life as if coming from an odyssey. She resumed normality, managing to hide her secret from her family during the day but succumbing to it at night when everybody was sleeping and she was able to escape to a place where beauty met her.

But soon, even during daytime, she couldn't control her thoughts anymore. She would blank out the whole world around her in a fraction of a second. She was present physically, answering questions and doing what was expected of her, yet her mind was elsewhere, back in the bedroom bathed in the afternoon sun. She would recall that scene as if it were a film she could replay as often as she wished on the screen of her memory.

She knew she couldn't retreat to the past. It was unhealthy and bad for her mental wellbeing. She wanted to fight it off and regain control of herself. After all, nothing had happened, nothing had been decided. Yes, really, she was shocked at how deeply involved she felt when, in fact, she had so little to show for herself: a brief encounter with a man in his house, a glimpse of his bedroom and a nice conversation. That was all. Was this the cause of so much heartache? Was it the reason why she was wasting away? However, she kept feeling the same and the longer it lasted, the harder it became to focus on anything else.

Then one day, something horrifying happened. Something that the world had not expected and therefore wasn't prepared for – the kind of event that changes the way we look at ourselves.

Sitting with her family watching television she witnessed, like millions of other people, the destruction of the Twin Towers in New York. One after the other the huge buildings were struck by the planes and collapsed in heaps of dust, debris and stones. The scene was in slow motion. It was like a movie, surreal and far removed. Only when she later saw the newspaper pictures and heard the news on the radio over and over did she accept the truth. A new and terrifying era had been born.

She was immediately overcome by fear: fear of a third world war; fear of the bomb; fear of violence and destruction; fear of the end of the world.

As the days passed and the magnitude of what happened sunk in, she thought with anguish, 'the world has turned upside down'. She felt as if she had to do something to change her life before it was too late. 'Will I ever see him again?' she kept asking herself. What was going on between them was so insignificant and she knew that soon their story would be swallowed by the tide. She was determined to take it to its logical conclusion, to make sure that something came out of it in one way or another.

She became increasingly restless, impatient with everybody. She had always thought she was a good mother, but now she felt that she was losing that too. She was not paying attention to her children, not hearing their calls, not acknowledging their needs. She had believed she would always put them first in her life, love them more than anybody else. But the reality was that she could feel herself slipping further and further away from them, experiencing a kind of estrangement she had never thought would be possible. Where was the closeness? Her children had become like little strangers. She got scared and attempted to erase that feeling but when she tried to get closer to them, they sensed her betrayal and recoiled from her touch. She was alone. Her obsession had destroyed the foundations of her life.

That's when she started having insomnia. She would wake up in the middle of the night, unable to go back to sleep. She was exhausted but all she could do to calm herself was read or walk around the house or eat all the food in the fridge. If she stayed in bed, each time she closed her eyes she would have the feeling that she was drowning. She gasped for air.

Her husband took her to the doctor. After running a series of tests, they were told that there was nothing wrong with her. 'I just want to sleep,' she pleaded with the doctor, 'just give me some pills so I can get my sanity back. I am so tired.'

She was given blue, yellow and red tablets.

Sometimes, she would awaken from her slumber and cry, wanting, wishing hard she could go back to her old self, before that sunny afternoon. It was hurting too much. She wanted to recover quickly, to stop that frightening feeling of estrangement. She thought she was failing everybody. She wanted her longing to vanish. But she couldn't help digging more and more into her memories.

Her husband tried again to help her, but she was unreachable. They could not communicate because she had closed her mind. He was unable to bring her back into the family. So, one day, he went to her and said, 'You cannot go on like this. If you need to leave, do so. Go wherever you want to if that is your wish. But make sure you know why you are doing this, why you are making us suffer so much.'

She packed up a small suitcase and left on the first plane.

Now, that was an extraordinary thing to do considering she had not been in touch with the man she dreamed about so much. She had had no further contact with him, even convinced as she was that he felt the same about her. 'Intuition doesn't lie,' she said to herself. 'It was all there. I saw it in his eyes, in the way he looked at me.'

For her, time had stood still. It had not altered anything. Her memory of that sunny afternoon was as vivid as ever, flowing in the same direction. Distance did not matter. In her heart she had not moved an inch.

She went straight to his house. She did not know whether he would be there but she was ready to wait until his return if necessary. And if he took too long to come back, she would simply ask the neighbours for his whereabouts. The taxi dropped her at his house. Suddenly she was seized by panic. What on earth was she doing coming unannounced? What madness had taken over her? Controlling her fear, she paid the driver, got out of the car and faced the entrance. The scent of the garden welcomed her. She pushed the gate with one hand, the other holding her small suitcase. In the driveway, her steps made crunching noises on the gravel. She thought, 'he must have heard me. He knows somebody has arrived.'

But no one came to the door when she pressed the bell. She waited a bit then stood there wondering what to do next. She was frightened like a little girl abruptly plunged into darkness. She had made herself feel quite helpless, more vulnerable than she had ever been for a very long time. But she said to herself with no apparent logic, 'I want to feel my body, not just bear it.'

She rang the bell again, this time a little bit longer.

She heard footsteps inside the living room. The next thing she knew, he was standing in front of her. 'Oh, is it you?' he said in a voice filled with surprise. 'When did you get here? I thought you had gone away.'

'Yes, I had but I have just come back. Look, I came straight from the airport!'

He glanced at the small suitcase and then looked at her again. That's when she noticed that his clothes looked like he had dressed quickly to answer the door.

'Well, come in,' he said after giving her a hug, 'don't stand here like this!'

She entered the house cautiously and dropped her suitcase in a corner. He enquired how she was and what she had been doing since he last saw her. They both looked up at the same time.

'Who was that at the door?' asked the voice. 'Why aren't you coming yet?'

Both questions were asked in an anxious tone by a man who was now standing halfway down the stairs, his right hand on the rail. He was tall and his trim body was fit and strong. He wore nothing except for a bath towel wrapped around his waist. He looked slightly annoyed. 'Hello!' he muttered, reluctantly looking at her. Then, talking as if to no one in particular, he added nonchalantly, before disappearing up the stairs again, 'I am getting bored in the bedroom. I won't wait for long. Hurry up, please!'

She kept her head bowed, refusing to show the confusion

that was overtaking her. Silence had fallen between them. He put his hand forward as if to touch her. His lips parted. He said, 'Listen...'

But she hardly heard, turning round and running out of the house before he could stop her. She ran up the driveway, through the gate and onto the road. She heard him call her name. She did not slow down. She ran straight ahead.

She ran and ran until she was completely out of breath. At last, she sat on a bench in a small park. She was incapable of moving anymore. She had difficulty breathing. Her chest was tight, hurting. Her head was throbbing. She closed her eyes. 'What a fool I am! What a fool I have been! How could I not see it?' she lamented. 'I was so engrossed in my own feelings, so shut up in my own world that I did not understand.'

It had seemed so easy, so natural. Yet, as she painfully realised now, she had been mistaken. She felt ashamed at her naivety – assuming that everybody was the same. She should have known better. She looked around her. A beggar was sleeping in the grass face down. She could see plastic bags filled with his few possessions lying next to him. His hair was matted and his legs were so dry they looked grey.

'We could remain friends,' she thought, trying to stir up some optimism in herself. 'But will I be able to put an end to the longing?'

She had to disentangle all the threads now and find a way to free herself. She had to shut down that part of her brain that made her see what did not exist. She had to remove her heart, clean it and place it back in her chest.

She got up, dusted her dress and turned round. She was feeling calmer, much calmer. Her breathing was steady. She needed to go back to his house to retrieve the small suitcase she had left behind when she ran away. What a silly thing to have done. Nobody escapes reality. Nobody can escape the truth. Her thoughts suddenly turned to her family. She wanted to see them. She wanted to recover the security of her former life.

The beggar was still asleep when she left the park. More

people were arriving. A group of children prepared to play a game of soccer.

She felt lighter, almost euphoric. She took a deep breath and smiled, thinking, 'we could have been so happy together…'

Chika Unigwe

Possessing the Secret of Joy

As she listened to the man beside her snore, like an airplane revving its engine for take off, she thought that she should never have allowed her mother to blackmail her into marrying him. She should have plugged her ears with her fingers or stuffed them with pieces of cloth when her mother – headscarf going awry on her head – had told her in a pained voice, 'Chief Okeke is our only hope. Don't you want to see me in nice clothes? And you, don't you want to be a madam? Have a driver? A big house? Servants? Don't you want to enjoy your life, *nwa m*?'

'But I don't love him, Mother. How can I marry a man I do not love? I can't.' Her voice was sharp, confident, daring her mother to contradict her. But her mother had contradicted her. 'Love does not matter, my daughter. There are things more important than love.' The older woman's voice was firmer, solid. It knocked the confidence of hers. As Chief's snore enveloped the entire room and kept her from sleeping, she whispered, 'Love does matter, Mother. You are so very wrong. It really does matter.' Her voice was weightless, floating like a ghost, hovering above her head. She would not have known she was crying if she had not felt the tears scarify her face.

Her mother had been persistent. She had been at it day after day, sometimes even crying, until she had eaten into Uju's reserves, corroding her confidence like acid on paper; until there was nothing left but consent. A heavy heart, a slight nod of the head, and a voice as still as the night. 'Yes. I will marry Chief. I will marry him.'

Chief.

Uju had just turned seventeen. Chief said he was forty-six. He looked older, closer to sixty. His stomach wobbled and preceded him whenever he walked into a room. It was like that of a woman on the verge of delivering quadruplets, but without the firmness of a pregnant stomach. The hair on his head was sparse and white, like cotton wool that had been haphazardly glued on by a child. His lips were huge and drooped as if they were implanted with lead that weighed them down. And when he spoke, he tended to send a saliva shower on those closest to him.

People said Chief had never married because he was too ugly to find a wife. She and her friends had made fun of Chief, laughing at his hair, his lips, his stomach. Yet now she was going to be Chief's wife. What fate could possibly be worse than that? She wished she could die. She desired, more than anything else, to just lie down and never wake up. To disappear. Vanish. Dissolve. Like salt in water.

Her mother threw herself into the wedding preparations with a ferocity that was not commensurate with her skinny frame. She whirled around the town, organising the caterers, the music band, her daughter's wedding dress. She settled herself in one of Chief's cars and sat in the owner's corner at the back while the driver called her 'Madam' and asked where she needed to be taken to.

Tonson's Supermarket
Fanny's Bridal Shop
Kenyatta market
Love is Blind Bakery
Your One Stop Tiara Shop
Wedding Specials
Mau's Cakes and More

She always came back, a huge smile on her face, her eyes shiny with new-found wealth and her mouth full of praises for her daughter who had made the right choice.

'Uju, you are a daughter to be proud of. You do not know

what a relief it is that you are marrying a man as rich as Chief. Poverty is not something to be proud of. *Afufu ajoka*!'

Uju knew all about poverty. She did not need to be told. She was the only child of her widowed mother. Her father had died when she was seven and all she remembered of him was a man as skinny as an *izaga* masquerade, dragging a battered brown briefcase out of the house every morning. When she tried to remember his face, she found that she could not. He was like an old Polaroid picture: defaced, effaced, without a face. She tried to recollect his voice but no matter how tight she shut her eyes and searched the crevices of her mind, she could not call up a voice. Her mother told her that he had been a quiet man. When he died in a road accident – the bus he was travelling in had been driving too fast and had hit a pothole, causing it to turn over and kill every passenger in it – his family had blamed his widow for killing their brother.

'A prophet told us that he saw you in a vision, chasing Papa Uju with a sharp knife,' his older sister announced. How could she have had a hand in it? the widow protested, crying. The roads were full of potholes which she did not create. Eye witnesses said the driver had been going too fast. How was she responsible for that? Her voice was weak and hoarse from crying. But her protests could not stand up to the prophet's believed infallibility.

Supervised by Uju's uncle, her father's oldest brother, Uju and her mother had been sent sprawling out of their modest three-bedroomed flat in New Lay Out, to a less modest one-room face-me-I-face-you flat on Obiagu Road, their property trailing behind them like unwanted children. The only things that the widow had been allowed to take out of the house were her clothes, Uju's clothes and the deceased's battered suitcase which had been discovered at the site of the accident, the lone survivor of the tragedy. Sometimes, Uju took down the suitcase from her mother's wardrobe and smelt it to catch a whiff of her father. But it just had that peculiar odour of old leather.

Uju knew how her mother had had to borrow money from a women's cooperative to start a petty business, selling *Dandy* chewing gum and sachets of milk and *Omo* detergent in her kiosk which was not actually a kiosk, but a wooden table set up in front of the house, right before the gutter which stank of urine and dying lives. Godfrey, the bachelor carpenter who lived in the same compound as they did, had knocked the table up for her at a really cheap rate. 'Neighbourly rate,' he had said, showing off his buck teeth as he smiled, his eyes taking in Uju's developing body, resting on her breasts until Uju's mother had asked him in a voice as cold as a harmattan morning if the rates included ogling the neighbour's daughter.

Uju remembered the days when all her mother could afford to give her for lunch was *abacha*, slices of cassava soaked in water, salted and, on lucky days, eaten with some coconut. She could never forget the day her mother told her she had to quit school as she could no longer pay her school fees. She had to help her mother out at her added business of selling *akara* and fried yam beside her kiosk. As Uju wrapped up the food straight off the pan for customers, she knew that at the back of her mother's mind lurked the hope that, one day, one of their richer clients would notice her daughter and ask for her hand in marriage. So, she knew that Chief's proposal was an answer to her mother's constant prayer. She almost hated her mother.

No matter how much Chief gave her, Uju could never forget being poor. It was inscribed on her, like *ichi* marks on an elder's face in her village, Osumenyi; marks to remind them of their status. No matter how low they fell, they could never rub off the *ichi*. She sat in her new house which reeked of luxury, but the smell of poverty never left her nostrils. And she knew that her new wealth would never make her happy.

Her mother told her she prayed for her to have sons for Chief. 'A wife with male children has her position secured. Nothing can shake that. If I had had a son, your father's family would never have thrown me out of our home. We would not have used our eyes to see the kind of suffering that we saw, *nwa m*. But there is a God, and he has brought Chief into our lives. So, I pray that that same God will bless you with *umu nwoke*, many sons. I pray that those who laughed at our misfortune will see us blessed. You shall have sons for Chief and our joy will be complete.'

Uju prayed fiercely in her mind as her mother spoke. She prayed that she would never have a son for Chief. She did not want her position crystallised. She wanted it to be shaky. She wanted Chief to find her wanting and set her free. Then, her mother would not blame her for leaving her matrimonial home.

On her wedding day, as Chief sat beside her, looking fit to burst in his three piece suit, she kept thinking, 'this man is an elephant'. When Chief slid a 24-carat gold ring on her finger, the ring burnt her and she was tempted to pull it off right there, with everybody watching. She was sure that the skin under the ring was welting. She cried throughout the ceremony, sniffing into a white lace handkerchief that Chief had bought her especially for the day – and her mother told her they were tears of joy. Uju did not tell her that the tears were gritty, like *garri*. She did not tell her mother that they rubbed into her skin, like a beauty scrub, breaking open her pores.

At the wedding reception later on in the day, her mother danced to the music being played by the live band. She glowed in her new George wrapper, singing Alleluia with a halo of wealth around her mighty, starched, silk scarf. She wriggled her buttocks to the music and came close to the new bride and enveloped her in an embrace that was so tight that it hurt the younger woman's ribs. Then she hugged Chief, her hands not making it around his enormous waist.

That night, when the new groom undressed and rested his weight on top of his wife she could hardly breathe and pushed her nose to the side to escape the assault of his breath. He heaved into her ears and called her name in many diverse ways. 'Uju m. Ju-ju. Ujay.' He parted her legs and thrust his manhood into her. In. Out. In. Out. In. Then he let it stay there.

Layers and layers of pain seared through her and when she thought that there could be no pain stronger than that, she felt his manhood bulge and explode into a million different types of pain between her thighs. And she felt sure that this was what it felt like to be dying. Then she heard him sigh and go limp. She turned her head into the pillow and he held her and told her she was young and she would learn. And it would get better with practice. 'The first time is always painful.'

Her mother had told her that she would fly. 'When your husband holds you for the first time, when he makes you a woman, *nwa m*, you will gain wings and fly and fly and fly. You will soar and never want to come down.' She had winked at her daughter as she imparted this piece of information.

But she had not flown. The pain between her legs made walking a chore. When she gathered the stained sheets to wash, she was aware even then that inside her a stain was spreading that she could not get to.

As her pregnancy grew and others noticed it too, she began to wish that she could reach into her womb and fling the baby out. She could not imagine having a baby that looked like Chief; a baby that would be one half of him. She wanted nothing of him, and definitely not a part of his flesh. With her stomach getting rounder and firmer, her mother's frequent visits became even more so. Often, she would stay for days at a stretch. She always found something to compliment. The leather sofa that swallowed her buttocks. The television set that she said was as huge as a cinema screen. The taps inside the house that answered to her command. The kitchen that was as big as their entire flat in Obiagu had been. The guest bedroom that was the size of their master bedroom in New Lay Out. The house helps that ran around dusting, cleaning, cooking.

'You are a lucky girl, Uju,' she told her daughter. 'All this, for you.'

When she said this, Uju grunted a reply that was swallowed up by the whirring of the air conditioner that the older woman had just switched on.

'*Negodu*, just look,' she exclaimed, giggling. 'The heat of outside does not touch you at all. White man's magic in my own daughter's house. God is great.' She stuck close to Uju, like a shadow, telling her what to eat and what to avoid.

'Don't eat okra soup at all. It will make your child drool like an imbecile.'

'Don't eat kola-nut. It will make the baby hot-tempered.'

'Don't eat *nsala* soup. It can cause a miscarriage.'

'Don't eat abacha. It will give the baby too much body hair.'

Uju listened and furtively ate okra soup and *nsala* soup and kola-nut. She waited with bated breath for the cramps that would expel the foetus in clots of blood, but they never came. Instead, her stomach grew and her skin shone and her husband remarked that she seemed to be getting more and more beautiful each day. 'My *mammy-water,*' he called her, 'my own mermaid.' He rubbed her stomach.

Her mother and a driver took her to the private hospital on Independence Lay Out the day her water broke. Chief was away in Abuja on a business trip, but his name was enough to gain her entrance into one of the best hospitals in Enugu. Nurses kow-towed to her asking, 'are you okay, Ma? Is the bed comfortable, Ma? Do you need anything, Ma?' Uju ignored them and her mother sailed on the attention they got, talking for the silent woman.

'Get us a big room.'

'Nurse! Let her have some water.'

'Nurse! This water is not cold enough. Does the fridge not work?'

'Nurse! How does this remote control work?'

'Nurse! Take this cup away.'

Her labour was long and hard. As the contractions squeezed her insides like a multitude of pincers, Uju opened her mouth and let loose a torrent of words. She shouted curses on the man who was responsible for all the pain. She cursed the baby who was dragging her to the very depths of hell. She cursed the poverty that made her marry Chief.

Her mother who sat beside her on her hospital bed tried to cover her daughter's mouth with her palm, as if she was trying to stuff the words back, to stop new ones from spewing out.

'Shh, *nwa m*, don't say these things, my daughter. It will soon be over. Swallow your words, *noda fa*.'

The gynecologist came in and smiled at her. She inserted a gloved hand into her and said in a loud voice, '8 cm dilated. We should get you into the delivery room right away.'

Her mother looked at the doctor and exclaimed at the miracle that allowed her daughter to be attended by the most reputable gynecologist that side of the Niger. She knew of women who gave birth at home, or in hospital corridors because there were no doctors to attend to them. Why, just three months ago, Mama Chinedu, their neighbour in Obiagu Road, had died from complications while giving birth in her bedroom. She had not gone to the hospital because the government hospital was on strike and she could not afford the exorbitant fees charged by the private hospitals. And here was her Uju, with a retinue of medical staff at her behest. 'God is good. *Chukwu ebuka*,' the older woman exclaimed as she followed the bed being rolled into the delivery room.

When the baby came it looked like an angry geriatric. It was bald and wrinkled. He let out a yell when the doctor, dangling him in one hand, spanked him on his scrawny old man's buttocks. The doctor laughed and said, 'this one is full of life! Hear him cry!' and handed him to the new mother. 'Here, hold him for a minute before we take him off to be cleaned.'

Uju held the baby close to her breasts. She felt its heartbeat, tat tat tat, like a tam-tam being beaten by a practised hand. She brought her face down to meet the baby's and then she felt something else. It started from the middle of her stomach like a tiny dot of warmth, and then it fanned out like an angel's wings spread vertically and touched her chest. She felt it flutter in her chest before it settled down. She closed her eyes and savoured the feeling; of being there, of smelling her baby. And then she knew that this was love.

She handed the baby over to the midwife to be cleaned and she thought, 'this is mine. He is mine. All mine. I, Uju, I possess the secret of joy.' She almost laughed out loud. Her legs twitched and itched to fly.

When the doctor asked if she had any names for him, she said the one name that came to her. 'Ifunanya.' Love. As she waited, counting the seconds until he was given back to her, she repeated his name, her voice soft and reverential, 'Ifunanya.' It was as if she was saying a prayer.

Wangui wa Goro

Deep Sea Fishing

He smiled at the thought of enveloping her, inhaling her as he often did when they spoke on the phone. Without turning, he felt her groping for him in the empty space beside her. He could see her fretting and watched her partly with amusement and partly feeling for her – with her – as she awoke.

She sat up, frightened at the thought that he was not there, at the thought that the magic had slipped and that it was only a dream, while realising that she was unclothed and shyly seeking to cover herself.

He had walked to the water's edge, holding his bottle of water. He was thirsty; she had made him thirsty; the heat made him thirsty. Even lying beside her could not seem to reassure him that she was here, was his for keeps, that he deserved this.

She smiled, as though she could read his thoughts although they had only met less than four hours ago. He melted her insides. She reflected his thoughts, thinking how lucky she was. He walked towards her, feeling her need propelling him towards her again. There was an unresolved, unspoken power between them that drew them together and, like the tidal waves, compelled them to different levels of madness, passion and calm. He had not known the 'right time' would come so soon.

She felt like an ocean, deep and wide, and this frightened and excited him, because he thought he was big and strong at heart as he was in soul. She was powerful and it unnerved him, not realising that he was the only man who could unleash such a force in her; that what he was experiencing was their power together, not hers alone. He had opened her to her core, made her want to writhe with unimaginable pleasure and desire – as she had imagined while they were apart – made her feel his deep need, his secret, sacred places of the body, her mind and soul.

This force had frightened them both then and now, this power, yet they lapped it up, with uncertainty, certainty. It was bound to be.

He leaned over to tease her earlobes then bent his head to kiss her, and he watched in awe as she stretched towards him like a cat, hungrily. There was no need to speak, to understand the world. 'Its OK you know, but you have to be very careful,' she had said, opening herself to him. Surprising themselves, they came to each other swiftly and gently and she surprised them both further still with her quick response. They felt complete. Then she started to laugh, deep from inside her throat... and then she calmed down, tears glistening on her lashes as she curled up beside him, and he could feel her gentle breathing as she drifted into a sweet sleep again, a smile at the corner of her mouth. What an amazing woman, he thought.

The preceding hours had been unusual. There was so much in the air and the wind, that had been howling madly, suddenly stopped leaving the glow of the hot sun on the whole landscape to shimmer and the sunlight reflected in the water jumped about madly in the ripples each time the fishing rods were disturbed.

It was awkward at first, as he tried to play the perfect host, tried not to ruffle her sensibilities that that was all he wanted from her, but it was playing on his mind, her mind; after all, it was a key factor in their wellbeing. They did not know what to do. Get it out of the way, at one level, just go for it, as they both so wanted to envelop each other, or wait, this itself being quite exquisite and sweet.

He had unpacked the picnic and passed her the various rods from the boot of his jeep. She said that she knew nothing about fishing. She knew that she was tired but she was so excited to be with him at last after all the months of talking on the phone since their first encounter twelve months before. They had promised that if the feelings they had first experienced on their initial encounter continued, they would meet in one year's time and then decide which way to go. It had been a long, tiring and expensive passionate year: phone calls, letters, emails, gifts, photographs, DVDs and more gifts.

They felt that they knew each other very well. They had been introduced to each other's families, by email and on the phone, and he had met all her family when he visited the city where they lived while on a work trip. He had introduced himself to her father as the future son-in-law although they had met for only one week before at a retreat far away from their respective homes. Her father did not seem to mind.

The week they met, they had each come away on a spiritual meditation on a silent retreat to ponder the meaning of life and seek direction for the future. They had met over dinner. As this was a silent meditation, all they could do was acknowledge each other with their eyes and all they did was look and look at each other, oblivious of everyone else present. On the third day they were already holding hands but not speaking, as this was not allowed, but on the final day they were finally allowed to speak. They decided to travel to the airport together and over dinner at a little restaurant on the way, they had agreed to the mad one-year trial plan. She had loved his voice and he loved her tinkling laughter. She loved his stature and he loved her curves. She loved his smile and his big gentle hands. He loved the nape of her neck and the texture of her skin. He admired the curve of her breast and she loved the curve of his rear. Most of all she loved his gentle laughter. They loved the taste of their mouths when they kissed for the first and only time as they said goodbye at the airport.

Now she sat quietly beside him with her book, pretending to read while he busily played with his fishing rods, wondering about the fish but still stunned at how beautiful she was, how soft her skin was and how wonderful she smelled. She looked more beautiful than he remembered, definitely better than the photographs and better than what he had imagined. Something had changed; she was more toned and had probably lost a bit of weight. Lenana was distracted for a while as he felt panic rising in his chest. He wondered whether he should have let her come... two delicious pleasures, fishing and her. He smiled at the thought. It was a tough one. She could hear him, he knew that she could hear him and she too was panicking but happy that she could read and be with him. What should she tell him about her life? That she was too scared? He did his slow laugh then, one which started from the back of his throat slowly rising while remaining deep in his belly.

She turned to look at him now, in wonder, pretended to silence him lest the fish got away and marvelled at his happiness. Did he know what she was thinking as he always did, especially through her silences when they spoke on the phone?

Shanti remained quiet for a long time. He thought that she was thinking that she might frighten the fish if she sushed him and watched him while he arranged the bait and the rods and sank the line and she wondered. He could not be further from the truth. She was worried about where to begin to tell him about her life.

He had chosen a perfect spot for the day and he knew that she was going to like it. He had made sandwiches earlier that morning and bought drinks and fruit on the way to pick her up at the airport.

She had woken up bright and early as a lark to catch her flight and he liked that. He liked her enthusiasm although she said she was scared of the sharks and did not want to go on the boat, which is why he had brought her here by the river, a peaceful secluded spot where it looked like a lake as it curved widely before heading for the falls. There were no sharks in rivers and if there was any shark around... He was going to bring her anyway as when they spoke on the phone often he had teased her that he would ravish her on the boat in the middle of nowhere and where all they had for company were sharks. He had seen her look at the falls in wonder as they had driven past them further below and decided it would be all right to bring her here. He knew that she would like it.

She still said nothing and he looked at her again. She somehow managed to amaze him with some unexpected thing even when they first met. Her surprises were swift and silent and he understood and enjoyed them.

She was trying her best to not talk to him or touch him on this warm sacred summer's day. Their first date. She could see that he was hot, but liking it. She buried her head in her book but she was not reading, she was thinking about their last evening together a year before, how he held her, squeezed her close and tight like the stars clinging to the night sky. This gesture had surprised her in its intensity. She had never felt like that before... tender and close to somebody, exquisite to the point of pain. He had done it again today when they met at the airport. She had allowed herself to drown in him, leaving nothing, nothing at all. He had felt it, this total surrender. It was both physical and spiritual and he had sighed deeply, contented that he had found heaven.

'My Shanti,' he said, several times, 'mine... '

He was at looking her intently now, aware that she had not turned a page for a long time. He put his hand out and touched her knee, dragging her out of her reverie, and his glimpse caught her look which she quickly tried to disguise but it was too late. She wanted him, but was afraid. He had caught a glimpse of it all right and smiled in resignation, reminding herself that she did not need to put up any barriers.

Just then, there was a tug on the rod and he stood up, excited to be 'caught' in this moment, wondering what he was going to say, what she was going to say. She closed her book in fascination, waiting to see what would emerge from the water at the end of the rod which curved so steeply now that it looked like it was ready to snap.

'It's a big one!' he said, a cheeky broad smile appearing on his face at the double entendre, as he finally broke the silence.

She suddenly felt the tremendous heat which she had not noticed and which seemed to consume the whole earth, although it came with clear skies and a stillness that she had never experienced before. The leaves were still, still, still. No rustle or movement. Even the birds knew to keep still. She smiled as she remembered the story that she had told him of when she was a child and she and her friends had wanted to run around the houses as a dare, to see who would survive the heat and how their grandmother had admonished them to keep still.

Those words now came in handy for this stillness. To do nothing. Nothing at all. Just keep very still, without the slightest movement.

Despite the heat and stillness, a storm seemed to be brewing. It felt as if it would break anytime, as if it sat underneath, waiting to explode. Break time and space. Break reality and dreams. Break... And she asked him several times, quite unconsciously, whether it was going to rain, and all he could do was smile indulgently. She later told him that she even thought she had heard a roll of thunder during the 'encounter', although he teased her that she had been so absorbed that it must have been subliminal wishful thinking. A thunderstorm in the middle of a heat storm! The records had been exceeded. Never had such heat been turned onto the unsuspecting dwellers of the city.

He had put his fish slowly on the ice, washed his hands and wiped his face with his wet hand while heading purposefully towards her. No escape.

It was reckoning time. She was waiting for whatever it was that was going to happen. She rose to meet him and he drew her blouse over her head to expose her light green camisole and matching briefs. She shivered involuntarily as her mind somersaulted in anxiety and excitement. Should she... ? Their lips met, leaving them both breathless and with no time for question or answers. Their hands were touching everything and everywhere. They gently lay down on the spread that she had brought. She listened to the songs of the universe, playing timbres, flutes, harps, nyatiti, mbira, a deep drum, the cora and the cow-horn. It was a peaceful melody and she decided to stay, stay with the stillness. It was a friendly stillness and there was no storm in store. It was the kind of stillness you felt before birth, between the tides of the contractions, a tough stillness, a lull before the storm. Still, peaceful in the midst of turmoil. Her head swam and she decided to close her eyes and luxuriate in the moment, with him, watch what it would yield in its own time, at its own pace and in its own rhythms. Not a word or murmur. Still. She decided to keep absolutely still as she had done on those long nights of waiting when she had quelled the panic, and the song that always came to her mind played louder still now.

Still my body lies
In a hammock in the skies
Swinging, I'm swinging
High up in the clouds
Singing, my body sings lows and highs

Still my body lies
Floating over the water

Still, still, floating down to the sea
Still my body lies
In the rafter in the reeds
Flowing down to the deep ocean
Open and wide

Still my body lies
In the vastness of time
I'm lying still
Waiting, waiting...

Still my body lies
I'm waiting for my love

Still my body lies, still my body lies
I'm like the ocean
Open to your love
Like the space above
Open to your love
I'm like the sky above
Stretching open wide

Still my body lies
Still my body lies
Still . . . my . . . body . . . lies.

Time stood still for both of them. They played for time, and she let him, let him be in control. He gave in to the deep impulse he had experienced since he had picked her up from the airport, an impulse to touch her, hold her, feel every inch of her. This desire of his turned her on because he did not seem to realise that it did not matter to her, she would surrender anyway, yield to him readily, at his asking, that asking was all he had to do. He did not care either. Just seeing her, smelling her, touching her was enough. They wanted to envelop each other.

It was overwhelming now, and he could no longer keep away from her. May I? She cleared her throat, 'yes please,' and his hand which had been touching her head, her neck, her belly, her back, everywhere descended.

She froze and this made him stop. 'I am sorry,' he said. She tried to clear her throat to say something, but it was too late. His lips covered hers. His hand found nothing, nothing at all. Although he was shocked and he felt like pulling back, he continued searching in case, in his excitement, he had missed something and he moved his hand lower down still. Nothing. He looked at her face, not comprehending, and saw her closed eyes, caught between fear and desire.

'Look at me,' he said, his voice filled with emotion, and he knew that she would not acquiesce. 'Look at me,' he said again gently, and she slowly turned her face towards him, a tear rolling down her face as she did so…

'Where is it?' he asked, tenderly, continuing to stroke her there gently while kissing her nipple. 'They sewed it in when I was young,' she answered in an anxious voice. 'Is it a problem?'

'No, it is not a problem for me, if it is not a problem for you, but I do want to visit there some day soon,' he said gently, trying to make light of the matter, while he wrapped her in both arms strongly, inhaling her and thankful that she was his and in his arms. She sighed and sank herself deeply into his body, enveloping him as she had promised him she would and as he had promised he would do her when they met. And she fell asleep, bare as she was born in the open space beside the river, her book and the fish forgotten.

The glow of the evening light shone gently on her brown curves, softening her tiredness which she had tried to conceal from him without success, softening her lips, her tips. She was so beautiful, even when she had been so nervous, so afraid. He hoped that he would please her; the day of reckoning was here. All that bravado on the phone could not conceal this secret and he had known that there was something significant troubling her, but not for one moment had he imagined that it would be this. He wondered what he was going to do to assure her that nothing in the world was ever going to part her from him, although the discovery of the absence of her special part had brought in him a certain sharp shock and realisation of what really mattered to him. His response seemed to be welcomed with a relief such as he had never experienced in anyone. He was proud that he had not reacted adversely, that the need in his loins was not the only propulsion in his desire for her; that he really loved her more than ever, if anything; that he could envelop her and kiss her every bit and it would be perfect. He realised that, in fact, what he wanted more than anything was to envelop her for life, through life, and that she, in turn, would envelop him. In that way they would deal with it – with whatever – together when the time was right.

Notes on Contributors

Leila Aboulela was born in Cairo in 1964 and grew up in Khartoum. She is half-Egyptian, half-Sudanese. She graduated from the University of Khartoum in 1985, later studying statistics at the London School of Economics. She is the author of *The Translator*, which was longlisted for the Orange Prize, a collection of short stories, *Coloured Lights*, and most recently the novel, *Minaret*. She is also a winner of the first Caine Prize for African writing in 2000. She now divides her time between Aberdeen and Dubai.

Tomi Adeaga was born in 1968 in Lagos, Nigeria. She obtained a Bachelors degree in German/French at the Obafemi Awolowo University, Ife, Ile-Ife and did post-graduate studies in Germany. She is a member of a number of organisations, notably the African Literature Association, the Modern Language Association and the African Concern Organisation (NGO) in Paris. Her current research interests include translation studies and studies of the African Diaspora in Europe. Her book *Translating and Publishing African Language(s) and Literature(s)* was published by IKO-Verlag in 2005. She has lived in Germany since 1992.

Chimamanda Ngozi Adichie was born in Nigeria in 1977. Her first novel, *Purple Hibiscus*, won the Commonwealth Writers Prize and the Hurston/Wright Legacy award, was shortlisted for the Orange Prize and the John Llewellyn Rhys Prize, and was longlisted for the Booker. A 2003 O Henry Prize winner, Adichie's short fiction has appeared in various literary publications, including *Granta* and the *Iowa Review*. She now divides her time between Nigeria and the United States, where she is a Hodder Fellow at Princeton University.

Sefi Atta was born in Lagos, Nigeria. She was educated there, in

England and in the United States. A former chartered accountant, she is a graduate of the creative writing programme at Antioch University, Los Angeles. Her works have appeared in journals such as the *Los Angeles Review* and the *Mississippi Review*, and have won prizes from Zoetrope, Red Hen Press, the BBC and the Commonwealth Broadcasting Association. She is the winner of PEN International's 2004/2005 David TK Wong Prize, and in 2002, the opening section of her debut novel was shortlisted for the Macmillan Writers Prize for Africa. In 2005, her novel entitled *Everything Good Will Come* was published in the United States, England and West Africa.

Yaba Badoe is a Ghanaian-British documentary filmmaker, journalist and fiction writer. She started her career in journalism as a general trainee with the BBC, where she trained in radio and television production. She has had short stories published in *Critical Quarterly* and is currently working on her first novel, *True Murder.*

Doreen Baingana is a Ugandan writer who lives in the United States. Her collection, *Tropical Fish: Stories out of Entebbe*, was published in February 2005 by the University of Massachusetts Press after it won the Associated Writers and Writing Programs (AWP) Award in Short Fiction in 2003. It has been republished in South Africa by Oshun Books. *Tropical Fish* won the Commonwealth Prize for First Book, Africa Region, 2006. Ms Baingana also won the Washington Independent Writers Fiction Prize in 2004, and has twice been a finalist for the Caine Prize for African Writing, in 2004 and 2005. She received the first Fairbanks International Fellowship for the Bread Loaf Writers' Conference, Vermont, 2005 and in the same year was a Writer-in-Residence at the University of Maryland, College Park. She received an MFA from that college and a law degree from Makerere University, Uganda.

Mildred Kiconco Barya is a writer, a poet and a member of FEMRITE, a Ugandan writers' group. She is currently working on her novel *Soul of Rivers*, which highlights major themes such as HIV/AIDS, religious cults and the quest for identity and belonging. She has written features for newspapers, travel articles, essays and short stories. Besides writing, she provides human resources advisory services and organisation development training to various clients. Her publications include *Africa Needs Her Promise*, *Women's Experience of War* and 'Raindrops', a short story published by FEMRITE in 2001 in *Words from the Granary*.

Rounke Coker was born in 1962 of mixed parentage and grew up in an African extended family in Lagos, with many white English mores and traditions. She came to the UK in 1978 to finish her formal education (Geography and later Development Studies). From 2000, she has facilitated the development of resources for Brighton and Hove LEA on issues around cultural diversity for school children aged five to thirteen years. In a project with new audiences, Liverpool Museums published in 2004 a Yoruba folktale she co-wrote for Diasporic readership. She is currently developing new work around experiences of family with a view to publication.

Anthonia C Kalu is Professor of Black Studies at the University of Northern Colorado in Greeley, Colorado, where she developed the Black Studies programme into an autonomous department. She has been teaching at UNC since 1989. She received her doctoral degree in African Languages and Literature with a minor in Afro-American Literature from the University of Wisconsin-Madison in 1984. Among her awards are a Ford Foundation postdoctoral fellowship, a Rockefeller writer-in-residence fellowship and a National Endowment for the Humanities summer fellowship for teachers. She spent a year at Connecticut College where, as a Distinguished Associate Professor, she helped define their programme in Africana Studies. She has also received Distinguished Scholar awards from the University of Notre Dame, Indiana and Spelman College, Atlanta, Georgia. Anthonia Kalu is a member of various academic organisations including the African Studies Association and the African Literature Association. She serves on the editorial board of several academic journals. Her research interests include African and African American literatures and literary theory construction, women in the African Diaspora, African development issues and multiculturalism. Journals in which she has published include *Africa Today*, *Research in African Literatures*, *African Studies Review*, the *Atlantic Literary Review*, *Seminar* and the *Literary Griot*. She has published two books, *Women, Literature and Development in Africa* (Africa World Press, 2001) and *Broken Lives and Other Stories*

(Ohio University Press, 2003). She is editor of the *Rienner Anthology of African Literature* (Lynne Rienner Publishers, 2006).

Antjie Krog is a South African poet, writer, journalist and Professor at the University of the Western Cape. She has published eleven volumes of poetry in Afrikaans, two volumes of verse for children, a short novel, a play and two non-fiction books in English: *Country of my Skull* (Random House, South Africa 1998), on the South African Truth and Reconciliation Commission, and *A Change of Tongue*, about the transformation in South Africa after ten years. She was also asked to translate the autobiography of Nelson Mandela, *Long Walk to Freedom*, into Afrikaans. Krog has been awarded most of the prestigious awards for non-fiction, prose and poetry in both Afrikaans and English.

Sindiwe Magona is an author, poet, playwright, essayist, story-teller, actor and inspirational speaker, recently retired from the United Nations and relocated to her home country, South Africa. Her published works include two autobiographical books, *To My Children's Children* and *Forced to Grow*; two collections of short stories, *Living, Loving, and Lying Awake at Night*; *Push-Push and Other Stories* and a novel, *Mother to Mother*, recently optioned by Universal Studios for a film on the life of Amy Biehl. She has also been published in the *New York TImes*, the *Cape Times*, the *Cape Argus* and the *Herald* as well as in magazines in South Africa and internationally. Several of her short stories, essays and poems have been anthologised. She is the recipient of several awards including an Honorary Doctorate in Humane Letters at Hartwick College, Oneonta, New York and Xhosa Heroes Award from the Xhosa Forum, Western Cape, South Africa. Sindiwe Magona is the founder and Executive Director of South Africa 2033, an NPO focusing on social transformation and the eradication of endemic poverty among the previously disadvantaged people of South Africa.

Sarah Ladipo Manyika holds a Masters and PhD in Education from the University of California, Berkeley. She is co-author of the Rockefeller report, *PhD Programs in African Universities: Current Status and Future Prospects*. Other scholarly works include published papers on race and class theory, as well as numerous conference papers and reviews in the area of African and African

Diasporan literatures. In recent years, she has convened roundtables of some of Africa's most prominent contemporary writers for the African Literature and African Studies Associations. She continues to work on such projects, facilitating dialogue between writers from Africa and the African Diaspora. She is an editor of the Weaverbird Collective for new Nigerian writings, and a long-time judge for the African Studies Association Children's Book Award. She has just completed her first novel, *In Dependence*, and is working on a second book of short stories from which *Modupe* is taken.

Blessing Musariri is a Zimbabwean award-winning children's writer who writes many other things besides. Her two publications to date are *Rufaro's Day* (Longman Zimbabwe, 2000) and *Going Home – A Tree's Story* (Weaver Press Zimbabwe, 2005). A sample of her poetry can be found in *New Writing*, Volume 14 (Granta Press, 2006). She currently resides in Zimbabwe and travels at every given opportunity. She mistakenly believed she would be a lawyer but came to her senses after sitting and passing the English Bar Finals in 1997. She is the first African e-intern for *Sable Litmag* and finds it an invaluable learning experience. She is single and, much to her disbelief, became a great-aunt last year.

Monica Arac de Nyeko is from Uganda. She was shortlisted for the Caine Prize for African writing in 2004 for her short story, 'Strange Fruit'. She is a member of the Uganda Women Writers Association (FEMRITE). Her works have appeared in several anthologies including *Words from a Granary* (FEMRITE Publications 2001), *Tears of Hope* (FEMRITE Publications 2003), *Memories of Sun* (Green Willow Books 2004) and *Seventh Street Alchemy (*Jacana Media 2005).

Promise Oguchukwu is a Nigerian writer who received the 1999 Cadbury Prize for poetry with her collection of poems entitled *My Mother's Eyes Speak Volumes*, while her novel, *Surveyor of Dreams*, obtained the 1999 Spectrum Prize for prose. In 2000, she was awarded the Okigbo Poetry Prize for poetry in Africa for her collection, *Canals in Paradox*. She was honoured with the Spectrum Prize for prose also in 2000 for her novel, *Deep Blue Woman*. In 2002, she earned the maiden ANA/NDDC Prize with her widely-acclaimed novel, *Hall of Memories,* and, in the same year, she won the Matatu Prize for children's literature with her children's book, *The Street Beggars*. In November 2003, she also bagged the Flora Nwapa Prize for prose with her novel entitled *Fumes and Cymbals*. Her novel, *In the Middle of the Night*, won the first Pat Utomi Book Prize in 2005, while her novel, *Swollen and Rotten Spaces*, won the 2005 Flora Nwapa Prize for literature. In the same 2005, her poetry collection, *Naked among These Hills*, was selected as one of the three best poetry books in Nigeria by the judges of the Nigeria LNG prize. She is also the author of the following collections of essays: *Creative Writing and the Muse, The Writer as God, Dreams, Shadow and Reality* and *Wild Letters in Harmattan*. Promise Oguchukwu is an Azikiwe Fellow in Communication as well as a Fellow of Stiftung Kulturfonds. She has enjoyed fellowships in the US, Italy and Germany and has travelled extensively in Europe, Africa and Asia as a scholar, a playwright and a poet. She has a PhD in Communication and Language Arts from the University of Ibadan. She is currently the Co-ordinator of the Wole Soyinka Prize for Literature in Africa instituted by the Lumina Foundation, which she founded. She lives in Nigeria.

Molara Ogundipe, also widely known and published as Molara Ogundipe-Leslie, is a critic, academic, editor in various capacities, essayist, media columnist and interactive poet in a mode of presentation she invented. She is a distinguished scholar in literary theory, studies of Africa and her Diaspora, and postcolonial studies. She is also one of the pioneer and leading African figures in feminist, women's and gender studies and activism. She is currently a Leverhulme Distinguished Professor in the School of English and Postcolonial Studies at Leeds University, UK. In 1986, she was nominated to be a national director for social mobilisation by the Federal Government of Nigeria to activate national and democratic awareness through politics, education and culture in preparation for civilian rule. A regular speaker at academic and other conferences and symposia, consultant and community builder, Molara Ogundipe is also a well-known and widely-anthologised poet.

Helen Oyeyemi was born in Ibadan, Nigeria, in 1984 and moved to London with her parents at the age of four. Her best friend is Mary Oyeyemi and her second best friend is (she wishes) Emily Dickinson. Helen is currently studying Social and Political Sciences at Corpus Christi College, Cambridge. Her first novel, *The Icarus Girl*, was shortlisted for the 2006 Commonwealth Writers' Prize's Best First Book for Eurasia, and has also been shortlisted for the 2006 British Arts Council's Decibel award. Her plays, *Juniper's Whitening* and *Victimese*, are published by Methuen. She is currently completing her second novel.

Nawal El Saadawi is one of the most respected and prolific Arab women writers widely published in the West, where her novels, *Woman at Point Zero* (1984) and *God Dies by the Nile* (1985), both translated into English by her husband, Sherif Hetata, are favourites. She was born in the village of Kafr Tahla, trained as a medical doctor and rose to become Egypt's Director of Public Health. *The Veil* was written in Addis Ababa in 1978, was first published in an English translation in Cairo in an anthology in 1987, and featured in the 1993 *Passport to Arabia.* In 1987 it was also included in the selection of her stories, *Death of an Ex-Minister*, translated by Shirley Eber. In 1989, the same translator also produced another selection of her stories, *She Has No Place in Paradise.* Nawal El Saadawi recently published her autobiography, *A Daughter of Isis* (Zed Books, London 1999). She lives in Cairo.

Véronique Tadjo is a writer and artist from Côte d'Ivoire. She was a lecturer at Abidjan University. Two of her novels are translated into English, *As the Crow Flies* (2001) and *The Shadow of Imana, Travels to the Heart of Rwanda* (2002), both published by Heinemann in the African Writers Series. Her latest book, *Reine Pokou*, published by Actes Sud in Paris, is about Abraha Pokou, Queen of the Baoule people who, according to the legend, had to sacrifice her only son to save her people. She is the 2005 recipient of Le Grand Prix d'Afrique Noire, awarded yearly to a French-speaking writer. Tadjo also writes and illustrates books for young people. She is currently based in Johannesburg.

Chika Unigwe is a Nigerian writer who lives in Turnhout, Belgium, with her husband and three children. She holds a BA in English Language and Literature from the University of Nigeria, Nsukka, and an MA from the Catholic University of Leuven, Belgium. She also holds a PhD from the University of Leiden, The Netherlands. She is the author of fiction, poetry, articles and educational material. She won the 2003 BBC Short Story Competition for her story, 'Borrowed Smile', a Commonwealth Short Story Award for 'Weathered Smiles' and a Flemish literary prize for 'De Smaak van Sneeuw', her first short story written in Dutch. 'The Secret', another of her short pieces, was nominated for the 2004 Caine Prize. Her short story, 'Dreams', was shortlisted for the Million Writers Best Online Fiction in 2005, and 'Thinking of Angel' was longlisted for the same award. Her story 'Confetti, Glitter and Ash' recently finished third in the 2005 Equiano Prize for Fiction. Unigwe's stories have been broadcast on BBC World Service, Radio Nigeria and other Commonwealth Radio Stations. Her first novel, *De Feniks*, was published in Dutch by Meulenhoff / Manteau in September 2005; it is the first book of fiction written by a Flemish author of African origin and has recently been shortlisted for the Dutch Vrouw en Kultuur debuutprijs, a bi-annual prize for the best debut by a female writer published in Holland.

Wangui wa Goro is a Kenyan and a public intellectual, academic, social and cultural catalyst, researcher, translator, writer and a campaigner for human rights in Africa and Europe. She is the translator of award-winning authors Ngũgĩ wa Thiong'o and Véronique Tadjo. Her forthcoming translation is Fatou Keita's *Rebelle*. Her publications include a short story, 'Heaven and Earth', edited by Ayebia Clarke and published in an anthology titled *Half a Day* by Macmillan Kenya in 2004; *Global Feminist Politics, Identities in a Changing World*, co-edited with Suki Ali and Kelly Coate (Routledge, London and New York, 2004); and *As the Crow Flies,* (translation) Véronique Tadjo, published by Heinemann in 2001. She was a member of the jury for *Africa's 100 Best Books of the Twenty-First Century*. She has also served on significant academic committees including the Executive Committee of the Women's Studies Network, UK, the translation advisory committees of the British Centre for Literary Translation and the Arts Council (of Britain), and PEN International Translation Advisory Committee. She currently works as a Research Fellow at the Centre for Social and Evaluation Research (DASS) at London Metropolitan University.

Acknowledgements

The publishers would like to thank the following copyright holders for permission to reproduce the short stories in this anthology:

Leila Aboulela for 'Something Old, Something New'; Tomi Adeaga for 'Marriage and Other Impediments'; Chimamanda Ngozi Adichie for 'Transition to Glory'; Sefi Atta for 'The Lawless'; Yaba Badoe for 'The Rival'; Doreen Baingana for 'Tropical Fish' which first appeared in *Tropical Fish: Stories out of Entebbe* published by University of Massachusetts Press; Mildred Kiconco Barya for 'Scars of Earth'; Rounke Coker for 'Ojo and the Armed Robbers'; Anthonia C Kalu for 'Ebube Dike!'; Antjie Krog for 'Three [Love] Stories in Brackets'; Sindiwe Magona for 'Modi's Bride'; Sarah Ladipo Manyika for 'Modupe'; Blessing Musariri for 'Counting Down the Hours'; Monica Arac de Nyeko for 'Jambula Tree'; Promise Oguchukwu for 'Needles of the Heart'; Molara Ogundipe for 'Give Us That Spade!'; Helen Oyeyemi for 'The Telltale Heart'; Nawal El Saadawi for 'The Veil' which appeared in *The Picador Book of African Stories* published by Picador, an imprint of Macmillan Publishers Ltd; Véronique Tadjo for 'A Sunny Afternoon'; Chika Unigwe for 'Possessing the Secret of Joy' and Wangui wa Goro for 'Deep Sea Fishing'.

Copyrights and Permissions

and publisher would be glad to hear from copyright holders they have not been able to contact and to print due acknowledgement in the next edition.